SIX ROOMS

by Gemma Amor

CEMETERY GATES
MEDIA

Six Rooms
Published by Cemetery Gates Media
Binghamton, New York

Copyright © 2021
by Gemma Amor

All rights reserved. Without limiting the rights under the copyright reserved above, no part of this publication may be reproduced, stored in, or introduced into a retrieval system, or transmitted in any form or by any means (electronic, mechanical, photocopying, recording, or otherwise) without prior written permission.

ISBN: 9798543045916

For more information about this book and other Cemetery Gates Media publications, visit us at:

cemeterygatesmedia.com
facebook.com/cemeterygatesmedia
twitter.com/cemeterygatesm
instagram.com/cemeterygatesm

Cover design by Chad Wehrle

PRAISE FOR SIX ROOMS

"Gemma Amor turns her keen eye for character and atmosphere to the nightmare land of ghosts—a gorgeous blend of historical horror and hauntings done right, *Six Rooms* is at turns chilling and heartbreaking, with enough scares to make sure you leave the lights on. A delight."

-Laurel Hightower, author of CROSSROADS & WHISPERS IN THE DARK

"Gemma Amor's *Six Rooms* is a chilling ghost story that is full of her usual prose magic and haunting imagery. This deftly crafted paranormal yarn will chill the very marrow of your bones, whilst the frenetic pace and readability of Amor's words will get your heart rate pumping until you turn that final page and can once more breathe easily. This is more than just a ghost story; this is a story about belonging, a story of finding one's place in the world, but above all else it is a unique and masterful book that takes the paranormal trope and crafts something truly magical... *Six Rooms* will leave its mark long after reading, mark my words."

-Ross Jeffery, Bram Stoker Nominated author of TOME, JUNIPER & ONLY THE STAINS REMAIN

"*Six Rooms* starts as an almost whimsical ghost story but devolves inexorably into a series of genuinely dreadful horrors. This descent into violence and greed and regret will leave you thoroughly unsettled."

-Alan Baxter, author of THE GULP & THE ALEX CAINE SERIES

"*Six Rooms* wraps its raw, corporeal fingers around the throat of the ghost story trope and pulls it inside out like a visceral magician's trick. The bloodied threads of past and present moments in Sunshire Chateau come together in a masterfully woven tapestry of greed, heartache, and the inhuman condition. One of her best works to date…"

-Michael Tyree, author of
POTTER'S FIELD BLUES & THE PALE HORSE

"What a ride. I've been a fan of Gemma Amor's work for years, and *Six Rooms* does not disappoint. A haunting, evocative story from start to finish that will leave you reeling. If you love emotional horror with realistic characters and settings so vivid you feel as though you're there, you won't want to miss this one."

-Briana Morgan, author of
THE TRICKER-TREATER AND OTHER STORIES

"Gemma Amor deftly takes you by the hand and leads you into this house of madness and mayhem, where nothing is as it seems. Twisty, compelling and masterfully crafted, the horrors in the Sunshire Chateau will haunt you long after you run screaming from its doors."

-Beverley Lee, bestselling author of
THE RUIN OF DELICATE THINGS

"*Six Rooms* will have you turning pages as quickly as its ill-fated tour group turns corners in this rich, contemporary Gothic haunted house novel. Amor weaves a character-driven ghost story guaranteed to chill you to your core, with a house you will love as much as you will fear it."

-Sonora Taylor, award-winning author of
LITTLE PARANOIAS: STORIES & SEEING THINGS

For my precious Nan, who went out through one door, and in through another, leaving me behind.

Keep chasing those patches of blue sky, and I hope that wherever you are, you can hear the sea.

My gratitude and heartfelt thanks to Laurel Hightower, wolf sister, who gave me honest, measured feedback that turned this book into a much better novel than it was before she set eyes on it.

    -G.A.

SIX ROOMS

RECEPTION HALL
(13)

THE BLUE ROOM
(49)

THE LIBRARY
(103)

THE ATRIUM
(139)

THE MASTER'S STUDY
(189)

THE MAP ROOM
(231)

FOREWORD

Just after I hit the halfway mark on this novel, already hugely delayed and horribly late due to the pandemic, my Grandmother died. She was living in a care home at the time, and struggling to recover after contracting covid. I think I knew in my heart that she was slipping from us, but, as with most painful things, I didn't want to admit this to myself, and so words, as they often are, went unsaid. Letters went unwritten. Phone calls never occurred. I never got to say goodbye to her before she decided to quit this troubling, marvellously unpredictable thing we call life, not in person, and this feels like the worst kind of injustice: not being able to tell the woman who raised me, nurtured kindness and warmth in me, taught me the value of compassion and unconditional love, how grateful I was to have her. A woman who wrapped me up in a blanket with a hot water bottle on days where I felt sick, a woman who used to load her CD player up with Rachmaninov and sit with me, enraptured, tears sliding down her cheeks as the music swept us along like a glacial torrent, off into a land of romance, where everything was seen through a soft-focus filter, because that is the sort of person she was. A dreamer, a romantic. A traveller, in her dreams at least—life did not allow her many opportunities to leave Britain. She was a gentle creature, and she hated the idea of violence, of conflict, of hurting anyone's feelings. She surrounded herself with cotton-wool comforts, with beautiful things, with art and music and animals and family and friends. She loved the sea, and she made a good life for herself, a life not without hardship, but a good, memorable life, which is all any of us can ask for, really.

It may come as a surprise, then, knowing what sort of woman she was, that I am dedicating this novel to her. Some of the characters who creep within these pages are not gentle, or kind, or compassionate, nor do they abhor violence, as she did. They do not experience the wonder and joy she did at daily, inconsequential things like a break in the clouds on a gloomy day or a bird on a branch in early spring or a bright dew drop on an unfurled fern. The characters within these pages have dark, blighted lives, and she would not have liked them very much. With that in mind, it goes without saying that there are, as usual, some strong themes in this novel: graphic acts of violence perpetrated on women perhaps being the most notable. There is also mention of suicidal ideation and self-harm, which doesn't feel very nice to write down, it never does, but sometimes the story comes out as the story comes out, and all I can hope is that you, the reader, know why we sometimes write about the darkness, instead of the light.

That being said, this is not just a book about death. It is also a book about life, and whatever lies after and between the two. More than that: this is a book about ghosts, and what it means to be haunted, what it means to stay behind, to remain long after our physical carriages have ceased to exist. I think about this a lot, as I wrestle with grief. I think about matter, and energy, and how Aaron Freeman wrote about asking a physicist to speak at your funeral, to tell those gathered that your energy 'has not died', that 'the warmth that flowed through you in life is still here, still part of all that we are', and I wonder if this is what we really mean when we think of ghosts and spirits. Do we mean the energy that is redistributed after our bodies rot? The rule of thermodynamics says that energy cannot be created, nor destroyed. Our bodies however, are open systems, by my frugal understanding of such things. We can lose energy and gain it, but that is not what matters here. What matters here is that once we die, all the little parts of us that go into composing the whole continue on. They are repurposed, recycled, and they find a new home. And when I think about this, I can see no better way of describing what a ghost could be. Energy, redistributed. Tiny little parts of us, mighty in their potential, unbound, disassembled, untethered, set free into the world once more, miniscule pilgrims seeking a new home. Like snow waiting to settle anew, for snow was once water vapour and dust, frozen to form a crystal, which crashed and collided with other crystals, which eventually fell to the ground, melted, and evaporated, so that the cycle could renew. I could go on, but my limited knowledge of science and physics will embarrass me even before we have even flipped to the first page.

So I'll slip away, as time slips away, as life slips away, but before I go I'll say this: this book is for you, Shirley, beloved, always, by me, by many, because in doing so, in placing your name in print, there is another part of you that will linger long after all else has gone back to the earth, and I can think of no better way to immortalise a precious person, for precious you were, and I shall love you always, and my love will linger long after I have also drawn my last, for love is energy, and energy, as we know now, thanks to scientists, can never die. It may disassemble, it may journey, it may even find a new home, it may, as you may, reappear as a rose petal or a snowflake or a leaf on the wind.

But it will never die, and that, dear reader, dearest Shirley, is all that is important.

G.A.

RECEPTION HALL

DOORS

They say that when one door closes, another door opens.

Certainly this is true of death, or so we have been led to believe. Whether life gently latches the gate behind us, or shoves us rudely out into the murky beyond, depending on the nature of our passing, death beckons, holding the door wide. We pass through and it is a simple transition, or at least it should be. A short, unremarkable journey. Out of one door, and in through another.

Easy enough.

Or is it?

What of those who lose their way between doors? Out through one, and then... Confusion. The opening behind slams shut, but there is no obvious path ahead. No welcoming committee, no sign post. No transition. What of these souls? Do they wander? Do they wander and find, after too long, that there is no way out but sideways, midways? Betwixt, between? Do they become the shadows that endlessly haunt the long, featureless corridors between life and death?

Maybe. Or maybe they slip through the cracks in the corridor walls instead, like water trickling through the fingers of a cupped palm, squeezing themselves between floorboards, wriggling through fissures in space, time, reality, and maybe they find themselves in other places, places with their own doors and windows and walls and rooms, places steeped in memory, places that straddle our long-clutched definitions of liminal space, places where the soul can roam, and search, and mourn, and rage.

Places where the echoes of people long gone still linger like woodsmoke in the tranquil air.

Places like the Sunshire Chateau, which sits high up on the brow of a hill, frowned upon by a brooding row of giant cedar trees that have been planted too close to each other.

A house the sunlight barely touches.

A house where, over the years, many a lost spirit has found a home, and made itself comfortable.

TOUR GUIDE

On an unseasonably warm, late summer morning in New York State, a small group of eight tourists waited near the massive front doors of an enormous, opulent yet rather grimly proportioned four-storey mansion known as the Sunshire Chateau, whispering amongst themselves impatiently. The tour was supposed to start at nine in the morning sharp, and it was now nine-twenty, yet the house remained silent and closed, with no signs of life.

The Sunshire Chateau offered guided tours infrequently. When tickets did become available at the tourist office down in the town of Lestershire, which lay at the bottom of the steep rock ledge that held the Chateau aloft, it was with little warning or fanfare. Thus, a tour at Sunshire was something of a prize, a rite of passage for any self-respecting tourist who managed to snag a spot at the last minute. The scarcity of tour tickets coupled with the rumors that lay thick like drifted leaves around the place—rumors of ghosts, treasures, violence, scandal and intrigue—meant the Chateau, when it was actually open, had taken on the dubious honor of being Lestershire's premier tourist attraction. For that reason, and because there was really very little else to do in town except drink bad, weak coffee and hike the nearby hill trails, every now and then at nine o'clock sharp, come rain or shine, a small gaggle of curious hopefuls (numbers were strictly limited for each tour, for reasons known only to the estate) gathered in the tree-lined driveway, whispering impatiently amongst themselves as they waited to be let in.

This particular group was a mixed bunch of the usual suspects: day-trippers and history enthusiasts, time-killers, nosey folk, retirees, and one small family made up of a mother, a father and their teenaged son, who were taking a shoulder-season vacation together and finding it an awkward, strained affair. The parents should have left the boy at home while they got away for some much needed alone time, for he was more than old enough to be left. But the boy, who was called Noah, was evidently not to be trusted, and so here he was, hair flopping down over his face, huge headphones clamped over his ears, hood pulled up over the headset and eyes firmly fixed on the ground where there was little risk of him accidentally making eye contact and having to engage with anyone else. Noah, who was always painfully aware of himself and those around him in the way that most kids going through puberty are, carried himself with the wounded grace of a natural-born martyr. The tour, and in fact the entire trip out of the city, was something to be suffered, to be borne, an injustice perpetrated against him by his parents, and shit, was he going to make them pay for it, in any way he could.

'Well, it's bigger than Biltmore House in Asheville, and that's sayin' somethin,' a squat old lady who stood knock-kneed a little way off from the boy said. She sucked on her gums as she gazed up at the enormous frontage of the Chateau. 'I ain't never seen anything so big!'

The Chateau was one of the largest privately owned historic properties in America, a solid brick and stone mass that was, even to the untrained eye, a hodgepodge of too many different architectural styles, an exercise in grandeur for grandeur's sake, as if the architect had simply been told to 'make it look expensive' (which was not too far from the truth of the original brief) and been given an unlimited budget and license to help enable this vision. The result was a peculiar blend of materials, features and design principles that was so immediately confusing no local historian had ever been able to fully agree on which style was the dominant style. Victorian English late gothic revival influences clashed with nods towards the Greek revival, Federal design aspects battled for attention alongside Second Empire flourishes, and the whole structure was capped with a chunky, four-sided double curbed Mansard roof with two levels of sloping sides punctured by ornately sculpted yet still remarkably ugly dormer windows. This last throwback to mid-nineteenth century Parisian architecture felt like it had only been implemented for the sole purpose of upsetting anyone who stood outside and stared at the Chateau for too long. Because it looked so wrong, and so out of place amongst the red-brick turrets and spires that vied for dominance around it like weeds reaching up for the sun around a large, ugly grey rock, as to be offensive. As if someone had trodden upon an exquisitely modelled statue of the Chateau with a much more appropriate steepled roof and flattened the top completely. It gave the house a brooding, hunched, unpleasant air. Visitors to the property often came away feeling like the Chateau had a chip on its shoulder, because of it.

And maybe it did, for all the money and all the contrived opulence in the world had still not been able to compensate for the mean-spirited nature of the Chateau's birth.

A person with an active imagination might have detected a hint of sadness about the place too, for this reason. Looking at the building for any extended length of time tended to give the onlooker a bit of a headache, for the eye was sent on an exhausting journey back and forth and up and down and across and around the exterior surfaces. The constantly warring design principles and clashing aspects manifested as a mess of angles, lines and perspectives that spoke a great deal about the mind of the man who originally conceived of them. A busy mind. An ambitious mind. A mind obsessed with wealth and the appearance of such. A mind that was educated, but unable to apply any of the lessons history sees fit to teach some of us: humility. Moderation. Restraint. Clarity.

'It's certainly big, Joan,' the old lady's companion agreed, sounding impressed. She, like her friend, was a little hard of hearing, and spoke too loudly to compensate for it.

'But it ain't as pretty as Biltmore, Mary. Kind of... second rate by comparison, don't you think?'

Mary nodded. 'Second rate, yeah. Still. Must take a whole army to run this place. You'd think they'd answer the door faster, though. I'm too old to stand around all day like this waitin' on other people.'

Noah, upon hearing this exchange, took a very deliberate step back to increase the distance between himself and the two women, turning his music up to drown out their high, insistent voices. Trance leaked from around the edges of his leatherette earpads, a tinny and irritating noise like a persistent mosquito that couldn't be swatted away.

The boy's mother frowned, leaned over and gently poked her son in the ribs, mouthing: 'You'll go deaf if you play that too loud.'

Noah scowled harder and shrugged her off, jamming his hands deep into his pockets and returning to his furious study of the ground.

His mother sighed. 'We *have* been out here a while,' she said to no one in particular, glancing at her watch. 'The tour office said nine o'clock sharp.'

'Why don't we ask that gardener?' An older gentleman wearing a bow tie said.

The group looked down the drive to where a young, broad-shouldered man clad in brown pants and old-fashioned braces was pulling weeds from a flower border that ran parallel to the drive. He had his back turned to them, and his once white shirt clung to it, soaked in creeping patches of sweat.

'Was he there before, Joan?' Mary asked, squinting in confusion.

'I don't remember seeing him when we walked up,' Noah's mother replied.

'Does it matter? I'm tired of waitin' around,' Joan said, irritably. She called out to the gardener, flapping her hands to get his attention.

'Hey there! Yoo hoo!'

'I don't think we should be bothering him,' Noah's mother said, uneasily. 'He looks busy.'

'Pshaw, he works for the house, don't he? It's his job to be bothered. Hey there! *Yoo!*'

The man paused in his work as the old woman's cries reached him, but he did not turn around. He simply knelt in the border, his tanned arm frozen in the act of yanking out an errant creeper.

'Hey! You deaf, young man?' Joan goaded.

Noah took another step back, glaring at her in disgust.

The Gardener continued to ignore them, and went back to his weeding, unperturbed.

'Well, *that's* rude,' Mary declared, and Joan sucked at her gums again.

'Maybe he didn't hear you,' Noah's mother said.

'Oh he heard me alright,' Joan snapped, and the old woman's face told a story of someone who was about to march on over there and dole out a piece of her mind.

Before she could do so, there was movement from within the house.

Sounds rang out from behind the thick wood of the massive front doors: a series of large iron bolts being dragged back into their sockets. A jangling noise followed, the unmistakable clunk of a large metal key slotting into a huge iron lock and turning. The tour group perked up—with the exception of Noah—and shifted back onto their heels as they waited for the doors to open.

After a prolonged and noisy interlude, followed by a pause, followed by another sequence of clicks and clunks and mechanisms sliding back and forth, the heavy oak portals finally swung wide.

The group held their breaths and peered inwards, curious.

And found the space behind the doorway filled by a tall, shadowy, indistinct figure.

Mary and Joan gazed up at it, unable to make out a face or anything much in the dense gloom of the Chateau's interior.

There was a further pause, during which the guests realized their pulses were beating rather fast, and then:

'Welcome, ladies and gentlemen, to the Sunshire Chateau.'

The shadowy figure stepped forward into the dull light of day, and the group found themselves looking up at a statuesque man who was aged somewhere in his late fifties, slender, immaculately dressed, with a neatly trimmed beard, a glossy head of dark hair and thick, straight brows that hung low over his eyes. From his belt, a giant mass of keys hung, and a faint jingling accompanied his movements. Pinned to his lapel was a shiny brass badge with two words engraved on it in capital letters: TOUR GUIDE.

'Well,' said Joan as she gathered herself quickly. 'Took ya long enough, dearie.'

The Tour Guide looked down his long nose at the old woman and grinned, switching his smile on like he was flicking on a light switch.

'Actually, madam,' he replied smoothly, checking an expensive looking watch strapped to his left wrist, 'It would appear that I am early, having opened the door thirty seconds before time, if we are being precise.'

Noah's mother looked at her own watch, frowning.

'Excuse me,' she said, in her quiet, breathy voice. 'But that's not right. It's nine thirty-five, by my watch.' She blushed after speaking, for she did not like to be a nuisance.

The Tour Guide flicked off his smile, glancing back at his own timepiece.

Then, he changed the subject.

'Is this everyone?' He asked, turning his attention to the rest of the group.

Noah's mother went slowly red as she realized she had been snubbed.

The Guide, oblivious to her discomfort, scanned each person in the group quickly in turn, processing those assembled and filing their faces away in his memory. 'I trust you all have your tickets to hand?'

Silently, each person in the group held up a yellow paper ticket with a crudely rendered image of the Chateau stamped on it in red ink, and the Tour Guide nodded.

'Very good, very good. In that case, it is my pleasure to welcome you all to the Sunshire Chateau, ancestral home of the Lester family these past many years.

Sometimes jokingly referred to as the *Sunshine* Chateau, because the trees, you see—they block the sun out almost completely.'

The Tour Guide waited for laughter. When none was forthcoming, he cleared his throat.

'I suppose it *is* a poor joke,' he continued, a note of bitterness in his voice, 'But it persists. As do the trees, which seem to get larger by the day. This particular variety is called *Thuja plicata*, otherwise known as the Pacific red cedar, or the giant cedar.'

Noah, bored already, turned away from the Guide to stare back down the driveway longingly. Maybe he could just slip away, without anyone noticing. *It's not like anyone would miss me much if I was gone,* he thought, and with that realization, his mood plummeted, sharply.

His eyes, which were suddenly scratchy and sore, lit upon the gardener, still busily yanking out weeds and vines with scarred arms that were heavily corded with muscle. The man heaved the unwanted plants out of the ground with methodical determination, shook the soil off the roots, and pressed them down into a large burlap sack, repeating this action over and over. Noah found himself watching intently, feeling his cheeks grow hot as he did so.

The gardener, perhaps sensing that he was being watched, stiffened slightly. His head turned, just a fraction. Noah flicked his gaze away, terrified he would be caught staring. Then, unable to help himself, he lowered his head and covertly peeked at the gardener again from beneath the shelter of his hood.

The man in the sweat-stained shirt had gone. Vanished, in a split second.

He was, impossibly, nowhere to be seen.

Noah blinked.

'This variety of tree can reach heights of up to two hundred and thirty feet, with trunks up to twenty feet in diameter,' the Guide said as Noah, confused, scanned the shaded drive back and forth, back and forth, wondering if the gardener was shy, had ducked down, or was hiding somewhere. He found no trace of movement, no glimpse of anything except trees, shrubs, gravel, and an abandoned burlap sack filled with weeds.

Huh, he thought, his mouth suddenly dry.

'Rather an impractical choice for so many of them to be planted so close to the Chateau,' the Guide continued, 'But here we are. I confess: it *can* feel a little like living in a cave, at times.'

'You live here?' Noah's mother asked, trying to redeem herself.

The Tour Guide hesitated before answering.

'Only as far as any man can ever truly live anywhere,' he replied, eventually.

'Oh,' Noah's mother said, bewildered yet unfailingly polite.

The rest of the group looked up at the trees solemnly, except for Noah, who jammed the toe of his left boot into the sand of the driveway over and over again in time to his music, which he had turned up louder still. The Tour Guide noted this, cataloguing it in his sharp, partitioned brain, and carried on smoothly.

'Still, it's not all bad. The lack of light is one of the reasons the antiquities inside the Chateau are so well preserved. We don't have to worry about harmful sun rays and ultraviolet light bleaching our delicate items. No small thing, for as you will see throughout the course of this tour: there are riches indeed to be admired within these walls.'

'Or there will be if you actually let us *inside* the darn house,' grumbled Mary.

The Tour Guide flipped his smile on once again, letting it stay on his face for thirty seconds, no more, no less, before it snapped off.

'Quite. Shall we?' He said, eyes hard as he stared at Mary like prey.

'Thought you'd never ask,' came the sarcastic reply. Mary was too old to be much bothered by the rudeness of others.

The Guide moved aside smoothly to let the tour group pass. One by one, they slowly filtered in through the front doors and were swallowed by the cavernous recesses of the house.

Noah, who was at the back of the group and therefore last to enter, threw one final long look over his shoulder at the spot where the gardener had stood only moments before. Still nothing.

Whatever, he thought, shrugging. He dragged his feet over the large stone doorstep and disappeared from view.

The Tour Guide stood alone for a moment, breathing in the cedar-scented air. He did not go outside often, and when he did, it felt strange to him, as if the air in The Outside were not as real and as sustaining as the air inside the Chateau. He knew this was absurd, but it remained the truth: he had grown too accustomed to his prison.

'Another day, another tour,' he said to himself, quietly.

Slight movement in the flower borders next to the driveway led his gaze to the familiar, sweat-stained figure of the Gardener, who had popped up suddenly out of the ground itself, it seemed, like a mushroom—something the Guide was used to, for he knew the other man was shy. The Guide watched him work for a moment. It felt as if the man had been weeding that particular patch of soil for all eternity, and maybe he had. The Guide considered waving. Then he remembered it was beneath him, and clenched his loose hands into tight fists.

He went back inside, dragging the doors shut behind him.

INSIDE

Once inside, the guests, who found themselves in a cavernous, quiet reception hall, clustered together like timid children as they stared up in collective awe at a pair of vast, spiraling twin staircases that dominated the entryway. Carved from mahogany, polished to a brilliant, chestnut gleam, the handrails were detailed imitations of pythons, complete with scales. The oiled snakes wound up lazily from the ground to the hidden recesses of the Chateau's roof, blunt, predatory heads at the bottom, tail-tips at the top, overlapping plates glinting in the light of an enormous electric chandelier that hung between each staircase.

'Well would you look at that,' an expensively dressed man with a thick Baltimore accent said, removing his branded baseball cap and scratching his head in wonder.

The Tour Guide was pleased with this reaction. His voice took on a different quality now that he was inside, a resonant quality, like the lingering echo of a cello in a concert hall.

'Yes, it is very tempting to let the eye rest on those staircases, isn't it? Reticulated pythons, in case you're wondering. But, as exciting as the bannisters are, I must encourage you to redirect your gaze to the floor, first.'

As one, the assembled tourists looked down at the highly polished surface under their feet.

'What am I supposed to be looking at?' Mary grumbled, removing her glasses and wiping them with a dirty handkerchief.

The Guide stiffened. A tiny note of ice crept into his voice.

'What you are looking at is, in fact, a tour de force of interior decoration and craftsmanship.'

'Jest looks like a shiny marble floor to me.'

The Tour Guide grew more brittle, and his voice grew cooler by a few degrees more.

'You see,' he said, intent on making his point, 'The space where we are standing now, formally known as the Reception Hall, is floored entirely in white statuario marble.'

A general silence betrayed that not a single soul present quite understood the significance of white statuario marble. The Tour Guide registered this and grew stiffer still with indignity.

'White statuario marble is one of the most precious and highly prized marbles in the world, ladies and gentlemen, and so I do hope you will appreciate that, for this reason, and to prevent wear and tear on the woodwork and carpets on the upper floors, we must ask you to kindly remove your shoes before we continue on the tour.'

'Shoes? Did he say remove our *shoes*?' Mary reared back, horrified.

'He did, Mary, he did!' Joan tutted, and shook her head.

'But it took me damn near ten years to put them on in the first place! I don't bend as easy as I used to, young man!' Mary waggled her finger at the Tour Guide.

'Me either, Mary, me either!' Joan said, in solidarity.

The Tour Guide spoke over the women, calmly ignoring their protests.

'There are alcoves over there to your left for you to place your shoes in, and freshly laundered and sterilized house-slippers on those shelves over there—yes, there—

for you to slip on afterwards. We don't want you getting cold feet, do we? The marble can get *very* chilly.'

'Chilly marble my sweet old wrinkly ass!' Mary spluttered. 'I ain't never heard of such a thing, taking your shoes off on a tour. It's absurd. What's next? Our panties?!'

The Tour Guide raised his voice a little.

'While you are doing this, ladies and gentlemen, I shall deliver some interesting facts about the house. Oh, and another thing—please do *not* lean on the walls while you are removing your shoes. The wallpaper, you see, in this part of the house—it is extremely valuable. It is fabricated from the finest handmade yellow velvet from China.'

The group turned their attention to the wallpaper in question, admiring its rich, pale mustardy color and velvety sheen.

'I've never seen anything like it,' Noah's mother said softly. 'It's beautiful.'

The Tour Guide puffed out his chest as if he had been personally complemented. Noah's mother felt relieved, glad to be back in the Guide's good books.

'It is, isn't it? It was specially manufactured for the Chateau in a remote village near Shaoxing, and its worth is unfathomable to the estate. But fingerprints are extremely damaging to our antiquities. Our fingers and hands are coated with natural oils, salt, dirt and grease, and this, as we have found over the years, does nothing for our wallpaper. So if you need to lean on something while you remove your shoes, you may use the bench we have provided over there, instead of our walls.'

Most of the group shrugged and began to obediently remove their shoes, either using the bench as instructed or leaning on each other to keep themselves steady as they did so.

The two old ladies, however, held their ground.

'I ain't taking off my shoes,' Joan said, folding her arms under her considerable breasts and lifting her chin up high. 'I don't care how old or how special the darn marble is. They're perfectly clean, they don't even have sharp heels on 'em, look!'

'I'm with her,' Mary agreed, nodding her head so fast that the jowls under her chin went into a wobbling frenzy.

'Well then ladies,' the Tour Guide said, striding back across to the now closed front doors and throwing them wide once again. 'I regret to inform you that here at Sunshire, we have rules. And I'm afraid that if you cannot respect those rules, I shall have to ask you to leave.'

'Oh no you don't!' Joan hissed back, venomously. 'That's discrimination! Pure and simple! It's...what is it, Mary? What's the word?'

'Ageism,' Mary confirmed. 'You should be *ashamed* of yourself.'

'Rules are rules, I'm afraid, regardless of age and mobility. No slippers, no tour. You can take it, or leave it.'

'I ain't taking off my shoes!' Joan repeated, firmly.

'Nor am I!' Mary said, although she looked suddenly a little less convinced than her friend did.

The Tour Guide stood resolute. 'No slippers, no entry.'

The others shifted uncomfortably as the drama unfolded. Joan sensed their unease and used it as fuel, puffing herself out and raising her voice further, cranking up the righteous indignation in her tone.

'I'll tell you what you can do with your stupid slippers, you horrible, rude man. You can take them, and shove them up your big long backside, is what you can do!'

'Now, ladies, ladies!' Baltimore, who seemed a reasonable, easy-going type, tried to intervene as the situation escalated. 'I don't think shouting and name-calling is going to help things much, is it? Let's try and remain civil.'

'Oh look, Mary, look at this would you, another man tryin' to tell us what we can and can't do with our mouths and bodies, would you just look at that!'

'Perhaps you could make an exception for them, just this once?' Noah's mother interjected, gently. 'It must be awfully inconvenient to have to change when you're...you're...' She faltered, unsure of how to continue.

'Old?' Mary snapped back.

'No, of course not, I meant...I...'

'Well shit, *yes* it is inconvenient!' Joan jumped in, excitedly. 'No use in sugar-coating it! We *are* old, and this man here is discriminatin' against us!'

The Tour Guide held up his arms abruptly, as if conducting an orchestra. Something about the way he did this, with such force and vehemence, very suddenly changed the atmosphere in the room. Things grew still, and quiet. The women's mouths snapped shut, and the rest of the tour group felt a heavy, sticky sort of inertia land on them as if from nowhere. They watched as the Tour Guide leaned down towards Mary and Joan, bending his long body at the waist so that his eyes were level with theirs despite the marked height difference between them. He spoke then, in a pleasant voice, enunciating every single syllable and drawing out his words in a lyrical, almost musical way. The overall effect was that of a snake-charmer fluting to a basket of unruly cobras.

'Thank you for your visit, ladies,' he said, allowing a full-bodied hatred to seep into his voice. His lips curved and twitched, and something about his face seemed liquid, slippery, somehow, as if his features were trying to figure out how to display themselves. 'It *has* been a pleasure to meet you. A real treat! But as I said, rules are rules, and if you have no intention of following those rules, then I rather think...'

The women waited, unsure of what he was about to say. Eventually, Mary cleared her throat, and said:

'Well? You rather think what?'

The Tour Guide flashed his teeth at her.

'I rather think that it is time for you to both fuck off.'

The tour group gasped. The color drained from the women's faces.

'I...beg your pardon?' Mary, flabbergasted, protested weakly.

'If you would be so kind.' The Tour Guide continued, and Noah, who had turned down his music and was watching this exchange intently, was reminded of a tiger in tall grass, tail switching gently from side to side.

'I don't understand.' Joan's defiance had evaporated.

The Guide leaned forward even further, put his mouth to Joan's ear, and whispered something the others couldn't hear. She flinched like a skittish horse and stared up into the face of the tall, bearded man who calmly unhinged himself, towering above her once again at his full height. Something passed between the two, some message conveyed and received, and Joan turned without another word, and shuffled out of the Sunshire Chateau as fast as her unsteady legs could take her, dragging Mary along roughly behind without looking back even once.

Soon, the sound of two pairs of feet crunching along the sandy driveway echoed back into the Chateau.

The Tour Guide smiled in satisfaction and dry washed his hands together, as if cleansing himself of the women.

'Well,' he said, turning back to the group and raising his eyebrows. 'Where were we, exactly?'

THE MASTER OF THE HOUSE

In the moments that followed, there was a stunned silence as the other guests processed what had just happened.

Then, Noah burst out laughing. He couldn't help himself. The sight of those two old crones getting their marching orders so definitively delighted him from the top of his head to the tips of his toes, and he laughed heartily into the thick quiet of the Reception Hall.

The unexpected expulsion of noise roused the rest of the tour group from their deep stupor, and one by one, they reacted.

'Say, I don't think you can really talk to people like that,' Baltimore stuttered, looking back and forth from the door to the Tour Guide in bewilderment. He had a slipper half-on, half-off his foot, and Noah's mother thought absent-mindedly how boyish this made him look, as if he had suddenly forgotten how to wear shoes, and needed help getting dressed. She shot a look at her own son, now more than capable of dressing himself, and felt a momentary flash of sadness for the helpless boy he had once been. He had needed her, then. He did not allow himself to need her now.

The Tour Guide cut Baltimore off with a raised hand.

'The last time I checked, it was a free country. And tell me you weren't thinking the exact same thing.'

Baltimore went red. 'Well, sure I was, I mean we all were, but I wouldn't have said it *out loud*, you know? You can't just go around cussing at old ladies!'

'Well,' the Tour Guide replied, examining his polished and trimmed fingernails with a graceful air of nonchalance. 'That appears to be your problem, not mine.'

'I agree with him!' The gentleman with the smart bowtie said, his bushy white eyebrows knitted together in outrage. 'You shouldn't talk to anyone like that, let alone seniors!'

'Swearing at an old woman because she won't take her shoes off!'

'Disgusting!'

'Unconscionable!'

The Tour Guide, now visibly irritated once again, clapped his hands. The noise belted out like a thunderclap, cutting the babble of protest in half. Silence reclaimed the room.

'Please continue putting on your slippers,' he said, as if nothing at all had happened.

And they all did, obediently, like well-trained dogs. Even Noah, who never did as he was told. He had secretly begun to crush quite hard on the Tour Guide, finding the older man's utter contempt for the rest of those present quite irresistible. He treated them like peasants, the lowest of the low in a bizarre sort of feudal system, and Noah found that incredibly appealing.

Noah wanted to be a king too, in his own way.

'Where was I? Oh, yes, that's right.' The Tour Guide straightened his badge on his lapel. 'I've been doing this for so long now, and yet I always lose my place at exactly this point. Senility beckons, I fear.'

'You're not the only one,' Baltimore muttered, staring after the two old ladies who could still be seen scurrying along the driveway, clinging to each other tightly as they went. Was it his imagination, or was one of them weeping? He thought he could hear something like crying, faint as it was. He also realized the gardener was nowhere to be seen, although his tools were laid out in the border next to the drive.

The Tour Guide ignored Baltimore and went back to his pre-prepared patter, clearing his throat first.

'Built by Charles Lester III in 1917, this house, designed by noted architect Frank Lloyd Werner, sits high upon Sunshire hill. From here, before the trees grew so tall, you could see almost all of Lestershire, such as it was back then, now rather spoiled by the ravages of industry, as well as a good swathe of the Quee-hana river valley as it meanders so pleasantly along the southern border of the Sunshire Estate. The estate itself is...*I SAID, NO LEANING ON THE FUCKING WALLPAPER!*'

The group jumped out of their skins as the tall man roared ferociously at Noah's mother. She, too intent on changing her footwear and more than a little rattled by events thus far, had forgotten the 'no leaning on the walls' rule and had been trying to balance herself against the nearest velvety surface whilst pushing a slipper onto her foot.

As the Tour Guide shouted at her, she yanked her hand back from the wall, almost toppling over as her balance shifted, and instantly flushed a deep shade of desperately embarrassed scarlet.

Further murmurs of discontent rippled around the group. Noah, already getting far more out of this tour than he ever could have hoped for, stifled back another laugh.

This did not go unnoticed by his mother, who felt a sharp pinch to her heart.

Sensing the mood, the Tour Guide flipped the switch again. Another smile snapped onto his face.

'Thank you,' he said. 'Do try to remember the rules, if it isn't too much trouble?'

Noah's mother nodded and went back to her slippers, shaken but too proud to make a show of it.

'Sorry,' she mumbled. Baltimore, who was wondering why the woman's husband had not spoken up in her defense, shot her a sympathetic smile. This made her flush an even darker shade of red, and they both looked away from each other awkwardly.

The Tour Guide noted her apology, and seemed a little mollified.

'Oh, please, try not to be offended. I did warn you. This house is brimming with riches, and it is my job to protect them from the clumsy advances of the general public to the very best of my ability. Just remember to keep your hands to yourselves, and follow my instructions to the very letter, and we shall all get along just fine.'

Noah's mother nodded. So did everyone else.

'Now, as I was saying.' The Tour Guide went back to his patter with the performative professionalism of a stand-up comedian used to being heckled on stage.

'The Sunshire Chateau was built in 1917, a curious year to choose to build a mansion, as by then, the First World War was well underway. The United States became actively involved in the war in April 1917. Construction on Sunshire started in *February* of 1917, and there is much speculation over whether Lester exploited his connections in high places and bribed the war department to allow him to keep his builders on site until the house was finished, rather than letting them be conscripted overseas to fight. Once the house was completed in late November—an astonishingly fast build time for a structure of this size and complexity—many of the workmen and artisans who crafted these incredible spaces around you then went on to die in the trenches and on the front lines, violently and without dignity, for such is war. Maybe this sombre history accounts for some of the rumors surrounding the Chateau today, rumors of ghostly figures in uniform who walk through the walls after dark. I have personally never encountered any soldiers myself, but then, it *is* a large house. Perhaps I just haven't been in the right place at the right time.'

Another humorless flash of white, straight teeth.

'Do you believe in ghosts?' Noah asked, surprising himself. His mother looked at him in shock. It was the first full sentence he had uttered all day.

The Guide examined Noah, an inscrutable expression on his face. Then, he smoothly moved the conversation on, as if the boy had never spoken at all.

'Is everyone slippered up?'

There was a quiet wave of shuffling feet to the affirmative. Noah, angered at being ignored, turned his music up to the maximum volume possible, and stewed in it.

'Excellent.' The Tour Guide pointed to a wall on the far side of the hall. 'Then let's begin with that portrait over there, shall we? Follow me'.

The group shuffled across the Reception Hall in their soft-slippered feet, making a rush of *swoosh-swoosh* noises on the polished, fabulously expensive marble. Noah, now nursing his bad mood like a hangover, noted that the Tour Guide himself was not wearing slippers. Simultaneously admiring and feeling piqued by this hypocrisy, he decided to keep his mouth shut about it.

For now.

The tourists came to a stop in front of a larger than life framed oil painting that was a portrait of a stern, tall man in his mid to late sixties who stood at three-quarters to the front, gazing into the middle distance with an expression of determination and pride and what could only be described as unadulterated confidence in himself and his place in the world. He was handsome, and held himself with a forced and somewhat regal bearing, the overall effect being stiffly formal and robotic, as if he were a statue merely playing at being a man. He clutched a long, black walking cane before him, the handle of which was fashioned out of ivory, and a pair of leather gloves were tucked awkwardly under the pit of his arm. Bright yellow cufflinks gleamed on his wrists.

'Ah, here he is. Charles Lester III himself.' The Tour Guide—who looked a little like the man in the painting, Noah realized—bowed, folding himself in half from the middle again like a door hinge. It was unclear if this was an ironic gesture or not, for there was a peculiar expression upon the Guide's face as he straightened up after his bow. For a brief second, the man gently cupped his hand and held his palm to the back of his head, checking for something. Then he caught himself, letting his hand drop down.

'A handsome fellow, if you can move beyond the rather cruel expression on his face, don't you think?' Bow-tie said, coquettishly. The older man seemed rather taken with the portrait, and fiddled restlessly with the collar of his shirt as he spoke, subconsciously checking his own appearance as he looked up at Lester.

'Kinda looks like he has a stick up his ass, if you ask me,' Baltimore replied.

'Was he really that tall? In real life, I mean.' Noah's mother fanned herself suddenly with her ticket.

'He was indeed an unusually tall man,' the Tour Guide confirmed. 'He measured up at over six foot five inches in his prime although, like most of us, he shrank as he grew older. He was down to six foot three at the time of his unexpected death—or so his wife wrote, in a letter to her sister.'

'Oh,' said the mother, absentmindedly, and Noah's father, who had thus far remained aloof from the tour, seemed to wake up a little. He frowned at her.

'Jesus, Barbara,' he muttered. 'Don't tie your panties in a knot over the dead industrialist.'

Barbara, who sometimes forgot that she had her own name beyond 'Noah's mother,' or 'Don's wife', blushed.

'Shhh, Don. People will hear you,' she said, feeling like a child.

Noah made a disgusted face. He hated the way his parents spoke to each other.

'And who is that?' Bow-tie pointed to another portrait, similarly sized, framed in a matching gilt surround, which hung next to the first. This was of a woman, and it was clearly painted by the same artist, although the lighting and pose portrayed a much softer personality in what felt like a deliberate attempt to highlight the contrast of character between subjects. The woman was seated, her shoulders rounded and angled towards the front. Her hands were hidden beneath a fur stole, as if she were cold, and her head was dipped forward slightly, in a gesture of humility. She smiled out of the painting with a tired, wan expression on her face. Streaks of gray hair winged out from her temples- she was older than her youthful complexion betrayed. A heavy pearl necklace ornamented with a red garnet pendant, that was more of a collar than an accessory, hung around her neck.

'That is Rose Lester,' the Tour Guide replied, so quietly he could barely be heard. 'Charles Lester III's wife. She inherited the estate after his death.'

Barbara considered the woman, wondering what it would be like to outlive one's spouse. Peaceful, she imagined. As she stood examining the portrait, taking in the careworn expression, the submissive posture, the tired eyes that had seen too much, an intrusive thought popped into her head. They did that, sometimes. She could be engaged in the most menial of tasks, mind in the safe, dull, automatic state it so often was, and then pop! The thought would leap out: *what if,* it would whisper, *what if you took that bread knife over on the kitchen counter, and dragged it across your wrist? What would that feel like? You're not going to do it, of course, we all know you don't have the gumption for suicide, but what if?*

This thought was different, though. This thought was not a remote, curious, blank thought like the others were. This thought was about Don.

Imagine if Don were dead, it said. *Just imagine the freedom you would have.*

Barbara ripped her gaze away from the painting and massaged the back of her neck, slowly. The thought would go away in a moment, or two, they usually did. She just had to ride it out, distract herself.

She tried to focus on what the Tour Guide was saying.

'For anyone who is not from around here, and therefore not acquainted with our local history, Charles Lester III was a wealthy landowner, farmer, and investor most famously known for his cigar factories. If you look over there in that cabinet hanging on the wall, you'll see some cigar molds salvaged from Lester's first operational factory. A nice little piece of memorabilia from a time when smoking was not considered the filthy habit it is today. Cigars used to be big business in America, and by 1895 there were reportedly around forty-two *thousand* cigar factories across the country. Lester took full advantage of this boom to cement his status as one of the wealthiest men in the state at the time.'

A bookish-looking woman wearing thick horn-rimmed spectacles and a bright green dress who stood at the back of the group and had, until now, purposely avoided drawing anyone's attention, snorted, cleared her throat, and spoke up.

'I bet he did,' she said in a voice steeped in sarcasm.

The Tour Guide blinked.

'I'm sorry?'

'Commercial tobacco production in America was founded on the blood and sweat of slave labor, an uncomfortable fact that most people leave out of these sorts of tours, I find.'

The Tour Guide's face suddenly resembled the polished statuario marble beneath his unslippered feet. Undeterred, the woman kept talking.

'Slavery kept costs down and profits high, so no wonder there were so many factories in existence across America at that time. I'm pretty sure old Charlie Lester up there was well-acquainted with that, even if he was born too late to have profited directly. I imagine by the time he came into his wealth, he was cooking with Cuban leaf imports, but the point stands.'

'The point?' The Tour Guide ventured, smoothly.

'This house was built with blood,' the woman replied, quietly.

The Guide stared at her, unblinking. Then he said:

'By your logic, most of America was built with blood, in that case.'

The woman remained silent, considering him.

The Guide took a moment to gather himself. It became obvious to all that a rule had been broken, a canon law carved in stone:

Never insult the house.

'You seem to know a lot about this particular topic,' the Guide continued eventually. A single vein popped on his forehead, and the woman in the green dress saw this, clocked it as a small victory.

The first of many, she hoped.

'Of course. I'm a historian,' she said out loud, cheerfully. 'I make it my mission to know a lot.'

The Guide stared with naked dislike as the woman calmly folded her own hands in front of her, twiddling her thumbs and smiling to herself. She seemed happy to have made ripples in his calm exterior.

'Do you have a name?' He questioned, languidly.

'My name is Linda Louise,' she replied. 'And yours is Mr. Tour Guide, apparently.'

He scrutinized her for a moment longer, his thoughts unreadable on his long, pale face, and then, as was his way, he smoothly pretended that the woman had never spoken up in the first place, erasure being the most powerful weapon he could lay his hands on at that precise moment in time.

'Yes, forty-two *thousand*,' he intoned solemnly, returning to his scripted lines, and the rest of the group let out a breath they didn't know they had been holding. Linda Louise, who was used to being ignored by men who felt threatened by her, was completely unfazed by his rudeness. She stopped twiddling her thumbs, and pushed her glasses further up the bridge of her nose.

'Cigar makers were so profuse back then, they had their own union. These days, cigar manufacturers are rarer, but there is still one of Lester's factories in existence and operational down in town, and I do urge you, if you like that sort of thing, to drop by and try a smoke if you have time after this tour.'

'Say, how long *is* the tour, exactly?' Baltimore asked. He was beginning to regret his decision to take part in what was turning out, in his estimation, to be a history lesson wrapped up in a soap opera. 'I gotta meeting in town at three.'

'I don't understand,' the Tour Guide replied, and for once, he was not being facetious.

'Well- how long is the tour? One hour? Two? Not three, surely!'

The Tour Guide lifted his chin. 'It will take as long as it takes. These things generally do.'

Baltimore shrugged, not getting it. 'Ballpark?'

The Tour Guide tapped his left shoe against the marble, *rap, rap, rap*. 'There *is* no ballpark, not at the Sunshire Chateau. We will finish the tour when the house decides. Not before, or after.'

'But...that doesn't make any sense.'

Linda Louise snorted again. 'Not the biggest problem we've got going on here, if you ask me.'

The Tour Guide smiled, and the conversation, like so many others, was over.

'How did he die?' Bow-tie asked, suddenly. He was still staring at the portrait of Charles Lester III with misty eyes.

'Die?' The Tour Guide grew still, which seemed to happen whenever he did not like the particular question he was fielding.

'Yes. You said 'unexpected death' earlier. So how did he die?'

'Ah. Well.' The Tour Guide let his own eyes linger on the portrait again. 'The commonly accepted theory is that he took his own life with a straight-razor in the bathtub one evening after a series of poor financial decisions led him to the brink of bankruptcy. His poor, devastated widow had him buried in town, in a small plot of land that later became Valleyview Cemetery, right in the middle, pride of place. Spent thousands on his memorial, and on getting various buildings and streets around town renamed in his honor. She never got over his death, apparently. Even had his suicide note framed. It hangs to this day in her bedroom.'

'Oh, is that part of the tour?' Bow-tie asked, grinning ghoulishly. 'I do *love* a good tragedy.'

'No,' the Guide replied, flatly.

'I heard another story,' Linda Louise interjected. 'I heard he just up and vanished one day, without warning, and was never seen or heard from again. I heard the wife was suspected of being involved, at one point.'

'Did you. How interesting,' the Guide replied, coldly.

'There is a petition to exhume his body, you know. Find out if whoever is buried in the cemetery is really him or not. Some distant relative suspects foul play, all these years later. There was a piece in the local paper about it last week. DNA profiling is a marvelous thing, right?' Linda Louise twirled a long strand of dark hair around her index finger innocently, examining the ends.

The Guide straightened his back, and stood very tall.

'Rose Lester was a good, honest woman.' The words came out harsh and hard. Linda Louise, it seemed, had touched a nerve. 'We don't speak badly of her, not in this house. Are we clear on that?'

'Perfectly,' Linda Louise replied. She did not sound contrite.

There was a moment's silence, broken by the uneasy shuffling of the guests' feet as they waited to see what would happen next.

'We have dawdled here long enough," the Guide said eventually, in a tone so loaded and poisonous it almost made the visitor's eyes water. 'Shall we move on?'

'Yes please,' Bow-tie did not like conflict. Barbara nodded in agreement.

'Now, if anyone needs to visit the bathroom before we set off, ask and I'll point you in the right direction, because there won't be another opportunity for quite some time. Anyone?'

Silence held court, and the Tour Guide shrugged.

'Suit yourselves. Follow me, then, and remember: keep together, and no dawdling. We wouldn't want you getting lost now, would we? The last tourist we misplaced, well...let's just say the Chateau had quite a bit of fun with them before it let them go. There are almost three miles of secret passages, tunnels, hidey-holes and corridors in this house, so when you get lost, you get *lost*, if you take my meaning. Is everyone clear on that?'

The group nodded their heads. The Guide, who looked suddenly tired, cricked his neck on one side, and then the other, a slow, deliberate series of movements that made distinct and unsettling crunching noises as his cartilage popped.

'Do keep up, and watch your step,' he concluded, turning smartly on his heel. 'The floors are rather uneven in places. Ready? Good. First stop- the Blue Room.'

And with that, the tour group moved off into the shadows of the Chateau.

Behind them, unnoticed, the heavy front doors of the house once again swung shut, slowly, seemingly of their own accord.

Anyone glancing out before they did so might have noticed the indistinct, motionless shadow of the gardener, standing amongst the weeds once more, his face, a blurred mess devoid of features, turned to the house, watching as the Chateau, and those that dwelt within, received its new guests eagerly.

THE BLUE ROOM

JUST NED

The Blue Room was artfully positioned so that any visitor to Sunshire had no choice but to notice it almost as soon as they left the Reception Hall.

Situated to the left of a long cloister that ran directly from the space between the giant python staircases in the Hall to the guts of the house itself, the door to the Blue Room was the first door open to the tour party as they shuffled along in their freshly laundered slippers, only half-listening to the Tour Guide's polished patter. As a bright glow of cerulean blue light gradually made itself known to them, a chorus of gasps and murmurs drowned that patter out almost completely.

'What is that?' Barbara said, girlishly excited by the bright glow. Baltimore, who kept sneaking looks at the woman when her husband's back was turned, thought how pretty she looked bathed in blue. He smiled at her, unable to disguise his attraction, but his timing was off. Don, who tried not to pay much attention to his wife until someone else did, caught the smile, squared his shoulders and moved to block her from view. He threw Baltimore a dirty look, and the other man shrugged, half-apologetic, half not.

'That is the Blue Room.' The Guide stepped back to allow the others to gawp.

The group crowded around the open doorway, their whispers filling the cloister from floor to ceiling. The Tour Guide soaked in their admiration for a moment. Despite everything, he remained proud of the Sunshire Chateau, even though he also hated it to his very core.

'It's so...so...*blue*,' Bow-tie said, impressed.

The Guide allowed himself a dry chuckle.

'Most of the rooms in the Chateau were built for the express purpose of impressing those who gazed upon them, rather than with any practical living requirements in mind such as comfort, space, light, or warmth. But the Blue Room in particular *is* possessed of a degree of ostentatious glamour that brooks no refusal when it comes to stopping and admiring it, I'll allow. It's why it always features as the first room on the tour.'

'Well,' Bow-tie said, blowing out his cheeks emphatically. 'I'm speechless.'

'Saying "I'm speechless" out loud in this context is something of a contradiction in terms, don't you think?' Linda Louise teased.

Bow-tie snorted in amusement.

'Okay, okay, you got me. Smarty-pants.'

Linda Louise laughed, and the noise carried.

'It's ugly,' Noah said out loud, suddenly annoyed at the good-natured banter.

His mother, shocked, poked him sharply in the back. 'Noah!' She said, and her voice was a politely constrained warning. 'Don't be rude.'

'Just saying. It is. Ugly.'

'Who is that man?' Baltimore asked, hurriedly trying to avoid another scene. He pointed into the room.

The Tour Guide, who had been glaring daggers at Noah, roused himself reluctantly. Easily a head and a half taller than the rest of the group, he peered over the top of Baltimore's baseball cap to where Bow-tie gestured.

His lip curled derisively when he saw.

'Oh, him?'

'Yeah.'

'That's just Ned,' the Tour Guide replied, dismissively, and Baltimore, who was getting tired of the Tour Guide's tricky ways, was none the wiser.

BOOKIE

In Ned's opinion, the Blue Room should have been called the Blue Glazed Room, because that was exactly what it was: a large, four-sided recreational room without windows, the walls of which were coated from floor to ceiling with a deep, azure blue ceramic glaze. Not glazed tiles. Not tile-effect wallpaper, or small patches of glazing here and there. No, this was the entire wall-space, every surface, from the ground up, fully glazed. Like a donut or a cake coated in icing. There was a name for that, wasn't there? *Mirror-glaze.* The words tugged at him. His fiancée Jo had been a pastry chef. She had broken his heart, but not before she'd fed him up nicely. He still had a hard time fitting into his best pants. The Blue Room reminded Ned of one of her confectionaries—brightly colored, a feast for the eyes, a saccharine, sugary space that was so over the top in its ambition and self-importance that it left him feeling a little nauseous if he spent too long in it.

It didn't help that the lighting was terrible. A lack of any windows meant a lack of any natural lighting, and the large, circular, stained-glass hanging lantern fixed to the ceiling did not throw out enough of a shine for him to work properly in. Ned was forced to use the flashlight on his cellphone and prop it up against a stack of books to illuminate his workspace better. It was about the only thing the cellphone was good for in the Blue Room, because the space was a communications dead zone, which made him resent using his battery power up on the flashlight function slightly less.

When Ned had first arrived in the Blue Room, he had not been overly concerned with the practicalities or lack thereof inherent in the decor. He had instead been blown away by the sheer scale of ambition the room represented. This was a sentiment that applied to the Chateau entire, for the whole building seemed to be an exercise in mind over matter when it came to architectural constraints. As if the brain behind the property had decided the usual rules of construction need not apply, not here. The Blue Room was a perfect example of this. Mind over matter, and style over practicality. As far as Ned knew, an entirely glazed room had never been done in a house before or since, and he could see why: ceramic glazing did not make for effective wall insulation. The room was constantly sweating, something he didn't appreciate fully until he had been in it for a while. Fully-glazed, non-porous wall surfaces left the Blue Room no space or ability to breathe, and this meant that in the summer, every surface—the shelving, the couches by the fireplace, the desk, the floor, even the wooden globe that stood in one corner—was covered in beads of condensation. His clothes always felt damp at the end of the day, damp and cold and clammy, and he could not wait to strip them off and shower when he got home.

During the winter, as he was informed by the Tour Guide, this condensation often froze. The house was not heated with a modern central heating system, only old-fashioned oil heaters or open fireplaces which were rarely lit because the chimneys hadn't been swept for some considerable time, and the extreme temperature fluctuations that marked the changing of seasons meant that the ceramic glazing coating the Blue Room was cracked and fractured as the winter cold made short work of the delicate material it penetrated. The resulting effect was that of a million deep blue spider-webs crawling across the walls, a frenzy of lines and patterns and threads spreading like a network of interlocking veins.

It was also a terrible place in which to store books, which was why he was there.

'So, who *is* that man?'

Ned jumped and groaned inwardly as a thick Baltimore accent broke his concentration, hissing the question at what the speaker imagined was a discreet volume. It wasn't. The harsh whisper hung in the air like an unwanted fly hovering over a fruit bowl, and Ned became aware of movement, of other voices, of shuffling feet behind him.

Another damn tour party, he thought, his brows beetling in annoyance.

He hunched his shoulders, refusing to turn around and engage. For one thing, he knew the Tour Guide would be with them, and the Tour Guide gave Ned the creeps like no-one else. He couldn't say why, exactly. The dapper, smooth-talking older man had been nothing but courteous to Ned ever since he had started working at Sunshire, but there was something in the set of his smile that Ned distrusted, a smile that appeared and disappeared too abruptly, as if only summoned for a purpose, rather than being a true expression of enjoyment or camaraderie.

'Ned is new here. He is our resident Antique Book Specialist and Conservator.' That was the Guide, and his tone was one that Ned was familiar with.

Baltimore snorted, but sounded intrigued. 'Bit of a mouthful, ain't it? As job titles go.'

'That's why we affectionately call him our 'Bookie',' the Tour Guide said.

At this, Ned broke his resolve, turned, and shot the Guide an incredulous glance over his shoulder.

Bookie? His look said. *Since when?*

The Tour Guide ignored him, peering instead over the heads of the tourists and into the Blue Room, scanning it quickly as if looking for something, nodding to himself in satisfaction on finding all as it should be, and gesturing to Ned, who had no choice but to nod and wave a hand in reluctant acknowledgment. The gaggle of assorted visitors waved back, cheerily.

'Ned is hard at work, as you can see, so we won't linger too long here, else we'll make the poor fellow self-conscious.'

'What is he doing?' A teenager standing out front said. If Ned had to place money on it, he would have put him at about fourteen or fifteen years old, maybe. His voice was mid-way through the process of breaking, and pitched and wobbled as he spoke. Ned remembered that phase. Being a teenage boy was a terrible thing, at times, a marathon of physical embarrassments.

'Well, Noah, the Sunshire Chateau is currently home to over thirteen thousand antique cloth, custom leather and calf-bound books of varying ages and importance, and they need a certain amount of love, attention and care to keep them from decaying or being eaten by parasites. Our esteemed Bookie over there has been tasked with individually cleaning and restoring every single tome and volume in this grand, if damp, old house. A rather thankless task, if you ask me, because by the time he's finished, he'll have to start all over again, poor man, ha ha. But, someone has to do it, and that someone appears to be Ned. Isn't he lucky?'

Ned gritted his teeth. The sheer number of passive aggressive digs in the Tour Guide's little introductory speech made his head hurt.

'Thirteen *thousand* books?' This was a woman standing behind Noah—his mother, most likely. Her manner was soft, timid, and rather nice.

'Give or take.'

'Yikes.' Another man in a bow-tie said, scratching a patch of dry skin on his elbow.

'Quite. As I told you, cigars were big business, and Charles Lester III was all about big business. But, I'll let you in on a little secret.'

So much for not lingering, Ned thought.

'What is less commonly known is that Charles Lester III did not actually make the majority of his fortune from cigar factories. He made it from lending the United States government considerably large sums of money—money he inherited upon marrying his wife. Rose Lester.'

A black woman wearing a bright green dress and large, stylish spectacles rolled her eyes, but said nothing.

'In 1917 federal government expenditure far outweighed its income, and financing our part in the exorbitantly expensive First World War happened in one of three ways: raising taxes, borrowing from the public, and printing extra money. Lester, who always had an eye for an investment opportunity, saw his chance and took it, loaning out enormous sums of cash and then charging the government even more enormous amounts of interest for the pleasure.'

'He was a war profiteer?' Bow-tie asked, looking shocked.

Figures, thought Ned, interested despite himself. It certainly stacked up with everything else he had learned about Lester during his short tenure at Sunshire.

'Not many people know that,' the Guide confirmed, 'Although Lester was hardly secretive about his dealings. He wasn't shy about his wealth either, building the

Chateau at the absolute peak of his prosperity. He spent the short number of years he lived here filling it with the valuables, collectibles and marvelous objects you'll see today on our tour—like the books Ned is restoring. Lester had a rather impeccable taste in books. I'm not sure he read many of them, but he had a collector's eye.'

Ned couldn't help but agree silently with the Tour Guide. The collection of books at Sunshire Chateau was the finest he had ever seen, if not the most extensive.

'Is it true that Lester hid his fortune in the walls of the house?' Noah asked, nonchalantly.

The Tour Guide paused for a moment, then smiled.

'People do love the idea of buried treasure, don't they?'

'But did he?'

'I suppose it depends on your definition of 'fortune'. One man's treasure is another man's trash, as they say.'

'That's not an answer.' Noah refused to be put off by the Tour Guide's riddles.

'Charles Lester III was many things, young man, but trusting was not one of them. It would not surprise me if, instead of hoarding his wealth in a bank vault like most rich people did, he had, instead, sequestered his fortune away somewhere in this house. It is full of secret spaces, after all, and Lester was clever, devious, and inventive. So sure, why not? Let's say there is treasure in the walls, if it makes you happy.' The Guide's eyes took on a faraway look as he said this, and he absentmindedly touched the back of his head again while Noah watched, fascinated.

Ned listened to this exchange with a growing sense of impatience. How long were they going to stand there, gossiping? Couldn't they see he was trying to work?

The Tour Guide shook himself back to the present moment.

'Now, you may see Ned wandering around from place to place with his canvas bag of tools as we move through the Chateau on our tour. That's because our books are spread out all over the house: the Blue Room, the Map Room, the Library, as you would expect, the Master's Study...even the attic above the east wing. I don't envy him that last one, I must confess. Very dusty, our attics. Haunted, of course. What attic isn't? Poor Ned. I'm sure the ghosts will get used to him, in time.'

Ned flinched as the tour group laughed politely.

'Now, if you're ready, let's move along.'

'Wait a moment- I thought this room was on the tour?' Baltimore protested. 'We can't leave yet, it looks so interesting! It's so...so...'

'Blue?'

The tourists laughed again, a genuine belly-chuckle this time that rippled through each person and made Ned's skin crawl.

'Well, yeah!'

'Oh, we can return here a little later on, don't worry. For now, let's let Ned work in peace, we've disturbed him enough.'

Enough to keep you happy at any rate, you old goat, Ned thought, blackly.

'Come along, remember to keep together, and please refrain from touching anything. The ghosts don't like it when you touch their things. Neither do I.'

With that, the Tour Guide and the group departed, the *woosh-woosh* of their slippered feet quickly fading away down the corridor.

A deep quiet returned to the Blue Room in the wake of their departure. It was both a blessing and a burden to Ned, because on the one hand, he was now alone again, which meant he could focus on his work without distraction.

But on the other hand…

He was alone again.

Or was he?

Probably not.

BOXES

Ned went back to cautiously cleaning and restoring the five hundred and forty-four page first edition of *Great Expectations* in front of him. It was the finest copy he had ever set eyes upon, and the book was, by his own admission, extraordinary in every sense of the word. Bound in full polished calf leather, it had gorgeous gilt triple ruled borders with green and red leather label bands on the spine that nestled amongst a row of three raised bands, in between which, the most incredible, intricate gilt tooling had been worked. Each edge was also gilt, meaning the contours of every page gleamed a rich, dull gold under the light of his cellphone, and the inner dentelles—ornamental tooling that looked a little like lacework—were also worked in gilt. There was hardly any wear to the spine, and not a jot of fading. There wasn't even any foxing on the paper, something that Ned found astonishing given the constantly sweating nature of the Blue Room. It was as if the book itself were immune to the effects of time, physics, and environment, and it excited him deep in his soul, as beautiful things always did.

The fact that this volume was, according to his research, one of only two hundred printed by this particular London based press in 1861, and was littered with a number of typos and rarities that he found endlessly charming as he worked through carefully, page by delicate page, made it all the more exciting, because the value of this artefact—and yes, it was so perfect that it transcended mere 'book' status and went right to hallowed 'artefact' in the museum of his mind—would have been considerable were it ever taken to auction.

He gently massaged leather cream into the cover of the tome, moisturizing the dry binding in its weakest spots and admiring the rich burnished reds and greens of the leather that seemed to wake under his ministrations. He tried to enjoy the process as he worked, but found himself unsettled in the wake of the tour group's departure. The interruption, albeit brief, had left him uneasy. The hairs on the back of his neck bristled, and he found himself holding back a series of involuntary shudders.

The guests had departed, but the sensation of being watched remained.

It was a feeling he was getting far too well acquainted with, working here.

He shifted in his chair, hating having his back to the room, to the door, to anyone who might walk past. It made him feel vulnerable, exposed. Defenseless.

But it was better than sitting the other way around. Something he had learned, from bitter experience, not to do.

Because facing the other way meant facing the Blue Room's ghost.

And Ned could not handle that, not today.

Not after last time.

Ned was, in normal circumstances, a cheerful sort of person with a pleasant disposition. He was well-liked and generally made his way easily through the world. This is not to say he had not had his share of ups and downs over the years, because he had, but Ned was not inclined to let life get the better of him. He was not built that way. Ned was a plodder, a trooper. Ned persevered, despite everything, even when his fiancée had jilted him at the altar. Actually, she had jilted him *before* she had reached the altar, but he could never find a better way to phrase it to those who asked. Regardless, he had tried not to let this catastrophic event affect the course of the rest of his life. He chose to deal with bad experiences as philosophically as he could, knowing that history is not a thing that can be changed just because a person is sad about what has happened to them. *No use crying over spilled milk*, and all that. *What will be, will be,* was his presiding rhetoric.

Or at least he told himself that, and anyone who enquired after his wellbeing, whilst quietly and secretly boxing his emotions away so that he wouldn't actually have to deal with them. There was a shelf in his closed and locked heart full of these boxes, boxes stuffed with memories of him and Jo and other feelings and truths Ned didn't want to face, and this process of compartmentalization, this rigid emotional filing system he maintained, allowed him to function on a daily basis.

I am so very sorry, Ned. I can't, she had said. Not even to his face—she had written a note, a note that he had found. Such a little piece of paper, yet such a large message.

I can't.

Spilled words, like spilled milk.

No use crying over them.

But it was hard for Ned to be that version of himself in the Sunshire Chateau. Something about the place got under his skin, found the hidden shelf in his heart, and began picking at the locks on the boxes. He struggled with himself when he was there. He found himself becoming insular, introspective, and he found that his diligently packaged memories bobbed to the surface stubbornly the longer he spent in the house.

He tried to talk to the Tour Guide about this in the early days of his employment.

'There's an atmosphere here, isn't there?' He'd said, wondering if he was alone in feeling that way. 'Something in the air. Makes it hard to think straight, at times. Know what I mean?'

The Tour Guide, whose real name Ned somehow still didn't know, despite the younger man's best efforts to wheedle it out of him, said nothing. This infuriated Ned, who had never had a problem getting someone to like him before. The Guide, however, remained staunchly impervious to his efforts.

The Tour Guide seemed to double up as an Estate Manager of sorts, when he wasn't conducting tours, and lived on site at Sunshire somewhere, although Ned had no idea which part of the house exactly. The tall man opened the doors wide to Ned each morning, smiling through his neatly clipped, silvery beard, a huge bunch of keys dangling from a large iron loop attached to his belt. Ned wondered that the keys did not drag the man's immaculately pressed pants down with them, but somehow he always managed to look pristine, like a magazine menswear model ready for a shoot.

Ned and the Guide, despite their obvious dislike of each other, had quickly fallen into an intimate daily routine in the short space of time he had been employed by the Sunshire Estate. Ned would arrive at the stroke of eight in the morning and rap on the enormous front door with the heavy brass knocker shaped like a winged harpy that hung at eye-height. This would summon the Guide, who always said the same thing to Ned as he opened up and greeted him:

'Gather ye rosebuds while ye may'.

It was a line from an obscure poem, an unnecessarily intellectual greeting, one designed to put Ned and the Guide on the same level as each other academically, he suspected. It came from a medieval poem by an English clergyman and 'cavalier poet' called Robert Herrick. The poem essentially told the reader to make the most of life before the roses wilted and died, a *carpe diem* school of thought that was popular in the Middle Ages and throughout the civil war in England. Ned knew this because he had spent a considerable period of time restoring an extremely valuable calf-bound collection of Herrick's poems entitled *'Hesperides'* for a Japanese collector who was also a loyal client and friend. Ned wondered if the Guide knew about this, somehow. Otherwise, it seemed like a terribly specific coincidence, his quoting that particular poem every morning upon greeting him.

But quote it he did, day in, day out. 'Gather ye rosebuds,' the Guide would say, and to this, Ned would reply, somewhat wearily, 'Old Time is still a-flying,' and the Guide would grin in almost genuine pleasure, which always gave Ned the impression that the older man was thirsty, no, *starving* for a little intellectual discourse, something Ned could sympathize more with when he heard the man wearily answering the same sorts of questions to the same sorts of people during the sporadic tours he conducted around the Chateau. Questions like:

'How much money did Charles Lester III actually make?'

'Is there really treasure buried in the walls?'

And:

'Is the toilet in the master bedroom actually made out of solid gold?' (It was, and it was obscene and extremely grotesque, although Ned had an insatiable desire to pee in it, just once, to understand how that would feel—a genuine golden shower).

Greetings exchanged, Ned would then be allowed inside the Chateau, where he would put down his canvas tool bag gently upon the incredibly valuable marble floor and take off his shoes, replacing them with the custom-made visitor slippers that waited in their designated, numbered alcoves to the left of the door. He would sit on the bench and slide the soft, freshly laundered footwear over his holey socks, hoping the Guide wouldn't notice how motheaten his clothing was, and knowing that he *had* noticed, noticed and assimilated this information, that Ned couldn't afford new clothes, and used this knowledge to keep Ned in his place. Perhaps that was why Ned struggled with the Tour Guide as much as he did, because he could tell, at heart, that the other man was a snob. An elitist. A lover of societal segregation. A devotee of wealth, status, power. Ned had no interest in such things. Book conservation was a career choice that filled his soul but not his bank account, and he had been okay with that, up until now. His current commission with Sunshire was about to change things for him financially by quite a long way. He had taken the job despite his reservations at the sheer scale of what the owners wanted him to achieve all by himself simply because the financial incentive attached to the commission had been so enormous.

Fifty grand's worth of enormous, in fact.

Fifty grand, for six months of work. A sum that Ned had never imagined possible in all his ten years of doing this job.

It was the main reason he hadn't turned tail and run screaming from the building when he had first seen the ghost in the Blue Room.

Because fifty grand, to Ned, was a life-changing sum of money.

Ghost notwithstanding.

GHOST

The ghost had come to him, as most ghosts do, when he was preoccupied, his guard down. Later he would wonder if maybe ghosts were always trying to get the attention of the living, but the living were simply too noisy and busy rushing about to pay heed. This thought made him sad, but then ghosts are sad entities by nature, something that Ned would come to understand more completely the longer he spent at Sunshire.

So engrossed was he in his work at the time, that he didn't notice the ghost until it was almost fully upon him. Ned often listened to music while he worked in those early days at the Chateau. His ear buds were noise cancelling, creating a cocoon of focus through which not much could penetrate as he spread himself out across an enormous old mahogany desk he had been told he could make use of and hummed along to Rachmaninoff's third.

Thus it was the smell that eventually got his attention, while his other senses were occupied. A blast of warm, fetid air that wafted around him, creeping along his skin like a wet summer mist. He first shivered and frowned as his arms pimpled with gooseflesh, then wrinkled his nose as he became aware of both the temperature shift and the odor. It was eggy and unpleasant, a smell he associated with rotting food, but there was a hint of damp about it too, the type of damp that sank into walls and stone from the ground up, a basement and hidden places sort of damp. He wondered if a drain had backed up somewhere in the house.

Sneezing, he noticed something else: a fluctuating breeze, which didn't make sense, because the Blue Room was windowless, a fully-glazed donut room, and the door to the room was currently closed and sealed at the bottom with a thick draft excluder.

Ned sneezed again, rousing reluctantly from his deep state of focus. He raised his head, wincing as his neck protested.

To find the ghost standing, or rather hovering, not three feet away from him.

Ned yelled, his heart very nearly exploding with shock in his chest, and threw himself backwards, a knee-jerk reaction designed to put as much distance between his body and the unexpected thing in the air before him as possible. It was an effective strategy: his chair toppled over and dumped him hard on the polished wooden floor beneath. The back of his head slammed into the ground with a meaty *thunk*, and he was momentarily stunned, his legs stuck up in the air like a turtle on its back exposing its soft belly, until he came to his senses. Yelling again, more in frustration this time, for he had made himself vulnerable at the worst time imaginable, he clumsily righted himself, surging to his feet and whipping around to face the figure that he was perfectly sure hadn't been there moments before.

Or had it? He had been preoccupied.

That somehow made him feel worse.

How long had it been hanging there, watching him?

As he confronted the thing again, his brain scrambling to catch up with the rest of his person, he knew instinctively that it was a ghost. Even as his throat seized with fear, even as adrenaline roared through every inch of him, he understood deep down in the parts of his mind that took care of things like this in a crisis that what he was looking at was supernatural.

This was for three reasons. First, the ghost was suspended in the air, not floating exactly, but rather hanging like a limp shirt from a coat-hanger. The tips of its toes came to rest a few inches above the honey-toned floor beneath it. Its toenails were long and dirty and jagged, its feet a purplish grey in color, as if the ghost had been suspended like this for some time, and blood had run into its extremities, collected there, as blood is prone to doing when a person dies. Ned thought instantly of an animal carcass on a hook at a butcher's shop, and the eggy smell only reinforced this impression. Like rotting meat. A bloating smell, a smell of decay. At once both sulphurous and sweet.

Second, the ghost's face was very nearly transparent, so much so that Ned wondered, for a second, if the whole thing were a projection or a trick of the light, a weird display or reflection from the polished ceramic surfaces of the walls. But the rest of it was too distinct for that, despite how hard it was to fix upon the face. Ned could make out long hair, and slim wrists, dainty hands with purpled fingernails, a suggestion of small breasts and a slightly rounded tummy under a garment that looked like an old-fashioned nightgown, frayed at the hem. Ned was fairly sure the ghost was a woman, although he couldn't confidently place an age on her. Not that it mattered, in the grand scheme of things. A haunting was a haunting, but Ned found this experience so much worse for not being able to make the face out, as if he were looking at an old black and white photograph of a person, one taken with a long exposure, where the rest of the body had been captured perfectly, but the head, whipping from left to right, had been caught only as a blurred smudge.

Lastly, the ghost moved differently to anything living that Ned had ever seen before in his life. It moved as if the laws of physics and the properties of matter did not fully apply, and he realized later, when he was lying in bed at home in a pool of cold sweat, reliving this moment over and over, that it made sense that they did not. No inertia, no momentum, no gravity. As a result, it shifted around in a way that was both terrifying and unique. It seemed to be both static, yet in a constant state of uncontrolled palsy, limbs twitching and trembling, the outline of the shape vibrating with uncoordinated motion, the form wracked with both accelerated and decelerated versions of normal human movement, as if the ghost had forgotten how to arrange itself within the usual, linear constraints of time. It undulated, Ned realized, a little like a long strand of weed stuck to the bottom of a stream bed, its form reacting to some unseen force that flowed around it and past it like water. Looking at it made Ned's stomach churn, made his eyes sting, and he wanted to blink, soothe the ache, erase the vision from his sight, but he dared not.

Because if he blinked, it might get closer to him while his eyelids were closed.

It might get closer, and it might attack him, somehow.

And so Ned just stared, eyes watering with stress, and as he did so, the thing began to rotate, slowly, so that the ghost's back was turned to him. Why it did this, Ned did not know, but the rear of the ghost's body seemed darker, more shadowy as it came into view, and Ned gasped as he saw the unmistakable pallor of blood spread across the back of the nightdress, blood that trickled down the ghost's spine and journeyed so far down the ghost's pale form that it dripped from the thing's toes and made a little puddle on the floor.

The blood came from a wound on the head.

And as Ned peered, his eyes almost popping out of his skull, his bladder on the verge of giving out through pure, unadulterated fear, he saw something flicker in and out of view, something shadowy yet distinct: an object, buried into the back of the ghost's head.

An object that looked familiar.

An object with a tail, and scales, and the distinctive, almost fish-like features of an Asian dragon.

An object the same shape and size as the heavy iron doorstop that he sometimes propped the door to the Blue Room open with when he needed a little air, or a change of view.

He dragged his eyes away from the ghost for a split second, checking for the real, worldly version of the object. Sure enough, there it sat, in its usual place next to a bookshelf near the door.

Ned snapped his gaze back to the dangling woman and realized, with a sickening jolt, two things. First, that he was observing both a past and present manifestation of the antique bronze doorstop at the same time, in the same place, and second, that the ghostly woman's face was transparent, smudged, blurred, not because it could not manifest its own features as completely as the rest of its body, but because someone had beaten her into a pulp with the doorstop, beaten her diligently and with the same dedication as a butcher tenderizing raw meat, and then finished the job by embedding the heavy object in the back of her skull.

What Ned was looking at was a portrait of violence, the ruins of a woman long since dead. Remains of remains.

A crime, frozen for posterity.

For this woman, whoever she was, whoever she had been, had been murdered, and he was being exposed to her memory: a morbid, incorporeal, supernatural time-capture of a crime scene. An echo of trauma.

Finally, no longer able to bear it, Ned squeezed his eyes shut, feeling completely overwhelmed.

And when he opened them again, the ghost was gone.

The doorstop, innocent and inanimate, remained.

Ned sank to his knees, and rested his hot, sore head in his hands.

'Fuck,' he had said out loud, and then he knelt there for some time, unsure of what else it was that he should do.

LUXURY OF CHOICE

That had been two weeks ago.

Since then, Ned had seen the ghost six more times. Always the same, always just appearing, suspended in the air like a leg of beef on a meat-hook, always dressed in the same ragged nightdress, with the same long, tangled hair, always twitching and trembling and rotating slowly as he watched, horrified, the strange, juddering form spinning about to reveal the blood on the back of the gown and the ghostly shadow of the Blue Room's doorstop in the back of the skull.

Ned did not know *why* the ghost appeared to him in this way, and he did not have any idea as to why it replayed the same short, grisly exhibition over and over again, only to disappear until it next decided to show itself, but he began to think of it as a recurring memory, one that the Sunshire Chateau had become rather stuck upon, like a needle stuck in a groove on an old vinyl record, replaying the same snippet of a forgotten tune over and over until someone came to knock the needle loose.

And eventually, as is the way with things when a person is repeatedly exposed to them, Ned stopped thinking about the apparition as something immediately dangerous and frightening and grew begrudgingly used to it. Although this did not mean he had become in any way comfortable with the ghost, for fifty-thousand dollars, he could certainly tolerate it, and so tolerate it he did. In some respects, the ghost was less disruptive than the tour parties that circled around at irregular intervals. It was certainly a good deal quieter.

He thought how curious it was that he had never for one moment questioned that he *was* actually seeing a ghost. It would have been the easier solution to his problems to assume he was hallucinating, that perhaps he had a brain tumor, or some delayed stress-response to certain events in his past, but he had quickly eliminated those possibilities from his toolbox of coping mechanisms by resolutely taking himself off to his Doctor the day after his first experience. He had told the Doc straight-up that he was worried he was having some sort of mental breakdown, for he had seen a ghost, just hanging there in front of him in broad daylight. He imparted this information in a weary, matter of fact way, but also took great care to mention that he had fallen backwards off of his chair with fright moments after, hitting his head upon the floor.

Upon hearing this, the Doctor kindly arranged a scan (this turned out to not be that kind of an act when Ned got his medical bill later in the week), and the scan came back clear: no masses, lumps, clots, contusions—just a sore little egg on the back of his head that hurt if he pressed upon it. After ruling out anything physically wrong, the Doc referred Ned to a psychiatrist, who, for an exorbitant fee, was able to see Ned at short notice. The shrink spent an expensive hour trying to get the progressively recalcitrant antique book specialist to talk about his childhood and his past relationships, only to determine, at the end, that Ned was largely sound of mind but perhaps a little exhausted and stressed, and could use a vacation. Ned thanked him for this analysis through gritted teeth and tried not to think about how much of the psychiatrist's hourly fee he could have used to pay for the aforementioned vacation instead. Or cover rent. Or buy food. Or new clothes. Or anything tangible to show for the sizable new dent in his wallet.

Bank balance aside, Ned now had no choice. Science had spoken, and he had to face up to the inconvenient and brain-pummeling fact that ghosts were real, and that he was indeed working in a haunted house.

His first instinct upon reaching that conclusion was to quit. If ghosts were real, and the Sunshire Chateau was home to one, what was to say it wasn't home to *more* than one? A place that big and old must have a convoluted past, especially when one considered the colorful family who had dwelt there for generations. The Lesters were known eccentrics with a chequered family history, and Ned, like most people who grew up locally, had heard the rumors of adultery, underhanded dealings, scandal and intrigue. Fertile soil for ghosts. A wise man would therefore steer well clear of such a place. A wise man would understand that the expression 'skeletons in the closet' was now no longer a mere expression, and sensibly take the money for services rendered so far and look for employment elsewhere.

Ned was not an unwise man, by any stretch of the imagination, and his sense of self-preservation was as well developed and healthy as anyone's.

His finances, however, were *not* quite so healthy. Ned was almost broke, through no real fault of his own, and he carried the weight of this knowledge heavily. He had lost a considerable sum of money on the sale of the house he had shared with his fiancée—*I'm sorry, Ned, but I can't*—and to other expenses that had piled up after Jo moved out. He had been forced to relocate, for one; he couldn't bear living in the place they had once shared together. Not after she'd done what she did. To add insult to injury, she had taken their only car, which meant he'd had to buy a new one. He had never fully recovered from this rapid succession of financial indignities, which hit him like a series of poison darts, a quickfire shower of barbed shit that immobilized him despite all his best efforts, and not knowing what else to do, he'd fallen back on the kindness of friends, accepting loans and opening credit cards in order to cover his needs. He was a hair's breadth away from bankruptcy, when all was said and done, and thus, halfway through the act of preparing his email of resignation to the Sunshire Estate (the manager of which he was yet to meet), he remembered that fifty-thousand dollars was a hell of a lot of money.

He therefore deleted the email, and started to rationalize the haunting.

Had the ghost hurt him?

No. It had simply appeared, and then...disappeared.

Had he been in any danger?

Probably not. He had felt afraid, but that was because there was a fucking ghost hanging in the air not four feet away from him when moments before, he had been completely unaware they even existed outside of the realms of fiction and folklore.

But it hadn't hurt him. It had simply popped into existence, spun around a bit, and then vanished.

What was so bad about that?

And if it wasn't dangerous at all, and he had to assume that it *wasn't*, both for his sanity and so that he could bring himself to actually go back to the Chateau and finish the job for which he was being so handsomely recompensed, then why had it appeared to him at all? What purpose did it serve?

Was it a thing that just happened, whether Ned was present in the Blue Room or not? Was it always there, and was it simply that sometimes, Ned could see it, and other times, he couldn't?

Or was it appearing to him for a reason? Like an SOS, a smoke signal in the sky? A message?

I died here. Look what someone did to me.

Was it even that conscious of an event? Or was the house simply lost in its own reverie? Memories could be fleeting and unpredictable, as Ned well knew. They could pop into a person's head without any warning. Maybe his presence in the Blue Room triggered the house, somehow. Maybe his work there reminded the Chateau of something else, of another time when the room was occupied, used, lived in, rather than an empty curiosity, a feature on a tour.

Maybe the house was lonely, and trying to communicate with him.

If that were the case, Ned could sympathize. He knew how that felt.

Did Jo see his ghost at all, when she least expected it? Did Ned pop into her mind when she was preparing pastry? Folding clothes? Walking in the woods?

Probably not.

Whatever the reasons behind the apparition, Ned knew that he would be returning to Sunshire regardless. If he had been a rich man, he would have had the luxury of choice, but he was not, and so he did not. He was reminded of a quote by Camus as he doggedly trudged back up the long gravel drive two days after the Blue Room ghost had first appeared to him. *'It is a kind of spiritual snobbery that makes people think they can be happy without money,'* he had said, and how much Ned felt this, in his bones. Because rich people were free, weren't they? Even if it meant they were only free to be unhappy. At least they had the choice. Ned didn't have a choice. He was both unhappy and poor, and so he followed the money, hoping that at the end of this, if he came out of it alive, he would at least be able to change one of those things for the better.

And so back he went, back to the house, back to the slippers, back to the robotic exchanges with the Tour Guide, back to the sweaty Blue Room, back to the books.

Back to the ghost.

And found that really, it wasn't so bad, being haunted.

At least, not at first.

DOORSTOP

Sighing, Ned carefully closed and set aside *Great Expectations,* taking a moment to admire the book as he did so, but feeling his joy for his work dissolve in the wake of the tour group's departure.

Life had been so much easier, before the ghost. Good, almost, or on the verge of being better, at least. Manageable, in a quiet, lonely sort of way.

Now, it was complicated again.

Ned was growing mighty tired of complicated.

Feeling antsy from the growing sense of unease that stubbornly crept up his spine, Ned got up from his seat, checking first for any ghostly activity, ears pricked, nostrils flared, like a rabbit scanning for predators in an open field. Once he was certain he was alone, both physically and spiritually, he crossed the Blue Room, poked his head out into the corridor, checked around quickly to confirm that the tour party and the Tour Guide were definitely gone, pulled his head back in, bent down, hesitated for a moment, then retrieved the doorstop from beneath the door, which he had decided to keep open since his return to work. The long metal dragon was much heavier than it looked, and he had to put his back into un-wedging it, bending at the knees for an extra boost. The thing was about as long as his forearm, and tricky to hold because of all the sharp lines and spiky parts, but he persevered until it came free with a sudden wrench.

Then he stood there holding the doorstop, as the heavy door swung to once more. He hefted the object in his hands, turning it over and over. A strange feeling came over him as the cold iron warmed slowly beneath his skin.

He envisaged the dragon, blood splattered and abused, embedded in the back of the shivering, ghostly woman's skull, felt his stomach turn as this idea took root, burrowed into his brain. He wondered why, if it *was* indeed a murder weapon, it had not been disposed of at the time. Why keep it? A grisly souvenir, hidden in plain sight? Or had the crime been carried out with a replica? Was there a twin to this dragon, buried somewhere on the grounds, secret and forgotten?

Ned chewed his lip. He didn't know the answer to any of these questions, but he did know that he was drawn to this object, and that by holding it, he hoped he might be able to shed some light on these things.

He brought it closer to his face, squinting in the dim light of the Blue Room. Would he be able to see blood? Brain matter? Tiny splinters of bone, wedged between the scales?

He hoped not.

Shaped like a Chinese dragon, it was a sinuous scaled design with sharp talons, antler-like horns, a large head and a wide mouth fringed with barbels that then bled into two florid pectoral fins. To Ned's eyes, it looked more like a carp or a strange, horned dolphin than a dragon. It was presented standing on its head with its tail raised high into the air, as if caught in the act of diving into a mass of stylized clouds that formed the wedged base. As it had been cast using a mold, the front of the dragon was detailed, and the reverse side was hollow, like an eggshell.

Inside the hollow, Ned discovered a curious hinged lever.

He grunted when he saw it, and brushed the lever with his thumb. It felt warm to the touch, warmer than the rest of the object.

It was an odd piece of engineering. Folded neatly into the cavity, it turned out to be an articulated arm attached by two brass screws, with three sections that folded outwards when manipulated. Extended, the arm looked a little like the branch of a tree, albeit very stylized, and it moved smoothly, as if it had been greased or oiled to allow it to do so. Ned could see immediately that the lever served a purpose, was designed to slot into something or attach to something, but he couldn't for the life of him figure out what.

As he stood there, working the lever by extending and collapsing it over and over, he began to feel strange. His posture changed, became more rigid, more straight-backed. He began to sweat, and felt the doorstop grow even warmer under his fingers, as if heated, left too close to an open fire, or a radiator. He frowned at it, but held on. Why did he feel as if the object were waking up, somehow? As if his handling of it had triggered a rush of awareness, of immediacy, of—

Charles Lester III, who found himself covered in blood and in a frustrating, almost delirious state of extreme fatigue tinged with euphoria, knew that to try and sleep in his current frame of mind, so soon after the murders, would be a waste of his time while his blood was so high.

He moved quietly to the Blue Room instead, where he kept his best whiskey stored in a bespoke, hand-made drinks cabinet that was also a beautiful wooden globe held up by a polished chrome tripod stand. The top half of the globe folded back on artfully concealed hinges to reveal a collection of mouth-blown Glencairn cut-crystal decanters standing in silk-lined recesses. There was also a selection of polished balloon tumblers, toothpicks and cigars held in place neatly by a series of gleaming chrome brackets. The glasses and accessories were monogrammed, of course, because Lester liked to stamp his ownership upon all he possessed—who didn't?

Lester, who had learned from bitter experience to close the doors in his house if he wanted to experience any true peace and solitude, marched over to the whiskey cabinet, lifted the lid, plucked a glass from its cradle, decanted two finger's worth of Macallan single malt, strode back to the doorway, and hauled the Blue Room's heavy portal shut. Then he jammed a solid iron doorstop that was cast in the shape of a Chinese dragon under the bottom of it, for good measure. He could have locked the damn door, had he the key, but keys (excluding the tiny golden key that sat in his waistcoat pocket) had been his Valet's domain, and the Valet was now...indisposed.

Lester would have to get new keys cut, he knew, at great expense. Murder was a costly procedure, when all was said and done.

For now, the doorstop would do.

Thinking himself finally, blissfully alone at last, he sank heavily into a leather armchair positioned close to the fireplace, where a dying grate of embers glowed and popped. He held his whiskey tumbler up to the light, examining the amber liquid inside before downing the lot in one, long, thirsty gulp. He felt the malt burn as it travelled down his gullet, felt himself relaxing, little by little, as warmth spread across his chest. For he was done. He had expended himself.

Who would have thought, he mused, enjoying the whiskey warmth, who would have thought, before this night, that I was a killer?

And an accomplished one, too. Having spent the better part of the night covering his own tracks, he felt proud of what he had achieved. All he had left to attend to were the minor details. All he left to do was spread lies about his Valet, and the Housekeeper he'd also disposed of.

And the Gardener.

Convincing lies, lies that would not lead back to him in any demonstrable way. He realized how convenient it was that they were two men and one woman, for he could much easier perpetuate the fallacy that they had run away together after stealing from him than if the Valet alone had vanished without a trace. He could spin a tale of a depraved love triangle, of betrayal and thievery and deceit. There was something more believable in a dramatic story of such a sordid nature, he knew, and Lester thought it rather poetic, too. Young love, and all that.

The papers would eat it up.

Details, details.

It could all be worked out later, once he had rested. For now, he was done, and could finally put the night behind him, and move on with his life.

He leaned back in the chair and closed his eyes, thinking that perhaps he could sleep, after all. Just a quick nap, just a moment or two to breathe, and recuperate, before he retired to his study, where his washstand stood ready to cleanse him of the blood, soil and filth that coated his skin. He would burn his usually spotless clothes in the fireplace there, and nobody would be any the wiser.

He took a deep breath, enjoying the quiet.

Then, feeling a deep sense of peace and contentment settle slowly into his bones, he took another.

'Master? Master, I need to speak with y—

Ned yelped, and hastily put the doorstop down on the floor. It now glowed a dull red, as if superheated, pulled straight from the furnace or forge. He half expected to see smoke rise from it as it charred the floor beneath, but none did. He stared at the object, his heart thundering in his chest.

'What the fuck was *that?*' He breathed, out loud.

Then, after a moment or two of eyeing the doorstop as if it were a live snake about to strike, curiosity got the better of him once more. He bent to retrieve the dragon.

As soon as his hands made contact with the hot iron, he felt different—warmer, more anxious, more—

Incredulous, Charles Lester III jolted upright. Had someone spoken? Or had he dozed off? Had he been dreaming, already?

'Master? If you please...wake up.'

Charles craned his neck around the edge of his chair, every nerve in his body suddenly on fire. He was greeted by the sight of a young woman dressed only in her nightgown. She stood in the middle of the Blue Room facing him and wringing her hands together. Her hair was long and unkempt, and fell halfway across her face as she spoke. He could tell, even in the dim light, that her fingernails were cracked and dirty. Her bare toes peeked out from beneath the frayed hem of her gown, and this small detail offended him most of all, for the rug in the Blue Room was extremely valuable, and if anyone was going to track their dirty, shoeless feet across his property, it should be him, and not this...this...

Scullery Maid, he realized.

'You,' he sneered, and he had not thought he could feel furious again, not after the Valet, not after the Housekeeper, not after the Gardener, but this dirty, unkempt creature arriving unannounced and uninvited in his private, personal quarters before the sun was even awake proved him wrong.

'How did you...ah. The servant's passage,' Lester continued, sighing and passing a hand over his eyes. 'I forgot

about the fucking servant's passage.' Looking past the girl, he could see a narrow black oblong yawning in the space between two large bookcases against the far wall.

Lester felt the ugly worm of anger stir in his belly. All staff were supposed to be abed by ten thirty, and they were supposed to stay there until dawn, not wander around the house at their own leisure. The staff should not have any leisure, that is not what he paid them for.

The Master did not like it when his rules were broken.

'What do you want?' He asked, in a dead, flat tone. Had she seen him, going about his grisly business?

'You said we could talk, Master. It's...it's important.'

Charles Lester III rose wearily from his chair and turned to face the Scullery Maid, looming up over her by a good foot, and then some. She shivered, cold in her flimsy gown.

'Now is not a good time, Isabelle,' Lester said, quietly, hoping that this would be enough.

It was not.

'But Master!'

He found her insistence offensive, and looked down at her as if she were a persistent smear of shit stuck to the sole of his shoe. Still, she stood there, wringing her hands, her eyes huge, pleading. Lester drew himself up, the fingers on both his hands twitching uncontrollably. He was itching for his cane, which, like the keys, like the Valet, was now missing. Lost. It had been his favorite cane, too. He found he needed it more as the years wore on, for his knees and hips grew sore in colder weather, despite the feather-stuffed mattress he slept upon. It had taken him time to get used to the idea of needing a cane, the effects of age not something that Lester had planned for—an oversight, born of an innate confidence in himself and his physicality—and even more time to find one that suited his particular height and personal tastes. It would take weeks to commission and receive delivery of a replacement. Lester would have to send word to his stick maker in Italy, which was, like most of the civilized world, currently caught up in conflict and nationalist agitation, the damn war having upended all refined society, it felt, so word would be slow.

He had other canes, of course he did.

But the one he had lost had been his favorite.

The night had been costly, indeed.

The worm stirred again.

When would these fucking people learn their place?

'I said, now is not a good time, Isabelle.' The words slid about between gritted teeth.

'But Master. I must. I must.'

Could the woman not understand plain English? Could she not see her Master was covered from head to toe in blood, earth, and dust? Perhaps not, the light was poor in the Blue Room and Isabelle had a queer, distracted, far-away look in her eyes that betrayed a confused state of mind.

Suddenly, Charles Lester III shook his head, understanding why she was here.

'Go back to the servant's quarters, Isabelle,' he said, and his voice became unsteady, strained.

'Master? I cannot. I...'

'I said go back to your quarters where you belong, Isabelle.'

And to think, he had momentarily lusted after this shivering, sniveling wisp.

'I'm with child, Master,' Isabelle whispered, and Lester realized then, with disgust, that the woman was crying. He watched her tears fall as the warmth in his chest evaporated.

'What did you say?' He asked, although he had understood her perfectly well.

'I'm...starting a child, Master.' She dropped her chin and gave into her tears, thin shoulders heaving beneath the yellowing cotton of her gown.

Charles Lester III almost burst out laughing then. Almost. The situation was so absurd, so unnecessary after everything else that had occurred that night, that he almost mistook it for a prank.

But the Scullery Maid's tears seemed real enough, and Lester was not so far gone that he could not remember staggering down to the kitchens late one night, whiskey-drunk, in search of what, he could not remember now, and finding the long-haired straggle scouring the floor on her hands and knees, her bony behind stuck up in the air, and he had not been able to help himself. He'd been down on his own knees without a moment's thought, fumbling at her skirts, his long, under-used prick eager for the dance, and afterwards he'd joked with his Valet, joked about what he would have done had he found her emptying the servant's chamber pots instead of scrubbing the floor, for Lester was a vulgar man, at heart, and no amount of money or decoration could disguise that.

'A child, Master.' The Scullery Maid wiped her nose with the back of her hand, and Charles Lester III suddenly felt nauseous. His eyes searched the Blue Room, darting about, looking for escape from her, looking for something, anything he could use to release himself from this situation.

He lit eventually upon the solid iron doorstop wedged beneath the door. It was fashioned in the shape of a Chinese dragon, a gift from a business associate in Beijing, and he knew it was plenty heavy, and plenty sharp in the right places.

A strange, prickling sensation crept across his scalp. The worm was now tying knots in his belly, writhing in and out of his guts, twisting, turning, roiling.

Yes, that would do.

His breathing slowed. His fingers twitched again.

He took a step towards the door.

'Master?' The Scullery Maid sobbed. 'Master, will you help me? It's yours, Master. It's your child.'

Charles Lester III took another step, and smiled. A strange, cooing sound came out of his mouth.

'Oh Isabelle. That is your name, isn't it? Or did I make a mistake?'

She nodded dumbly, then shook her head, confused.

'Isabelle, Isabelle. You had to pick tonight to tell me this, didn't you?'

'I don't understand.'

Another step, and Charles Lester III moved incrementally closer to his fourth murder of the day.

'You had to pick tonight, of all nights. Perhaps there is something in the water, eh? Or maybe the moon is waxing gibbous, as my wife would say.'

Another step.

The Scullery Maid, who had not a clue what Charles was talking about, resumed her sobbing.

'Master I...I don't know what to do. Will you help me, sir?'

'There, there, don't cry Isabelle,' Lester said, his voice dripping with false reassurances. 'Of course I will help you.'

'You will?' The woman's tears cut short and she faltered, her puffy eyes opening wide. 'But your wife, Master. She'll-'

'My wife?' An image of Rose sprang to mind: her benign, lined, plain face, always turned from him, as if admiring a view he could never see. He had no hate in his heart for his

wife, but no love, either. She existed for him in much the same way that the furniture of the Chateau existed: it was there, and sometimes he used it, and sometimes he didn't.

That didn't mean he wanted her to find out about his indiscretions.

Another step. Two more, and the doorstop would be within arm's reach. His fingers ached to grab hold of it.

'Yes, Master,' the scullery maid whispered, hiccupping with stress and clasping her belly with thin, grubby hands. 'Your wife, she won't...'

'My wife will never find out,' Lester said, and as his fingertips brushed against cold, reliable iron, he thought: Once is a mistake, twice is a coincidence, thrice...

Thrice is a habit.

But what about four?

He could not remember how the saying went.

And where to hide the body? A small voice whispered, in the back of his mind.

Details, he told it firmly. Details. I can deal with those late—

Suddenly, without warning, the doorstop grew so hot Ned could no longer hold onto it. He yelled and hissed as his skin began to sizzle, and dropped the dragon, breaking the possession that had settled on him like a fog. The heavy object hit the floor with a solid, loud *thunk!* Ned kicked at it with his toe, wanting to remove himself from the thing. It refused to move, and his toe caught painfully against one of the dragon's spiky horns instead. He cursed, and hopped backwards, feeling sick, sick to his very stomach. His toe throbbed, and he wondered if he had broken it. His hands throbbed too, the skin on his palms and fingertips raw and hot. He remembered things that did not belong to him, scenes of violence, sensations of pleasure, of anger, and disgust. He shivered and shook with the force of these feelings, and dragged his shaking, sore hands through his hair, over and over, trying to soothe himself.

And it was while he was in this state, vulnerable and preoccupied, gaze turned inward, that Alice introduced herself.

ALICE

She did this by approaching Ned silently from behind and touching him lightly on the shoulder while he was in the throes of shaking off the long-dead Charles Lester III's memories.

'Are you alright?' She asked, politely. She had bright red hair that stood out against the blue surroundings like a flower in an otherwise barren meadow.

Ned jumped violently as he felt her fingers brush against him, and rocketed across the room away from her touch, stumbling sideways and almost falling headlong into the nearby fireplace in the process, only stopping himself at the very last moment by putting his arms out and grabbing hold of the padded guard-rail that encircled the Blue Room's sizeable hearth. He stayed like that for a moment or two, holding himself taut as a plank as if he were doing push-ups on a park railing, and it was while he was staring into the maw of the fireplace, breathing heavily, abs quivering, hands raging and sore, that he spotted something in the very back of the hearth.

It was a narrow, soot-blackened groove, virtually invisible unless someone were staring right at it. It cut across the rear of the only visible part of the flue above the firebox at a right angle, and formed a rectangular, distinctly shaped furrow that was segmented into three parts.

Ned knew instantly what would slot into that furrow.

Having more important fish to fry at that particular moment however, he righted himself awkwardly, and turned around, fully expecting the specter of the murdered, faceless woman to be looming over him once again, arms outstretched, grasping.

Isabelle.

He pictured her as she had been when living: shivering, pitiful, cradling her belly. His stomach roiled as he recalled the sensation of gentle flesh giving way to cold, unforgiving iron.

The ghost, he thought frantically, *has tolerated me long enough. I know her secret now. I know what he did to her.*

Now he was to be strangled, or clawed at, or disembowelled, or at the very least screamed at, or whatever it was ghosts did when they decided to terrorize the living with the injustices of their death. Ned knew he would have to face it, just like most terrifying things in life must be faced, just like he had faced that room full of people in dresses and bow-ties on his wedding day. He had survived that day, hadn't he?

Yes, yes he had, he reminded himself.

One either survived, or one didn't.

And so he turned, mouth slack with fear, tensing himself for a vision of terror, and found instead a pair of wide brown eyes and mass of glowing red ringlets that sat in a perfect cloud around soft, pretty features.

It was not the ghost of Isabelle. It was a young woman, very much alive in appearance, dressed in a spotlessly clean and pressed Housekeeper's pinny that was a crisp, clean, flawless shade of white.

'Fuck,' Ned said out loud before he could stop himself, because for a split second, he thought his Jo had come back to him.

But Jo is married to someone else, you idiot, he reminded himself. His locked memory-box, the one that held all things related to Jo, boomed once upon its shelf,

92

and a deep blare of pain sounded out in his heart, which was only just returning to a normal rhythm as the effects of the doorstop dissipated.

The woman in the tunic chewed her lip, blushing.

'I am *so* sorry,' she apologized, wringing her hands. 'I didn't mean to frighten you. Are you quite well?'

Ned said nothing, trying to get his emotions under control.

'I should know better than to creep up on anyone in this place, but you were so engrossed, I couldn't get your attention at all. I did try.'

Ned remained silent, trying to calm his breathing down. He didn't trust himself to speak, not yet. He realized then what a toll the hauntings had taken upon him. No matter how hard and how often he had tried to normalize the sight of a bloody, battered corpse dangling in the air before him, a ghost was still a ghost, and ghosts were, by essence of what they represented, terrifying. The constant stress of waiting for the next appearance had worn away at him more than he had appreciated. That, coupled with the unexpected trip down Lester's memory lane, and the stubborn, unwelcome flashes of Jo, had put him in a dire state.

The house is trying to push me over the edge, he thought, bleakly, not knowing how close to the truth he really was.

And here he had been telling himself that he was 'getting used to it'.

The woman, oblivious to all this, dry washed her hands in a contrite gesture of anxiety. 'You fell pretty hard. Are you sure you're alright?'

Another vivid memory came to Ned as he stood facing the woman. It hit him with such force that he nearly sat down on the floor. Jo, standing in the kitchen of the house they had bought together, wearing an apron a little like this one, wringing her hands on a wet tea towel, flour smeared across her left cheek. He couldn't remember what she had been saying, but she'd had a concerned expression on her face, almost identical to the look on this woman's face, and he wondered how many conversations there had been with Jo like this, conversations he had blanked out of his recollections, exchanges where the clues had been obvious and plain for anyone who was looking to see. Because Jo had often been anxious, and worried, and had wrung her hands so much at times that the skins on the back of her fingers had chapped, an occupational hazard for a woman who baked and therefore washed her hands a multitude of times a day, but still. He understood then that he had exacerbated her stress, somehow, he had been responsible for the raw patches of skin on her knuckles, and for that, he instantly hated himself.

Until, that is, he managed to seize the feeling by the throat and wrestle it into another iron lock-box.

Why are memories like this? He wondered, slamming the lid down furiously. *My memories, another man's memories, they are all the same. They come at you like ghosts come at you: when your guard is down.* Anger washed through him, and the woman watched as he wrestled with himself, a dozen fleeting feelings playing out on his usually open, pleasant face. Her nervous expression intensified. Ned knew he was being weird, and tried to get a handle on it. Tried, and failed.

'It's fine,' he said out loud, but it sounded anything but fine.

'I'm sorry,' the woman replied, awkwardly. 'You're... I'll come back later.' She turned as if to leave.

Ned cleared his throat.

'No, don't...it's okay. I'm sorry. I overreacted. It's been a day. I'm fine now.' He forced himself to smile.

'Are you sure? You've gone as white as a sheet.' The woman chuckled softly. 'And I'm an expert in sheets, trust me. Do you know there are seventeen beds in this place? Seventeen. And they all need clean sheets, once a week, even though nobody sleeps in them anymore.'

Ned struggled to catch up. The pinny finally made sense, finally slotted into place in his comprehension.

'You work here?'

The woman nodded. 'I do, but I keep odd hours.'

'I've never seen you before.'

'Well, that is partly deliberate. I've seen *you*, a few times, when I've passed this room, but...you always seem so deep in your work, it felt wrong to interrupt you. Besides, this place is big enough that a person can go days without seeing another soul. Trust me, I have.'

Ned laughed politely, and the sound made him feel a little better. The memories of the doorstop retreated a little further. His hands still throbbed, though.

'Lucky you. I can't seem to escape the incessant tour parties that circle the place like flies. The only other member of staff I've met is the Tour Guide. I was beginning to think the place was run by robots, so you're...you're something of a relief, actually.'

'Oh, him.' The woman wrinkled her nose. 'I try to avoid him as much as possible. He's a strange man.'

'Do you have a name, or is Chief Expert in Sheets your official title?'

She made a face, halfway between approval and annoyance. 'Funny, are we? Wonderful. Just what I need right now.'

Ned shrugged. 'I'm just trying to make up for being a complete idiot earlier.'

She grinned. 'You did jump rather a long way. Impressive, really.'

Ned groaned. 'If you don't tell me your name soon, I'll give you one, and it won't be complimentary.'

'Fine.' She chuckled, and it was a nice noise. 'I'm Alice.'

'I'm Ned,' he replied, noticing that the maid was younger than he initially thought. 'I'm...the book guy.'

Alice smiled and shook his offered hand, which he stuck out without thought. Her skin was icy cool and dry where he was hot and sore and clammy, and he fought the urge to yank his hand back as their palms touched, for the pain was intense.

'I suppose you could call me the resident House-keeper,' she continued, not seeming to register his discomfort, for Ned had become a master of disguise, and allowed none of his pain to surface, ever. 'Only it's not that glamorous. I'm more of a maid, really. I used to have other duties, but times change, and now I just keep the place clean. Hard work, but there are worse jobs, I suppose.'

Ned blinked. 'All by yourself? There must be over fifty rooms, how do you manage it all on your own?'

Alice nodded. 'Well, not so well, as it happens.' She laughed uncomfortably. 'Which is why I'm disturbing you. I'm so sorry, but if it isn't too much trouble...'

'It isn't,' Ned blurted, and then, a little warning light went off in his head.

Careful Ned, it said, as it blinked on and off.

Careful. You like her.

And liking people is a good way to get hurt.

Besides...don't you have other things to worry about right now?

He looked to the doorstop, which once again appeared innocuous and innocent, an inanimate object only, and then to the fireplace.

'What did you need?' He murmured, but already he had accepted the warning that had been delivered, accepted it and made a pact with himself, his momentary happiness at finding someone normal and nice to talk to in the aftermath of all the strangeness he had encountered faltering. Whatever Alice needed, he would help with, because Ned was a helpful sort of person, but then he would find a way to retreat, to absent himself, because he wasn't ready, not really. Wasn't ready to laugh with a woman, no matter how innocently.

He certainly wasn't ready to add any more boxes to the shelf in his heart.

Alice continued. 'I need to clean the crystal chandelier in the Library, and I can't stand going up the step-ladder by myself without someone to hold it steady for me. It's a big room. The ceiling is a long way up. The last Housekeeper...well. I keep imagining myself falling like she did, or breaking something, and no-one finding me until days later. Would you...may I ask you for your help? I sure would appreciate it.'

Despite himself, Ned smiled, and turned his full attention back to her. She was so polite it almost made his teeth hurt. This softened him, for Ned had good manners too, and he could tell when someone had been brought up with the same respect for courtesy that he had.

'I would be delighted to hold the ladder for you, Alice,' he replied, honestly. 'I need a break from this room anyway. It's been...it's been a day.'

Alice brightened. 'Thank you,' she smiled.

'It's my pleasure.'

'Can I ask you something?'

'Sure.'

'Did something happen to you before I showed up? You seemed...well. Preoccupied.'

Ned sighed. 'I *am* preoccupied. And yes, to answer your question. Something did happen. Well, not just one thing. More of an...ongoing situation. A puzzle, I guess. But I don't know how to elaborate without sounding like a mad man.'

'I like puzzles.'

Ned shook his head. 'No, I'd rather not. Not yet. But can I ask *you* something?'

'Of course.'

'Do you know much about the history of this place? I know there's talk of bad things happening here. Scandals, rivalries, disappearances...murder... that sort of thing. Have you heard anything like that?'

Alice winced, then blew out her cheeks. She looked pained, suddenly, and Ned regretted asking her.

'What?' He prodded, for it was obvious his question had triggered some emotion in her.

'Nothing.'

'Are you sure? I don't want to-'

'It's fine, I promise. And, in answer to your question: take your pick. The stories are so varied, I wouldn't know where to start.'

'Any stories about a young woman? Maybe going missing? Suspected foul play?' He tried to make his voice sound casual, but didn't quite manage it.

Alice's eyes narrowed.

'What are you asking me?'

Ned didn't reply, just stared at the doorstop, wondering what temperature it was at that precise moment. His fingers twitched, and he realized he couldn't leave the room without testing something out first.

'You can tell me,' Alice prompted, softening. 'I won't judge. This house...it has a lot of secrets.'

Ned held up a finger. 'Hold that thought,' he said. 'I'll help you with the chandelier, but I just...I just need to do one thing first. Won't be a moment.'

Before his nerve gave out, he crossed the Blue Room and grabbed the dragon doorstopper. It was cool to the touch again, but Ned did not want to risk more burns, so he dragged his shirt sleeves down over his hands and used that as a wrapping, then hauled the object over to the fireplace.

Alice watched him, frowning, but saying nothing.

Ned unfolded the strange articulated arm from the back of the dragon, then got down on his hands and knees, dragging the padded fire guard out of the way first, and crawling into the fireplace so that he could reach the back of the flue where he had spotted the strange groove. He took the doorstop and pressed it arm-first into the groove, where, sure enough, the segmented arm fitted perfectly. Ned felt it slot into place, a little like a key slotting into a lock. Something clicked, and he felt a small release of tension, as if something had been sprung, or unlocked. Acting on instinct, he applied pressure to the dragon, turning it as one would turn a door knob, and it rotated. The unmistakable sound of gears turning and a mechanism operating came to him, muffled through the brick of the flue.

'I knew it,' he breathed, and for a second, he was flooded with triumph. The doorstopper was not only a murder weapon, but a key to something, and this also explained the random hotness of the thing. Because maybe the object had been left in place, at times, wedged into the back of the chimney flue. Perhaps when the fire was lit, or not long after, and so no wonder it was warm. The object was recalling a particular state, perhaps recollecting the temperature it had been at a certain

99

moment in time, and Ned knew that this was another memory manifested, a remembrance poured into an everyday, commonplace object.

'What have you found?' Alice murmured, from close behind him. She spoke directly over his shoulder, and he felt her breath on his cheek momentarily. Unable to help himself, he shuddered and said:

'I don't know, but I'm pretty sure I opened something.'

'I'm pretty sure you did too.'

She moved clear, and he backed out of the fireplace and straightened up, dusting his now blackened hands on his knees.

'But opened what?' He mused, wondering what this woman thought of him as he stood there with ash on his clothes and hair sticking out all over the place.

She said nothing. *Keeps her cards close,* he thought. *That's not a bad thing.*

He pivoted slowly on his heels, scanning the entirety of the Blue Room for anything outwardly or noticeably different, out of place, or remarkable, while Alice stood demurely by, watching him, as if waiting for him to discover something.

It only took Ned a moment to figure out what had changed, and where the sudden breeze that now drifted through the room had come from.

It came from the large, narrow doorway that had opened up on the far wall between two bookcases. A doorway that had been completely concealed, until now.

The fucking servant's passage, he remembered. Lester's memory, not his.

Ned felt violated, and shook his head as if trying to dislodge water from his ears.

Alice, meanwhile, was nodding, her red curls bouncing, as if this was all perfectly normal.

'You know there is a secret network of passages built into the walls of Sunshire Chateau, don't you?' She said, matter-of-factly.

'No, no I did not know that.'

She folded her arms, sighing. 'The Master of the house used to say that menial, everyday tasks and necessities were ugly, base things that people like himself should not have to be subjected to. So he built a series of service tunnels and passages to keep us hardworking folk out of sight.'

Ned walked over to the yawning, black doorway, peering. It was dark, in the tunnel, and he could not see more than a foot or so beyond the door's mouth. He could feel the air within, however, on his face: musty, alternately cool and warm, and tinged with a faint eggy, sulphurous smell.

One mystery solved, he thought.

Out loud, he mused: 'I suppose that's not unusual for an old house of this size. A lot of historic properties had hidden doors and servant's passages, wallpapered or papered so that they blended in with the surrounding decor. It was a common practice in many of the large old houses and stately homes in England. So the hired help could come and go without cluttering up the aesthetics of the house with their 'common' appearances, I suppose.'

Alice snorted.

'Behind green baize doors,' Ned continued, thoughtfully. Alice looked at him.

'It's an old term for the divide between domestic servants and their masters,' he explained. 'It was common in houses this substantial to have a specific door that acted as a divide between the domestic half of the house and the resident part of the house. The haves, and the have-nots. The door was often covered with a thick green baize cloth, pinned in place with brass tacks. It insulated the door, you see. From noise. From any kitchen smells.'

'There is a door like that near the stairs in the entrance hall.' Alice kept her eyes lowered, so he could not tell what she was thinking.

'Is there? I've never seen it. Huh.' Ned shook his head. 'I'm always too busy changing my shoes.'

Alice sighed.

'I really do need to clean that chandelier, you know.'

Ned looked at the servant's passage. 'Can we get to it this way?' He asked, and she laughed, thinking he was joking. Then she read the expression on his face.

'You're serious,' she realized, and Ned nodded.

'About most things,' he replied, 'But don't tell anyone- I like to keep that a secret.' A weak attempt at a weak joke, but he was trying, at least, and that was all anyone could do in the face of difficulty: try, try, and try some more.

'It would be much easier to go the other way,' Alice said, shaking her head. 'It's easy to get lost back there.'

Ned snorted. 'I could do with getting a little lost, to be honest with you,' he replied, knowing that the statement made absolutely no sense whatsoever to anyone but him. Then without waiting, he switched on the flashlight app on his cellphone, and plunged headfirst into the gloom.

Alice, who understood the dark only too well, sighed, and followed him.

THE LIBRARY

RUMORS

'And this, ladies and gentlemen, is the Library.' The Tour Guide ushered his party into the next designated room on the tour, glancing at his wristwatch and performing a silent headcount as each member of the group walked past him. *Nobody missing, not yet,* he thought, then tapped the glass watch face, for the second hand needle had frozen on its circular route, and was now ticking back and forth, back and forth, back and forth across the number '8'.

Give it time, give it time.

The Sunshire Chateau Library was situated in the far reaches of the east wing, a good fifteen-minute walk from the Blue Room. Getting there involved climbing a lot of stairs and navigating a lot of corridors and hallways to the point that the guests, who had no prior experience of a house that shifted and stretched and changed at whim the way that Sunshire did, began to find it hard to distinguish one passageway from another. The Guide, who was familiar with the place, knew that this inability to gain a sense of direction was deliberate on the part of the house: the architect, upon advisement, had devised a floor plan that assimilated as many twists and turns and angles as physically possible in order to create the impression that the Chateau was bigger than it actually was, and to disorient visitors as they moved around.

As a result, the party was slightly breathless when they eventually reached the Library, and they stood in a little cluster in the middle of the book-lined space, panting and mopping at sweat-beaded brows and looking about themselves in wonder.

'Well, that is somethin,' Baltimore said, taking off his cap to scratch at the top of his head.

'It really is,' Bow-tie replied, in vehement agreement.

The huge Library soared up and around them with the assured extravagance of a palace ballroom, and climaxed with an enormous vaulted wooden ceiling that was heavily decorated with gothic carvings, inscriptions and delicate frescos. Linda Louise, who was more awake than the others, realized as soon as she entered the room that it being this size and shape was a stark impossibility. The Library was situated on the second floor of the property, she was sure of it, which meant there must, owing to there being another story above, therefore be a room sitting directly on *top* of the Library with a large hump in the center of it to accommodate the high arch and pitch of the ceiling in the room below, which she knew was a ridiculous idea. As this sank in, she began to feel strange, and a little giddy. The space in which she stood, the space available, was not commensurate with the dimensions and proportions of the Chateau itself, and Linda, being a fan of facts and certainties, did not quite know how to deal with this. So she chose silence, as she so often did, but she made sure she could see the door at all times, in case she needed to escape the room at any point. She was not claustrophobic, precisely, but she was something, and that something had a real hard time coming to terms with impossible spaces.

The rest of the tour group, being generally ignorant of such things, did not notice the anomalies in design that Linda Louise noticed. Instead, the group noticed other things as the Tour Guide coolly pointed them out one by one, like the large bay window with molded mullions and rectilinear bar tracery in the English perpendicular gothic style. Beautiful, vividly colored stained glass decorated the gaps between the tracery, and let in a weird, scattered luminescent light that fell on the room in showers of blue and scarlet and gold, casting glittering tattoos upon the furnishings and people within, despite the heavy shade thrown by the trees outside the Chateau.

They saw the huge marble fireplace, polished and colossal, also resplendent with tracery that was inlaid with semi-precious stones: colored Blue John's stone from Yorkshire in England, Jadeite from Burma, Rose Quartz from Madagascar.

They also saw a giant oriental carpet, hand-knotted with the unique 'Senneh' or Persian knot that made it so desirable, the wefts and warps richly colored in various shades of claret and mauve, the fringes a clean ivory, despite its age. They saw paintings from the masters, hung high on the walls in heavy gilt frames: a Turner, a Constable, a particularly fine Jan Steen. They saw pottery and curios, glassware and earthenware, a giant copper incense brazier, chairs, a chaise longue, footstools, a selection of desks in different woods and finishes. They saw a huge crystal chandelier, suspended from a long rope hung from the apex of the vaulted ceiling. The chandelier was cobwebbed with delicate white strands of silk that looked like intentional decorative strings, rather than the result of neglect and time.

But above all, they saw books.

Row upon row of books, books as far as the eye could see, books from the floor up to where the ceiling began to vault. Displayed on warm, honey-colored oak shelving, the wood complimented the gold tooling on the thousands of assembled book spines in a way that gave the entire room an air of peace, and warmth, and welcome—a rare thing to feel at the Sunshire Chateau, for the building, being at once both hungry for new visitors and wary of them, had, up until this point, felt rather unfriendly.

Not that the Tour Guide expected any of his guests to understand much of this, nor fully appreciate the finer details of the things they were looking at.

But he knew. He appreciated it, all of it. He liked this room.

Rose had liked this room too, he remembered.

'How many books are there?' Noah asked in his relentlessly unreliable voice that hitched and plummeted in equal measure. The Guide nodded his head in acknowledgement, for this was usually the first question anyone asked upon arriving in the Library. *How many books,* they always wanted to know. As if it mattered how many. What they should have been asking was what was *in* those books. But nobody ever asked that question. People were so caught up with the idea of owning things, that they only ever cared about quantity, not quality.

Still, the Tour Guide found himself duty bound to reply.

'There are over four thousand books in the library, or at least there were the last time we counted,' he replied.

'Four thousand?' Barbara repeated, and the Tour Guide looked at her as if he were thinking: *Moron, that's what I just said, isn't it?*

Outwardly, he nodded, politely.

'And that poor sap in the Blue Room has to clean every single one?' Baltimore continued, removing his cap once more and scratching his head for the hundredth time.

'Yes, yes he does.'

'I suppose a job is a job, but phew,' Baltimore said, shaking his head. 'Rather him than me. I like my job better.'

'What do you do?' Barbara asked, curiously, and Don, who had been staring at a long, ebony walking cane propped up against one of the writing desks, stiffened.

Baltimore drew himself up a little, pleased to have been asked.

'Well, Barbara—can I call you Barbara?'

'Of course.'

'I am the Vice President of Operations for a well-known fulfillment center that I won't name here, for several reasons. But it's a highly complex operation, and the job takes skill, leadership, and a fou-'

'We know which company you mean, asshat,' Noah said, rolling his eyes. Don, who had been about to jump in with his own thoughts on the matter, smiled and patted his son on the back. Noah flinched under his touch and sidestepped the next pat, loath to be touched by his father. Don ended up patting the air Noah left behind, then sliding his hand awkwardly into his jeans pocket, while Barbara stammered out an apology to Baltimore, mortified.

'Aw, it's alright,' Baltimore said, shooting Noah a look. 'I got a teenager myself.'

'You do?' Something in Barbara's eyes revealed an eagerness to trade war stories.

'A girl,' Baltimore continued, and he smiled wistfully as he said it. 'She doesn't much like me either, at the moment. It's why I travel so damn much.'

'Oh,' said Barbara, softly.

'I don't know why I said that. Why did I say that? I'm not usually one for sharing, but there's something about-'

'What does that mean?' Barbara interrupted Baltimore, trying to save him from further embarrassment. She pointed at some ornate lettering that decorated the arched ceiling. It was a slogan, painted meticulously in red and gold script:

This was a question the Guide was actually happy to answer. He translated the phrase for them with relish.

'*Written words remain, spoken words fly away,*' he said.

Baltimore made a face. 'What's that supposed to mean?' He asked, and Barbara was relieved, for she also wanted to know, but was too intimidated by the Tour Guide to display her ignorance.

'It means that books are powerful things. They remain long after a person has died.'

Bow-tie sighed, the romanticism of it all exciting him again. The color was high in his cheeks, and his eyes gleamed with a memory.

'My mother used to tell me that books were the ghosts,' he said, 'of people who had once lived like we did, only they wrote their lived experiences down, ensuring they would never really die.'

'Of course,' the Tour Guide replied, taking the statement at face value. There was no bitterness or sarcasm present in his voice, for once. 'That is why people write books, I imagine. Immortality via creation.'

Noah said nothing, turning up his music once again. The idea of immortality suddenly made him very tired, and very sad. A while ago he'd told his parents that he wanted to be a writer. His father had laughed the idea right out of the room.

'No kid of mine is going to tie himself to poverty for the rest of his life,' he'd said, shaking his head. 'Not if I can help it. Write a book when you're sixty, like most of 'em do. Until then, what's important is paying the bills.'

Barbara had kept quiet, knowing that an intervention on her part would have repercussions that would not have been good for any of them. Noah, who understood little of the complicated dynamic that existed between his parents, largely because Barbara did her very best to protect him from it at all costs, had seen her lack of support as a direct assault on his whole being, and it had set him on a downward spiral: if his own mother could not stand up in defense of him, who would?

Might as well accept that his life was not his own to live, and probably never would be.

Noah was having a hard time accepting that, however. He had given up on a part of himself in the face of his father's derision, and that part had been an important piece of him. Shutting himself off from it hurt, every day.

Every single day.

He snuck a wounded look across at Don, who had distanced himself from the conversation going on around him, as he so often did. He'd gone back to staring at the long black walking cane leaning against the desk, eyes fixed on it as if he thought it might move, or something.

One day you'll get it, Noah thought to himself, his mind potent and rancid with rejection and frustration.

One day.

But Don, who had other things on his mind, remained oblivious.

WALKING CANE

Don was oblivious to everyone, in fact, not just his son. He found himself rooted in place, staring at the slender, polished ebony walking cane somehow so alluring. He thought the cane looked familiar, but couldn't be bothered to try and figure out why. He retreated into himself instead, feeling his vision filling up with this one, singular object, and, moving as if he was in a dream, he edged closer to the desk.

Distantly, Noah's father heard the others gathered nearby talking, heard them as if hearing them from beneath the water in a large warm bath, for the babble of conversation was distorted and muffled, but he was fine with that. They all talked too much anyway, and none of it was about anything he considered worthwhile.

That walking cane, however...it was weird, because it seemed to *want* his attention, somehow, and even more strangely, Don got the impression that this object was actually *worth* his attention. He knew this was a dumbfuck stupid thing to think, but he couldn't shake the feeling that it had been put there for him, and him alone, ivory handle smooth and worked like something edible, like candy, or half-melted butter, and he knew he wasn't supposed to, but he wanted to touch it. He wanted to reach out and let his fingers slide across the glossy bone handle, and whenever Don wanted something, he generally went right ahead and took it, so he crept closer to the desk, moving slowly until it bumped against his hip, then pretended to lean against it for support. He snuck a look at the rest of the party as he did this, saw they were still engaged in the act of staring up at the stupid, fancy ceiling, the Tour Guide included.

And so he took the opportunity as presented. He pulled his right hand back out of his jean pocket, and slid it carefully and slowly over the handle of the walking cane, which was leaning right next to him, waiting. He almost sagged in pleasure as his rough skin hit smooth ivory.

The conversation in the room dampened down further, as if he had suddenly moved very far away from them all. For a moment, Don wondered if he was, in fact, moving, although he knew he was also standing still. It was a weird feeling, but not an unpleasant one, a bit like the feeling you got if you were sitting still in a train, and another train moved past yours, and for a split second, there was no way of knowing who was moving: was it your train, or the other one?

It felt kind of exciting to Don, and not much in Don's life excited him anymore.

He tightened his grip. The cane felt good in his hand, *right* somehow. Ergonomically matched to the contours of his palm. He closed his eyes and let his thumb caress the handle's nub, which was inscribed with some more fancy lettering: *CLIII*. As he did so, he felt the ivory warm up beneath his skin, as if it was responding to him somehow, as if—

Charles Lester III tried to get his breathing under control, attempting to slow the rampant thunder of his runaway heartbeat. This was proving difficult, for he was not as young as he used to be, and the adrenaline was high in him. Besides, it was hard to think of anything much with the smell of fresh blood so thick in his nostrils. Fresh blood, and fresh brains, for Charles Lester III was covered from head to toe in the tissue and matter and dust of another man. A man who had stood in his way. A man who had transgressed, after years of loyal service.

Charles looked down at the ruined body lying on the floor of his study. He tried to make sense of what he saw, and found that he couldn't, not really. What remained of his former valet's face was an indistinct smear of flesh mashed into an expensive oriental carpet, one of several around the Chateau, but that was hardly the point.

If he squinted and used his imagination he could just about make out the shell-like shape of an ear, emerging from the pulpy mess like a little fungus, and resting on the floor an inch away from the polished patent leather of his left shoe, he could see two broken teeth. From his viewpoint, they looked like dropped cherry-blossom petals after a heavy rain, only the rain was red, the floor was red, the walls were spattered with red, in fact everything was red, just the way he usually liked it, only—

Don jerked himself away from the desk, and the walking stick slid out of his grasp, clattering to the floor. He shook his head, as if trying to dislodge an insect from his ear canal. What the fuck had that been? What? He could still smell the unmistakable scent of blood in his nostrils, still feel how wet and heavy his skin had been, how red, how—

'I told you not to touch anything, didn't I? I was quite clear, I remember.'

The Tour Guide appeared before him, and he did not look happy. Don blinked and rubbed his eyes. For a moment, when looking at the Tour Guide, he thought he had seen...he thought...

'Sorry,' he mumbled, and he bent quickly to pick up the cane before the Guide could interfere and confiscate it from him. As soon as his fingers connected with the ivory handle once again he felt a thrill of energy coursing up his arm, and his heart, already racing along, skipped a beat, and he bowed his head as he tried to fight off a surge of dizziness that assaulted him out of nowhere. Beneath him, the intricate pattern of the Persian carpet swum and danced, and he—

Charles felt increasingly annoyed about the carpet the longer he stared at it. It would have to be disposed of. There was no one alive who could work all the blood out, no matter how hard they scrubbed. He realized with a steadily mounting fury that his outburst of violence had cost him thousands upon thousands of dollars in lost investment, for he considered every item he collected and installed in his house an investment, an addition to the estate, an extension of his wealth and status, even if he did not consider the people who worked for him in the same light.

'Bastard,' he muttered to the Valet's corpse. 'You ruined my fucking carpet.'

He could taste blood on his tongue as he spoke. It tasted foreign, exotic. Exciting. It spurred him into another frenzied bout of violence.

'Bastard!'

His arm, which was raised high above his head, came down in a vicious, swooping arc. A glint of yellow streaked past: a glittering cufflink, punctuating the crisp sleeve of his white dress shirt, a dress shirt his Valet had starched and pressed for him only that morning.

'Bastard!'

Clutched tight in his slick wet hand was a long, polished gentleman's walking cane fashioned from polished ebony. The handle of the cane was carved from ivory, worn smooth by years of handling, and embossed with the initials 'CLIII' in florid gold lettering.

'Stupid, ungrateful bastard!'

With a disgusting, nauseating whump, the end of the cane, which was now encrusted in brain matter and strands of glossy, dark hair, came down upon the lifeless body, striking the ribcage, needlessly shattering yet more bone. Charles, intent on breaking everything encased in the useless sack of flesh below him, cared not for what was necessary or needful. He cared only about the raging fury in his head, for the dead man who had been alive only ten minutes prior had betrayed him. The greedy dirty bastard Valet had put his disgusting, worthless hands upon his property, taken what did not belong to him, and so to his mind, overkill was perfectly justifiable.

'Bastard! Bastard! Bastard!'

He battered and thrashed at the corpse until suddenly, with a distinct crack, the end of the cane snapped off and went flying across the room, hitting the far wall and rolling to a stop near the door, which Charles had foolishly left open.

Near the door, or more precisely, near the feet of a woman who stood, terrified in the doorway, unnoticed until now.

Charles, who had until that moment been a frenzied blur of a man, froze.

The woman, who was dressed in a Housekeeper's pinny and cap, red tufts of hair peeking out from beneath, clutched a pail and mop in one hand. The mop handle rattled against the metal pail. The fingers of her other hand were clamped firmly over her mouth, stifling back a small, strangled scream as she absorbed the scene before her.

For a second or two, there was silence. The two observed each other.

Then:

'Master,' the Housekeeper said, from behind her fingers. She shivered from head to toe in shock, the mop handle rattle, rattle, rattling away into the morbid quiet.

'Master...what have you done?'

Charles Lester III was across the room in four long, quick strides, before the woman had time to drop the pail and run. He snatched at her wrist and dragged her into the room, heaving the heavy door shut behind them. The Housekeeper, who was stronger than she looked, struggled in his grip, but the Master was fueled by desperation and righteous anger and self-preservation and adrenaline, a potent cocktail of stimulants. He tightened his hold on her wrist, dragging her over to the horrible, saturated scene in the middle of the room and flinging her hard in the direction of the body.

Propelled by his fury, she flew forward, stumbled, tripped over the pulpy mess, and landed on her rear beside the body, legs and arms akimbo as she struggled for purchase on the slippery, sodden carpet. The sight was so pitiful and absurd that it drew Charles up short, and he let out a sharp snort of laughter.

'Please,' the woman begged, clumsily scrabbling backwards, her hands slipping on the little treacly messes that were the Valet's brains. 'Please, don't!'

And Charles, who liked it when people begged, could see from the look on her face that she could not believe this was really happening to her, he could see that her grasp of reality had slipped to the point where she was unable to process what was about to occur: the inevitable.

Don realized, distantly, that the Tour Guide was trying to pull the walking cane from his now sweaty hands. Not being able to give the man his full attention, owing to the drama playing out in his mind's eye, he instead tightened his grip, became a vice, became a locked box, and the cane, which felt slick and greasy, remained his. Because he was stronger than the Guide, despite their mismatched heights, and Don was by far the more alpha of the two—and he knew it. He knew it as surely as—

The weak can never quite believe it when they find themselves prey, Charles thought. *They think they can eat grass in the sun and never become food, do they?*

How can people let themselves live this way, as lesser creatures? How?

Charles' rage, already a huge, high, towering thing, taller than the cedar trees outside, taller than the Sunshire Chateau itself, tall enough to brush against the very moon, continued to stretch and swell until it became a rod he could threaten gods with, although Charles did not believe in gods or God or in anything much except for money.

Money, and violence.

Charles Lester III hefted his cane in his right hand, filled to bursting with the type of uncontrollable anger that sets a man apart from his peers (although this, of course, is what Charles Lester III craved—to be set apart, and above, and beyond all those around him) and the Housekeeper flinched and cowered, bringing her own arm across her face protectively. This only served to make her Master madder still, as if the weakness and vulnerability of others was his responsibility somehow, his burden.

And even though his cane was broken, now snapped in two, he knew it had just enough life left in it to finish one last job, an important job. A job that the Master of a big house such as he was familiar with: to remind his employees, his inferiors, his lessers, of his weight in gold over theirs, which was insubstantial, for they were, after all, smaller creatures. It was his duty to remind them of their righteous place in the scheme of things, and to protect himself at all costs, because he was the Master, and his life was worth so much more than the lives of those who had been stupid enough to be born the wrong side of money and smarts.

'Bitch,' he snarled, and his face contorted with the force of the word.

The cane swung high up into the air, the jagged, splintered end pointing skyward for a moment like a righteous finger, and then it descended, and the woman screamed, and screamed, and then screamed once more until suddenly, there were no more screams.

The Sunshire Chateau fell quiet as yet more blood sank down through the rich weft and warp of the large carpet beneath Charles' feet. It was a carpet that had come all the way from Persia, a carpet he had hand-picked himself after much searching and haggling. The sickle-leaf, vine scroll patterning drank thirstily of the red nectar spilled upon its design, and the blood worked its way past the hand-pulled knots, of which there must have been thousands, tens of thousands, asymmetrically woven because it was Persian rather than Turkish which also added to its value, and it began to soak into the tiny gaps in the polished parquet wooden floor that sat beneath the carpet.

And the Chateau, ill-fated and ill-conceived from the day the very first foundation brick was laid only a few years before, accepted the gift of blood with a slavish thirst, drinking deep, while the Master of the house straightened his cuffs, upon which yellow stones glittered, smoothed back his disheveled, sticky hair, and tried to think of a good place to hide the bodies.

'DON! What are you doing?'

Barbara's shocked voice eventually brought him back into the room with a jolt. Brimming with anger, with fury, with power, with righteousness, he raised the cane, which was still in his hand, high above his head, and things swam back into view slowly: the members of the tour group, staring at him, his wife, raising an arm to shield herself, his son, a shocked, blank look on his face, moving to intervene. The Guide, grimly determined to wrest the cane from Don's hand. Baltimore, rushing to help. It all looked like a tableau or a painting from a fucking museum, and he was in the middle of it, and the cane, which had grown almost too warm to hold, was starting to come down, down upon his wife, down upon his misery, down upon...

'Don!'

He blinked, and the cane was still in his hand, but he was not towering above her anymore, ready to thrash the living daylights out of her, but rather standing, gripping the cane as the Tour Guide tried to take it from him. He came fully back into his own consciousness then, aware that something else had been living inside of him, even if for a short while, and the residue it left on his brain was slimy, and fetid, like garbage juice.

Don, realising that he had been occupied against his will, and understanding at last what it meant to be controlled, coerced, invaded without permission—even though his wife had been trying to tell him for years—let go of the cane by suddenly springing his fingers open. The Guide, who had been braced against a tug-of-war, almost fell backwards, but managed to recover at the last moment.

'Thank you,' he said, smoothing his hair back. 'That belongs to the house, not to you.'

Don looked down at his hands, which were suddenly raw, red, and blistered, as if he'd thrust them into an open fire.

'I'm sorry,' he replied, dully. 'I don't know what came over me.' A fog began to settle on his mind, damp, and thick. It made him feel confused, dislocated.

What had just happened to him?

The Tour Guide wiped a bead of sweat from his brow with his index finger. 'Apology accepted,' he replied, and he put the walking cane back where Don had found it, leaning it carefully against the edge of the writing desk. He stared at it for a moment or two as he once again touched the back of his head with tender fingers.

The rest of the group, who had been sure they were about to see Don evicted from the Chateau, exchanged stunned glances with each other, glances which the Guide noted, and chose to ignore.

'Shall we move on?' He said, brightly. 'We've still got a lot left to see.'

SECRET DOORWAYS

'I'm so sorry about my husband's behavior,' Barbara said quietly, while Don stood gazing out of the Library window with a vacant, zombie-like expression on his face, as if he were reliving something, a memory perhaps, and not a good one.

'I really don't know what's wrong with him.'

This was a lie, for there was a lot wrong with Don, and Barbara was well acquainted with his faults, for that was what marriage felt like, sometimes—an enforced, protracted analysis of another person's weaknesses. Still, her contrition was genuine. Truth be told, she'd been worried about something like this happening before now, only she'd expected such acting out from Noah, not her husband. Not that spoiling things wasn't a specialty of Don's, because it was. Parties, meals out, school events, family barbecues...but Don usually chose to disrupt things in less dramatic ways, with sneering, sarcasm, recalcitrance and a general moodiness.

Not whatever that display had been.

Barbara turned to check on her son, wondering if Don's little exercise in rule-breaking had inspired her son to break a few rules of his own, but she found him where she'd left him, hood up, eyes on his feet, looking bored, but still behaving himself. Looking at him, she realized what a mistake she'd made in booking this tour. A tour that Don had not wanted to come on in the first place. Don had wanted to take a drive out to the mountains, or the lakes, maybe try some fishing. Barbara, who was not fond of boats, bait, or fish, knew that trying to take their son fishing in his current frame of mind would have been a disaster, so she'd suggested the Sunshire Chateau instead, largely because Noah didn't appear to hate that idea quite so vehemently. After several attempts, Barbara had finally managed to talk Don out of the fishing idea, citing all the usual reasons—not wanting to encourage any more conflict, needing to keep Noah in sight all day so he couldn't get up to mischief, the weather, how tired they were, how they didn't have the right clothes for a trip out on the water, Noah's intense dislike of fish...Don had given in, eventually, but sulked about being outnumbered from the second he agreed to do something else to the second they set foot in the property they now toured.

Barbara found this behavior, and her husband's existence generally, quite exhausting, akin to having a second child, and she was starting to show it. She felt like the portrait of Lester's wife in the Reception Hall: tired, stretched, and worn.

So she apologized on Don's behalf, although she needn't have worried. The Tour Guide seemed curiously unruffled.

'Think nothing of it,' he replied, nonchalantly.

'Wait a moment, wait a moment,' Bow-tie said, and the color in his cheeks was no longer due to excitement. 'You booted those two darling little old ladies off of the tour because they wouldn't wear these hideous slippers, but when a man breaks one of your rules, and touches something he has been told not to, it's alright?'

The Guide sighed. 'It's different,' he said, not elaborating on this statement.

'Different how? I fail to see any difference except the obvious one,' Bow-tie replied, crossly. The petite older man folded his arms and beetled his brows. 'I'm not fond of rules, at the best of times, but if you're going to have them, at least be consistent.'

The Guide did not like being challenged in his domain. He puffed out his chest and drew himself up to his full height. Bow-tie, aware that he was attempting to intimidate him with his superior tallness, yanked at his shirt collars, making sure they were straight and sharp.

'I suggest, sir, that if you-'

'Did you hear that?' Linda Louise asked, cutting over the conversation and taking a huge amount in pleasure at being able to do so.

The group went quiet, and listened.

'Hear what?' Bow-tie asked, and the Tour Guide echoed this question by raising his eyebrows.

'I heard a noise, a weird...'

Before she could continue, a grinding and grating filled the Library. The floor under the tour group's feet rumbled as something heavy worked in an unseen part of the Chateau.

'What on earth?' Bow-tie muttered.

By way of a reply, a section of the left-hand Library shelf nearest to the bay window suddenly popped open, swinging wide to reveal a black space behind. The group saw then that the end section of the giant bookcase was actually a cleverly disguised and concealed door, perfectly camouflaged by a thin line of dummy books cut neatly in half. Attached to the shelves around the outline of the door in such a way that when the door was closed, the books looked complete, but when it was open, they bifurcated, they were brilliantly effective, and the tour party were delighted by this new development.

'Is that a secret door?'

'Cool.'

'Where does it go?'

'Is there a secret vault down there?'

'Servant's passages? I know they have those in the big fancy houses in England!'

'Oh, I wonder if it's where Lester kept his treasure!'

'Or a body, ha ha.'

The Tour Guide let the tide of banality wash over him, thinking: *Ned.*

Ned had been investigating the Blue Room, it seemed. Ned had discovered that the doorstopper had a dual purpose, and by some miracle of observation, Ned had found the operating mechanism in the back of the fireplace.

This led the Tour Guide to wonder, had Ned met Alice yet?

The distant sound of footsteps approaching the Library by way of the passage, echoed out, and the Guide could tell there was more than one set of feet making their way in his direction. This answered his question.

Well, he thought, bleakly. *Well.*

If Alice had introduced herself to Ned, then the house was working faster than he thought it would. Maybe it had warmed to the irritating man, and if that was the case, the Tour Guide hated him even more for it.

He hung this hatred out on his face to dry.

It was the first thing Ned saw when he popped his head out of the servant's passage to find himself in the Library.

MEMORIES IN BOXES

'Not you again,' Ned grinned, enjoying the dark look on the Tour Guide's face. He held his phone out before him like a flashlight as he emerged and stepped to one side to allow Alice through the space behind him. Fumbling with the phone, he tapped at the screen until the light went off, and nodded another greeting at the tour party.

The Guide curled his lip in disgust. 'I see you found a new friend,' he said. This was not directed at Ned.

'Ned offered to help me clean the chandelier,' Alice offered, meekly. 'We can wait, if it's a bad time.'

Don, who felt as if his entire head were encased by resin, blearily clocked Alice's red curls and flinched in distant recognition. Did he know this woman? Had he...

Please, don't!

Don suddenly understood the expression *'you look like you've seen a ghost'*. He made an odd croaking noise deep in his throat, but that was all he could manage. Everything else was too much, too much effort.

'We were just leaving,' the Guide countered, and he proceeded to round up the chattering guests like a mother hen rounding up chicks. 'Plenty more to see,' he said, hustling them along and tapping his watch for emphasis. 'Time is ticking on.'

Except it wasn't, not on his wrist.

'Don't let me stop you,' Ned said, delighted to be the one interrupting the other man's day, for a change.

'Can we see the secret passage?' Bow-tie asked, eagerly. Barbara did not look so sure about this suggestion, but the others seemed keen.

The Guide thought about it for a moment. He knew exactly where the passages led, how far they stretched, and the dangers inherent in taking the guests into them, but he also knew that it made no real difference, in the end, which way they went. A tour was a tour when all was said and done, and if they wanted to see the innards of the house instead of the dermis, that was their problem.

He shrugged.

'Why not,' he said, 'but if one of you gets lost, don't blame me.'

The guests assured him they would stay together. The Guide knew that assurances meant nothing at Sunshire. Promises were as reliable as dust, between these walls. Why make promises the house had no intention of keeping? It was a waste of everybody's time, as he was well aware. The house would decide who became lost, and who remained found, just as it always had.

'Come along,' he commanded, taking a hold of Don's elbow and steering him along. The other man now had a blank, empty look in his eyes, and an odd half-smile on his lips. His hands tensed and released, making fists that relaxed and clenched and relaxed over and over again, and the Guide knew without looking that the skin on those hands would be burned, sore.

He cast a final look at the walking cane, touching the back of his head.

Then he ushered the tour party out of the Library and into the servant's passage by way of the secret door, one by one, like children into a classroom. The guests filed into the narrow space beyond, ducking their heads and jumping at cobwebs and stumbling in the shadows as Alice and Ned, who stood quietly side by side, watched them go, until only the Guide was left.

He turned to them, and Alice made a show of examining her hands, her face turned down, avoiding scrutiny. Ned did not like this, did not like the effect the other man had on the polite, cheerful woman he had known for such a short time, but then there was not much about the Tour Guide he *did* like.

'Behave yourselves,' the Tour Guide said, blackly.

'We won't,' Ned replied, under his breath.

The Tour Guide bent his head and retreated into the dark passageway, which Ned now knew to be cold, damp, narrow, and poorly lit. Without waiting even a moment, he closed the secret door behind the Guide, obscuring his retreating form from view, and watched in admiration as the outline of the doorway seemed to dissolve seamlessly into rows of leather bound books.

'Clever,' he said, and Alice breathed a sigh of relief.

'I really don't like that man,' she said, and then she spotted something, and froze.

'What?' Ned asked, following her gaze. He found himself staring at a long, polished wooden walking cane with an ivory handle inlaid with gold, tooled letters. He knew instantly who it belonged to, for he had seen the exact same item in the portrait of Charles Lester III that hung in the Reception Hall.

Alice swallowed, and ran a hand gently down the side of her face. For a split second, Ned thought the outline of her cheek shimmered faintly, flickered, became something else, but then the moment passed, and she was solid, peachy flesh again.

Peachy?! Ned thought to himself. *Get a grip, man.*

Then he allowed the grandeur of the Library to sink in. 'This really is a fantastic collection,' he said, running a finger along a shelf lined with theology texts, the most comprehensive array he'd ever seen, including several first editions of *Tracts for the Times*, a series of ninety Anglo-Catholic revival tracts that were of enormous value.

'Why didn't you start in this room? With the books, I mean. That would have made more sense. Why the Blue Room?' Alice asked, her composure recovered.

'I went where I was sent, I guess,' Ned replied, distracted. 'The Guide took me straight there and set me to work.'

'Yes, he would, I suppose,' Alice replied.

'He looks a bit like Charles Lester, don't you think? The Guide, I mean.' Ned made this realization as his train of thought was interrupted by a miniature portrait of the man in question, framed in velvet and silver and resting on one of the bookshelves he was examining. He almost reached out and picked it up for a closer look, but the stinging of his palms and fingertips stopped him: *The ghosts don't like it when you touch their things. Neither do I.*

Alice stayed quiet, but Ned didn't mind. She was a quiet, shy sort of person. *The exact opposite of Jo, even if they look the same* he thought, but swiped that idea away.

He continued, working through some things in his head.

'I've never seen a house with this much ego, you know? Everywhere you look, there is some reminder of Lester's wealth and success. Do you know how many portraits of him there are in this house? I counted once, on my lunch break. Fifty-three. Imagine living in a place with *fifty-three* paintings of yourself hung on the walls. That's without the mirrors everywhere. Walking around, looking at yourself all day long. The man made a religion out of himself, like this house is a giant shrine or something.'

Alice sighed, and went over to the large bay window, where an antique wooden and brass step-ladder was folded and stowed in an alcove, awaiting use. Ned saw it was a book ladder, meant to allow people to reach whatever was on the higher shelves, but Alice dragged it over to a spot beneath the chandelier. It took Ned a second or two to wake up to what she was doing before he went to help her.

'Successful men rarely are nice,' she said, panting a little. 'It takes a certain type of person to build an empire, doesn't it?'

'I suppose you're right. Nice men finish last.' Bitterness came through as he said this, and memories of Jo began battering at the lock-box again. He ignored them as best he could, but the memories were getting louder, more insistent by the hour.

Alice finished wrestling with the ladder, having set it up to her satisfaction. She looked at Ned then, and she seemed so serious, so earnest, that he was completely taken aback.

'You're nice,' she said, simply.

Ned felt a little surge of excitement in the pit of his belly, and squashed it down quickly.

'Maybe, but I am also extremely unsuccessful, by modern standards. No real home to call my own, a specific but wholly unprofitable career path, not even...' He grimaced, feeling the old wounds throb. 'Not even a girlfriend.'

Alice said:

'No sweetheart?'

Ned's eyes locked onto hers, and he found himself smiling. Her turn of phrase was so formal, so old-fashioned, he thought she was teasing him.

'No sweetheart,' he replied, and it hurt to say.

The last time Ned had really smiled at a woman properly, really relaxed into it, really put his whole soul out there and open for business in his eyes, had been the night before his wedding.

Jo, his fiancée, had taken a room in a hotel across town, citing superstition, tradition and 'bad luck' as a good reason not to see each other right before the big day, but Ned couldn't stand being away from her at such an important moment in their lives. For months he had been dreaming of this day, months and months, and even a few hours separated from her felt like a waste. So, he flipped superstition the birdy and drove to see her, a cold bottle of Moët and a bunch of roses in the crook of his arm as a surprise. When he knocked on her door, he was surprised not to hear the sound of laughter within—he had thought she was spending the night with some girlfriends, watching stupid movies and getting tipsy, but all was quiet. He knocked again. Eventually, Jo answered. She was dressed in a bathrobe, and makeup-free, her hair scraped on top of her head in a messy bun. When she saw Ned standing there, arms full of champagne and roses, her face had crumpled.

'Oh,' she said, voice cracking. 'It's you.'

'Were you expecting someone else?' He chuckled, feeling a slight twist in his guts.

'No, it's just...you shouldn't...' The words tailed off, and she covered her eyes with her hands, a sure sign that she was about to burst into tears.

'Hey, come on now, what's the matter?' Ned looked at Jo in confusion, putting the gifts down on the floor by his feet and scooping her into an embrace. She'd gone to him reluctantly, her body taught with emotion, but eventually she let him do what he did best: stand strong while she leaned on him.

'What's up, baby?' He spoke softly into her hair, which always smelled like coconut shampoo.

Jo shook, unable to reply. Then the tears came, as he knew they would. She cried into his shoulder for a solid ten minutes, he out in the hall, she half-in, half-out of her hotel room. Ned didn't bother trying to get anything out of her until she began to dry out, until her body stopped quivering. He felt a damp patch spread on his shirt, ignored it. He was used to soaking up her tears. Jo cried easily. He liked that about her. It meant she cared about things. She was soft, in the middle, something that had surprised him when he first met her, because she was loud and brash and kind of brittle on the outside. He used to joke that she was like a crème brûlée, that he had cracked her hard surface with a silver teaspoon. She would roll her eyes at him when he said that.

'You going to tell me what's up?' He prompted, when her sobs had calmed to small hiccups.

She pushed herself away from him, examining the soggy patch on his shirt with a rueful expression. Even with a face swollen and blotchy from crying, she was still beautiful. He had no idea sometimes why she had decided to hitch her wagon to him. He had learned not to question that, too much, because therein lay madness. He simply learned to enjoy the fact that he was her cart horse.

Or so he'd thought.

Jo sighed, and straightened her back a little, a subconscious gesture that indicated her resolve to deal with whatever was bothering her. A little outburst here and there, and then on with the day, that was her style.

Except Ned wasn't completely sure if that *was* what was happening here. Something had nagged at his sense of equilibrium, an instinct, or sixth sense.

Surely she shouldn't be this sad on the night before their wedding?

'I'm alright,' she said, and he knew it was a lie.

'Anything you want to talk about?'

'Just nerves,' she replied, dropping eye contact and staring at her fingernails, which were immaculately manicured. 'I'm just nervous about the wedding. You know I'm not good around so many people, and it's a big day, right?'

He nodded. 'Right.'

'I'll be okay. It's just a last-minute panic. I think it happens to all brides, right?'

'Right,' Ned repeated, feeling like a parrot. A rather awkward silence followed.

Is she getting cold feet?

He dismissed the idea, annoyed with himself.

'I'm fine,' Jo said, and she forced a smile onto her face.

But behind her, on the bed in the hotel room, Ned could see Jo's phone lying face up on the bed. The screen glowed with notifications, one after the other, a little display of anxious communication that made him feel itchy, without knowing why.

'Are you sure?' He said, feeling suddenly less sure of himself. 'I can come in, if you'd like, run you a bath, maybe a...'

'No.' She cut him off, a little too sharply. Then, her voice calmed. 'No, it's okay, Ned. I'm honestly okay. I'm just tired and a bundle of nerves. I'll be alright, I promise. Besides, it's bad luck for you to see me like this, before the wedding. So scoot, okay? I promise I'm fine.'

After, Ned would wish he had insisted on spending the night with her. He wished he'd found a reason to go into her hotel room, get a look at her phone screen. He wished he'd probed further, gotten to the bottom of her weird, sad outburst.

Instead, he'd smiled at her. 'I can't wait to marry you tomorrow,' he'd said, offering the roses and champagne once again. And he meant it. He put everything into those words, and everything into his smile.

Turned out, everything wouldn't be enough.

'Ned? Where did you go?'

Ned focused on Alice, and realized he wasn't smiling anymore. 'My fiancée jilted me at the altar,' he blurted, and then slapped a hand over his mouth, thinking *why the hell did I say that?*

'I'm sorry,' he apologized, after a moment. 'I'm not sure why I told you that.'

'It's the house,' Alice replied simply. 'The house gets under your skin, after a while. It likes to play with your secrets, Ned. Play with them, and make them its own.'

'I...I have no idea what you're talking about,' Ned said, but all he could think about, now that he had allowed the memory to get a foothold, was the note Jo had left.

I can't, it said.
I am so very sorry.
This is not what I need.
We both know it is for the best.
Jo.

But what about me? Ned had thought, crushing the letter in his fist, feeling his fingernails cut a row of tiny half-moons into the tender flesh of his palm.

What about the room full of guests waiting for us downstairs, expecting me to return with Jo on my arm?

What about my Mother, who had her suit freshly tailored and her hair cut especially for this day?

What about my Father, pacing the halls with the ring in his pocket?

What about the cake?

And the eighty-five bottles of champagne chilling in the kitchen?

And the honeymoon?

Fuck...what about the mortgage?

And the kids we talked about having?

What about...

Me?

He'd sunk slowly onto the large double bed that she'd been in, only hours before. Had she slept here? Or gone as soon as he had left?

He should never have left her.

Then he'd thought:

What about me, Jo?

Do I get a say in this?

I guess not. He had felt cold seep into his very core.

I guess I can't force someone to marry me if they don't want to...can I?

Before he could continue with that fuzzy train of thought, there had been a knock at the suite door. With a lurching heart, thinking it was Jo, thinking that she had changed her mind, he'd staggered up from the bed.

'Jo?!' He'd fumbled with the handle like a drunk man, his fingers slick and clammy. But when he yanked the door wide, he found only his father outside. The last few dregs of hope that he had subconsciously nursed up until that point dissolved in an instant, and he'd stood, waiting for his heart to slippery-slide back down his gullet while it dawned on his father that something was terribly, terribly wrong.

'Everything okay, son?' The other man asked, gently, knowing already what the answer would be.

And there was something in his father's eyes that had brought it home for Ned, then. It was the kindness that shone there, and the deep, deep sorrow. For Jo was gone, she really was.

And today was no longer their wedding day.

Ned had leaned forward, like a tower slowly collapsing as rotten foundations sank and gave way, and his father had caught him, and held him, and Ned had cried then, the first time he had cried for years, because he had always been told that to cry was to be weak, and not wanting to appear weak, he had instead wreathed himself in smiles and the disguise had been a good one up until this point. Maybe it had even deceived Jo for a while, but not enough.

He had not been convincing enough.

While his father tensed and then softened, began to stroke his back, the hotel door closed behind them, slowly, and it felt, at the time, as if that door closed on Ned's very soul, and it would take a house full of ghosts to unlock it again, and to show him that some doors are meant to be closed, and others...

'Ned?'

'What?' He replied, dully.

'Can I show you something?' Alice asked, abandoning the idea of cleaning the chandelier.

'I should be getting back to my work,' Ned replied, and his voice was cold, colder than he'd intended.

'You have plenty of time for that later,' Alice replied, and again, for a tiny, confusing moment, the outlines and contours of her face seemed to blur, shift, and he was reminded of the ghost of the Blue Room, who he'd almost forgotten about, as incredible as that seemed. For his brain was a mess of thoughts and feelings, of memories that belonged to him and to someone else, of ghosts both real and rooted in the past, and he was beginning to feel strange, and unpredictable, and overwhelmed.

He was beginning, for want of a better word, to feel haunted.

'I'm...I'm sorry, I can't.'

But Alice took his hand in hers, gently this time, and he found it didn't hurt as much as he thought it might.

'Yes, yes you can,' she said, and her tone brooked no refusal.

THE ATRIUM

PASSAGES

The tour party traipsed through the servant's passage, keeping close together as they promised they would, and keeping their thoughts closer still, for the strange, narrow space they now found themselves in did not invite conversation, although it did invite a lot of other things, like curiosity, anxiety, and even a touch of wonder as it suddenly branched out, and became one of several narrow alleys.

For there was a world behind the walls, a world of forks and angles and curves and smooth, neatly laid bricks, drainage and ventilation shafts, staircases, dumb-waiter shafts, rotting electrics, doors, handles, alcoves, passing places, and unexpectedly, little spaces here and there with chairs and tables arranged, sometimes even a shelf or two of books, thick with dust and cobwebs, neatly arranged: resting spots for weary staff who had been run off their feet. Unobtrusive yet functional, the passages were part of a network of tunnels at Sunshire that, the Guide informed them, stretched for miles, acting like a plexus of veins beneath the skin and connecting every single part of the house together, including the attic, cellars, grounds and gardens.

The guests pondered this as they walked, Noah up front, the Guide bringing up the rear, prodding at Don, who shuffled along as if sleepwalking. Every now and then, Barbara would turn and poke at him, her mouth drawn tight. 'Don?' She would ask. 'Are you okay?'

But Don was lost in a world of his own, and would not, could not answer.

The odd book nooks served as natural pause points for the group as they wound their way slowly towards their next destination. Rests were frequent, for the guests were getting tired. They would walk for what felt like a long, long time, simultaneously covering huge distances yet hardly moving at all. Quick, concerned glances at cell phones and watches revealed that time was being deceitful, and their progress was no slower than it had been on the other side of the walls.

The third time the passage widened out into a resting alcove, Linda Louise dropped to her ankles to scratch an itch on the arch of her foot beneath the slipper sole. She used this as an opportunity to let the Guide and the others move ahead after their quick break, for she was struggling with feelings of claustrophobia and anxiety the more grouped and squashed together they were. She was also tired of having the Guide behind her, for some reason. It felt better to let him move ahead, let him lead, than to let him follow.

She waited until there was a decent gap between herself and the last of the party, and then followed at a slower pace, admiring at the feat of engineering and design the passages represented. She had known of their existence before coming on the tour, but they were still remarkable. Not so much in what they represented—that people of a certain status should be neither seen nor heard—but a valuable slice of local history nonetheless.

There was, she noted, as her feet began to protest at the amount of ground she had covered, a system of bells and buzzers laid out along the passage walls, for what mysterious purpose, Linda could not tell—perhaps for a member of staff to sound and raise the alarm if they got lost, which, now she was deep within the house, she could understand as a feasible possibility. At least it wasn't as dark down here as she had first feared: the narrow, cool spaces between the walls of the Sunshire Chateau were lit at intervals by lamps fitted with Mazda half-watt electric bulbs, sent over especially from a factory in Rugby, England, if her memory served correctly. Linda had memorized a lot of things about Sunshire, from the type of perfume Rose Lester liked to wear to the exact amount of money spent on the giant cedar trees planted in the drive—Lester had had them shipped over and transplanted almost fully grown, at massive expense. Linda remembered poring over the old house receipts, now kept in an archive down in town, and shaking her head at the extravagance. But then, she had shaken her head at a lot of things, when it came to Sunshire. The Chateau was in thrall to the whim and greed of Charles Lester III, and in that respect, was a wounded, abused place, a layered oil painting, just like the paintings in the Reception Hall, only instead of paint, it was daubed with secret after secret, lie after lie, and Linda Louise knew, deep down, that her work in the archives had only scratched the surface of the place. That was why she had been so keen to see it in the flesh, so to speak. She knew that if she could soak up some of the atmosphere of the place, she could put visuals to some of the facts and data she'd been collecting.

She was determined to peel the veneer off of Sunshire, if it killed her. Rewrite history a little, make it fairer. More representative of how life had actually been, instead of the universally accepted, sterile version the local schools currently fed students.

She dropped a little further back from the group, enjoying the quiet as the other feet shuffled ahead, their ridiculous slippers catching on the rough flooring of the passages—no Persian carpets or polished parquet here, thank you very much. Just bare brick, bare cables, spiders, mildew and—

A cupboard. Large, a rusty padlock on the handle, indicating that something of value had once been stored inside, was *still* possibly stored inside.

Is it true that Lester hid his fortune in the walls of the house?

The teen's voice came back to her. An annoying kid, for sure, but he asked the right questions.

Hid his fortune...walls...

Linda Louise stopped in her tracks. Surely not, not in a cupboard this scrappy. Still, it was well concealed, out of the public's eye, unopened for years, it looked like. She couldn't have explained what it was, exactly, but something about the sealed alcove called to her. An energy, perhaps, or maybe a small detail that she couldn't quite make sense of. Something.

Who are you kidding, girl, she told herself, smiling. *You know exactly what's calling to you. You know he must have hid his fortune somewhere, because the accounts and the receipts didn't add up, did they? The ones you found down in the archives, at any rate. It was all supposed to be made public, wasn't it?*

But she knew enough about Charles Lester III to assume that it hadn't.

The closed door was suddenly the only thing she could think about. It seemed to grow in size before her eyes, as she imagined lock-boxes full of gold and jewels inside—or at the very least, a safe. The handle to the cupboard in particular seemed to want to be touched, held, pulled upon, and Linda decided, in a rare moment of impulse, to try it.

First, she took a moment to orient herself, for the tunnels looked eerily uniform in every direction, and she did not want to get lost. Scanning left then right, Linda Louise made a note of how far ahead the tour group were—far enough to be a little concerning, but not so far that she could not hear them further along the passage, or make out the retreating, looming figure of the Guide in the distance, his size highlighted by the cramped space around him.

Then, she turned back to the cupboard. *Maybe,* she thought, *there is something important in there. The padlock looks old, and unreliable. I should just give the handle a quick rattle, see if anything comes of it.*

So she did, and her assumptions were correct. She grasped hold of the long metal handle, braced herself by rooting her feet firmly into the ground, and pulled. The padlock, which was threaded through a rusted iron hasp, resisted, but Linda could see the hasp was loose, the screws holding it in place unthreaded, almost ready to drop to the floor.

Linda pulled again, and the padlock hasp popped out of the old wooden frame it was attached to, and swung loose. The padlock dangled from it heavily.

The door began to swing open, but then stopped. The wood of the door was swollen, warped and caught against the uneven floor of the passage. Linda Louise renewed her grip on the handle, grounded herself once more, and—

Charles Lester III had not been in the servant's passage for long before he managed to find a place to dispose of Isabelle's body. After closing the door to the Blue Room quietly behind him, he took a moment to let his eyes adjust to the new lighting and then travelled left, where the tunnel departed from the contours of the room he had entered by and branched off into multiple directions. Lester grew suddenly annoyed with himself, the deeper into the guts of the house he travelled, annoyed that he had not made the effort to inspect these passages earlier. He had considered this a space beneath him, but he realized now how foolish that presumption was: there should be no part of his house that he was unfamiliar with, not when he was the Master. To know your dominion was to rule it more effectively, and he realized, as the body on his shoulder began to weigh down on him, compressing his spine, swelling his knee and ankle joints, that any and all manner of mischief could have occurred in these tunnels and he would have been none the wiser.

Well, not anymore.

In the meantime, the servants' passages, to Charles' immense relief and delight, presented several choice opportunities and locations within which he could conceal a corpse. After much deliberation, having walked for what felt like miles up and down and in and around the confined brick and stone shafts that seemed to stretch on into eternity, he settled on a cool, narrow, concealed alcove built into a passage wall not far from the main kitchen. Purpose-built for hanging, storing and curing meat, the alcove had a lockable cupboard door, from which a padlock dangled, its shackle wide open. Lester made a note to find out if the cook was stealing from his meat supplies whilst simultaneously feeling enormous relief that she had left the alcove lazily unlocked.

On opening the alcove door, he understood why it was not secured: the alcove was an overflow alcove, only used for surplus stock at the times of the year when meat was in glut—Christmastime, and after harvest. Now, it being high summer, it only contained a few legs of salted and smoked beef, and a couple of large, wrapped hams which dangled from solid iron hooks set into the ceiling of the alcove. The prime meat—venison, bacon, poultry, tongue, the good quality beef for braising, and lamb, Lester's personal favorite—was in a special cold-room elsewhere, he knew.

Lucky for him.

Smiling at his continued good fortune, Lester rolled the dead maid off of his shoulder. She landed on the floor of the passage with a heavy, appropriately meaty noise, long dark stringy hair flopping out like the tassels of a dust brush, and Lester took a moment to mop his once again sweaty brow with a now filthy handkerchief.

After this, I am done, he promised himself. No more. I am too old for such foolery and nonsense.

Thrice is a habit, four times is...?

Better hope for no further interruption, Charles thought.

Once he had caught his breath, he rolled the Scullery Maid over with his toe, wanting another look at her. She flopped onto her back, and greeted him with an inside-out face.

Lester surveyed the damage he had wrought with the Chinese dragon doorstop. It was substantial. Isabelle's face was now concave, her once soft, almost-pretty features flattened against the bloody depression the iron dragon had left behind. He had a momentary flash of regret as he looked at the remains of her, for she had, underneath all the dirt, been a halfway handsome woman, if you liked that sort of thing. A little too winsome, a little too thin and far too artless to be truly interesting, but appealing enough to have caught his eye, if only for a moment. A regrettable moment. A moment of weakness, when he had been deep in his cups, where whiskey had helped him to gloss over the dirty, unkempt parts of her that resulted from her servitude, but a moment nevertheless. Charles Lester III's wife, Rose, was fond of saying that life was a collection of mere moments, strung upon a thread like a sequence of pearls ready to be worn. Charles Lester III's wife was fond of saying lots of things, probably owing to all those books she read. Books he *collected. His property. He had told her time and time again that they were not for reading, that they were an investment, but he knew she disregarded him. He had never caught her in the act, but he knew it, just as he had known he would find his Valet digging around in his best things shortly before the evening had taken a turn towards the violent.*

Sometimes, intuition kept a man ahead of the game.

Linda Louise let go of the handle and fell back against the far passage wall, chest heaving. She felt as if a giant hand had flipped open the top of her skull, plucked out her mind, and replaced with the mind of another, only this was a horrible mind, a swollen, dark, angry thing bloated with self-righteousness and rage and a cold, hard desire to rule over everyone and everything around it. She felt both hot and cold at the same time, and the hand that had gripped the cupboard door felt blistered, as if burned.

Pushing herself upright, away from the wall, she stared at the alcove, which was now open for her to see, understanding none of what she had just been shown.

Shown?

Or relived?

Linda Louise did not believe in ghosts, or in nonsense of any description.

And yet the feel of the Master still lingered in her brain, a scummy residue after a sink had been drained.

The cupboard yawned in front of her, and she felt disappointment knocking at the edges of her confusion. There was nothing secret or exciting inside, only a few shelves off to one side that held old dusty jam jars and an ancient wooden rolling pin, and a few large meat hooks hanging from the ceiling.

Pantry, she thought, feeling like an idiot. *You went through all...that, whatever it was, for a pantry.*

The door, which hung on old, loose hinges, began to close again, slowly, slowly. She swallowed, and realized she had let the others get too far ahead, now. If she wasn't careful, she'd be lost down here alone, lost in the endless brick corridors, and the idea suddenly terrified her.

She turned and put her right foot out, meaning to get as much distance between herself and the cupboard as possible. Instead, the cap of her right slipper found an uneven spot in the floor and she tripped forward, twisting awkwardly as she tried to avoid falling. Her arms went out, but too late, and as she toppled over, her hands scrabbled for something to slow her descent.

The edge of the cupboard door, still making its steady way back home, smashed into her face before she could find anything. She saw stars as the solid wooded edge connected with her nose, square in the middle, and she cried out, grabbing the door, hurling it backwards again and knowing as she did so where she was about to land, and being suddenly desperate but unable to avoid it. As her body came down fast and hard, she managed to twist and contort herself, narrowly avoiding one of the meat hooks that dangled from the ceiling, and her right hand, the hand that was now inexplicably blistered from the cupboard handle, came up to grab at the hook, instinctively knowing it would be a way of anchoring herself and halt her trajectory, and as her fingers snatched at it, fumbling, closing around the curved, cold, heavy thing, she—

Not so pretty now, Charles mused as he stared down at bludgeoned, damaged flesh and bone lying by his feet. The grisly scene was surprisingly easy to absorb, a fourth time around. It seemed to make more sense to him, the mess and blood. He examined his handiwork like a jeweler looking for flaws in a diamond: peering intently at the body and scrutinizing it from every angle. It did not cross his mind for even one second that the woman lying before him had been carrying his child. Not for want of trying, for his brain definitely tried to skirt around the edges of the idea, but Lester ultimately found the notion of a filthy bastard scullery child too unpalatable for his distinct tastes, particularly as he was father already to a grown son, Harry, and starting another, legitimate child with his wife, whom he had thought too old, certainly too old to bear him another son, but she had, at the last threshold of fertility, borne fruit after a drunken night of aggressive fumbling on his part four months prior. And so he rejected the thought of this other parasitic child outright, although his eyes did linger for a second on Isabelle's belly, which was not yet round enough to be noticeable, but certainly displayed a rotundness at odds with the rest of her frame.

His eyes travelled back to his hands, which were layered in red: old, new, and in between. Once is a mistake, twice is a coincidence, thrice is a habit. Four is a...he still could not remember. It was his wife's saying, not his. His spouse was full of clever phrases like that, wisdom dressed up as rhetoric. Most of the time he let her prattle wash over him, but for some reason those words now bounced around like a dropped glass marble in the echoey chasm of his brain, which had emptied itself of coherent thoughts and feelings in the aftermath of his third kill.

'This was your fault, you know,' he said to the body, and he meant it with every fiber of his being. Absurdly, as he addressed her, Charles Lester III could just make out the swollen lumps of her tonsils, peeking through the remains of her shattered jaw, glistening in the light of the electric

lamps in the passageway. The sight should have made him feel something, but he didn't, and, being finally bored of such exertions, he made one, final effort to put his misfortunes to bed, heaving the pale, nightdress clad body upright, wrapping his arms around her middle as if in some terrible, perverted dance, hoisting her upright as sharply and with as much force as he could muster, and then bringing her down hard upon one of the meat hooks. He left her dangling there like that, her head and shoulders hidden by the swinging hams, her bare, dirty feet poking out beneath, almost brushing the floor, but not quite.

Then he closed the alcove door, and pushed the padlock shackle into place in its hasp, where it rested. Not locked, but it would give the appearance of such, and that might be enough to dissuade someone from going into the meat cupboard, at least for a little while.

And a little while was all Charles Lester III needed, for once time had passed between the Scullery Maid's disappearance and her eventual, inevitable discovery, he would have been able to distance himself appropriately from her, his crimes, and this godforsaken night, which had now cost him a Valet, a Housekeeper, a Gardener and a Scullery Rat, and was fast turning into a new, godforsaken day.

And now I am done, he told himself, shambling along the corridors as the sun rose, unseen, beyond the windows of the Sunshire Chateau.

I am done, and I am free.

Or at least, that was what he thought.

He was rudely disabused of this notion when he stumbled wearily to his—

Linda Louise let go of the hook and scrambled out of the cupboard as fast as her body could carry her. She was dimly aware that her nose was bleeding, but she ignored it, and ran after the tour group, sobbing, hoping against hope that she would be able to find them again, because although she was confused, her mind babbling with the crazed thoughts of another, she understood one thing, one simple truth:

She no longer wanted to be alone in the Sunshire Chateau.

STATUES

The group, now more than a little fatigued and yet thoroughly ensnared by both the Tour Guide and the Sunshire Chateau (who were both, as individual entities reluctantly entwined for many, many years, too many for the Guide to recall with any true clarity, rather skilled in the art of entrapment by various differing means) funneled slowly down a long winding Gallery that greeted them as they emerged from the servant's passage, blinking.

It was an impressive display of art and grandeur, a high-ceilinged corridor clad in framed paintings, portraits, tapestries and ornate crystalline light fittings that cast a warm, bright glow into the space, a glow that was illuminating but demure enough to not obliterate the detail in the paintings with any overbearing glare. Interspersed between each painting or hanging was a polished white marble sculpture, displayed upon a pedestal, and these lined the Gallery for its whole length, as far as the eye could see and beyond, for the Gallery curved and disappeared around a corner, rather than ending definitively as most corridors do with straight lines and clear horizons, or at the very least a doorway or wall.

But then this was the Sunshire Chateau, where nothing was as it should be, and the guests were slowly beginning to realize this.

As they moved along the Gallery proper, the door to the passage closed behind them with a soft *shunk,* and then seemed to melt away, the line denoting its existence barely visible against the clean stone of the Gallery wall.

'Huh,' said Don, who was beginning to rouse from his stupor. He tried and failed to hide how impressed he was by the ingenuity of design on display. 'Neat trick.'

Then he looked ahead to the Gallery itself, and Barbara, who could not quite bring herself to stand next to him anymore, experienced a low, sinking, familiar sensation of intense dislike. It crept over her slowly and grew stronger the longer she looked at him, for her husband, chest out, legs braced wide apart, fingers tapping a little irritated tattoo against his waistband, was clearly struggling with himself. The reason for this was evident, to Barbara at least.

Don was enjoying himself. Whatever had been bothering him before was clearly no longer an issue, and he had emerged from his stupor like a man waking up from a long, delicious sleep. He looked refreshed, renewed. The opposite of how Barbara felt.

Yes, Don was secretly enjoying himself, she could tell, and for this reason, Barbara, who knew him far too well after so many years of marriage, began to feel nervous.

Because when Don enjoyed himself, he over-compensated for it.

Enjoying things put Don in a quandary, enjoyment not being a natural emotion for him to experience. This plunged him into a state of both happy-and-not-happy that played havoc with his carefully guarded misery equilibrium. He couldn't regulate when he was having fun, and this meant his mood would swing wildly from port to port. He cycled through curiosity, annoyance, admiration, envy, wonder, and repulsion, all in a matter of moments. Barbara could see the cocktail of feelings swirling around in his gut like fermenting apples, bloating him out with a near convulsive type of turmoil that he was grappling to keep a lid upon. The Sunshire Chateau tour was the sort of thing he usually hated, being generally ill-disposed towards antiques, history, other people's money and anything that required effort to learn about, but Barbara knew the Chateau also appealed to Don for precisely those reasons. Opulence and grandeur, masculinity, hard-won spoils, pomp, formality. It was all Don, down to a 'D'. She had a feeling that had Charles Lester III himself appeared in the midst of the tour group at that very moment, dressed in his finest suit and sucking on a giant hand-rolled cigar, he and Don would have exchanged pleasantries and gotten along just fine.

Yes, it would not be long, she knew, until Don started acting out again.

Her eyes wandered across the Gallery to Baltimore, who had slipped his cap off his head and was scratching at his scalp once more in the distracted gesture that she had already become familiar with, even though they had only been exposed to each other for a relatively short space of time. The feeling of dread and dislike sloshing around her own guts faded as Barbara assessed Baltimore, who spun on his heel to admire a large tapestry depicting a woman sitting astride a unicorn with a large weeping willow forming the backdrop. There was something about the delighted appreciation in his posture, how his mouth hung ever so slightly open, how his eyes scanned every surface they could find, how he folded his arms so that he could better lean back to admire the view, that was so different to her husband's way of presenting and holding himself it was almost breathtaking. One could look at both men, side by side, which is exactly what Barbara *was* doing, and understand with an immediate instinct that one man was someone with whom you could relax and have a good time, and the other…

Well, the other was Don.

Barbara found herself blushing, and averted her gaze away from Baltimore, ashamed at how her mind was running off.

'Where are we now?' Asked Bow-tie, also admiring the unicorn tapestry that hung just to their left.

'This is the South Gallery,' the Tour Guide replied. For a moment it seemed that he was not going to elaborate on this, and Bow-tie's face dropped.

'Oh.'

'You are now in one of the most celebrated sculpture galleries known to America,' the Guide continued, turning back and looming over Bow-tie by a good four or five inches. 'Curated and assembled, of course, by Charles Lester III himself, who had particularly refined tastes. The wealth of items assembled in this space, which, by the way, is also the longest display gallery of its type in any historic property in the country, perhaps the *world*, is unfathomable. It is a privilege for you to see this, for it is a part of the house that has been closed to visitors for many, many years.'

He stopped momentarily to flick an invisible crumb of dust off the shoulder of a statue of Hercules, huge and bearded, who was leaning against his own upturned club. The sculpture towered above the Tour Guide, who was no short man himself, and seemed to be judging them all with blank marble eyes.

'Is that a copy of the Farnese Hercules?' Bow-tie asked, eyes wide with approval. 'It's remarkable.'

The Guide stiffened. 'We do not like to use the word 'copy' at Sunshire,' he said coolly, and he began walking along the Gallery.

'Does that mean it *isn't* a copy? I don't understand,' Bow-tie persisted. Bow-tie was a warm and lively sort, and he was getting more than a little tired of the Tour Guide's attitude towards everyone, which was markedly less polite than Bow-tie was accustomed to in his everyday life.

'What's the Farnese Hercules?' Baltimore asked, gazing up at the bearded hero.

'This, apparently,' Bow-tie replied, tartly. He twiddled on the corner of his moustache, which was styled a little like a certain Colonel's, an impression heightened by how snowy Bow-tie's own facial hair was. 'Although last I heard, it was safely ensconced in the Museo Archeologico Nazionale, where it rightfully belongs.'

'The Farnese Hercules,' the Tour Guide shot back, through gritted teeth, 'Is an ancient roman sculpture of Hercules thought to have been fashioned in the year 216 A.D. However, as I'm sure our illustrious enthusiast is aware, that statue is, itself, a copy of a much older Greek work of art fashioned from bronze by Lysippos, one of the greatest sculptors and artists of his era. As with most things in Rome, they built upon the skills of a greater civilization who came before them. For this reason, and many others besides, the word 'copy' is not one we favor here.'

Bow-tie sighed. 'But this entire house, on that reasoning, is a copy, if you look at it like that. And replica or not, the original statue is in a museum in Italy. So what is this? Because as replicas go, it's extraordinary.'

'You are assuming that there can only ever be one certified copy of a famous statue in existence at any one time, sir?'

'My name is Terry. And no, no I'm not saying that, but are you telling me this is a contemporaneous copy of a copy, or-'

'I've got a headache,' Baltimore said, a bemused look on his face.

157

'He's got nice muscles, hasn't he?' Terry added, in a mischievous, appreciative voice. 'What's that he's holding behind his back?'

'Plums,' Barbara replied, her mouth twitching. Baltimore shot her a surprised, appreciative grin, and Terry laughed out loud. It was a lascivious sound, and it lightened the mood of the tour party instantly. Barbara realized she liked Terry. He was smart and inquisitive, and had a warmth to him that she missed about people.

The Tour Guide quivered with restraint.

'They are apples,' he said, sounding strangled. '*Apples*. Shall we?'

It wasn't a question.

'Well,' Don blustered, finally settling on a single mood as he weather-vaned through every available emotion. He threw back his head as they walked on down the Gallery, and looked down his nose at the statues as if his elevated chin could somehow help him save face and protect him from the fact that he was about to say something complimentary. Don was not a man who ever praised things or displayed appreciation, and it was for this reason, first and foremost amongst so many reasons, that Don and Barbara were extremely ill-suited to each other. Barbara was an optimist at heart, a woman who would always try and find the good in any given situation, although that optimism had been well and truly abraded by her husband over the years. Don didn't even seem to know he was doing it at times, she suspected. Negativity was just a habit for him, and this habit was something her son seemed to have inherited.

Speaking of her son, where was he?

Barbara looked around in a sudden panic. Where was Noah? She could have sworn he was right behind her as she left the passage. She made sure to keep him in her sights at all times, and had no idea how he'd been able to sneak off in the few moments she was distracted. If he was somewhere he shouldn't be, she would lose her shit, she knew she would. It was not his safety she was worried about, well, that was not true, of *course* she worried about him, but she was also worried about the safety of the objects and valuables housed in the Sunshire Chateau, valuables that Noah sadly couldn't be trusted around, as much as it hurt her to admit that. Noah had sticky fingers, and while she was sure it was a behavioral thing, a protest thing, Noah simply trying to get her attention rather than being an inherently bad kid, it was a problem that she simply didn't know how to deal with. There were only so many letters of apology a woman could write on behalf of her son before people started to blame the Mother, not the boy, and that thought made her want to weep, because Barbara had always fought to be a good sort of person, to follow rules, and stay out of trouble, and she thought she had taught her son to do the same.

And she loved Noah, fiercely, even if that love was roundly rejected on a daily basis. Maybe that was what hurt above everything else.

Perhaps if she stopped showing him she loved him, he would stop stealing things. Perhaps.

Perhaps not.

But then, that would not be true to herself, and she knew it.

Besides, what was so wrong about openly loving someone? Isn't that what a Mother was supposed to do, love, unconditionally?

Eventually she spotted her son lurking at the back of the group and staring at the naked, cold breasts of what Barbara assumed was a Venus or an Aphrodite. Relief washed over her, and she did a quick scan to see if his pockets were bulging with anything they shouldn't have been, or if his hands were closed around something that was not his. Once she'd satisfied herself that everything was as it should be, she relaxed, and then felt instantly guilty for thinking the worst of him.

No wonder the poor kid is a fuck-up, with a mother like me, she thought.

He'd be much better off without me.

So would Don.

So would everyone.

I wonder what it feels like to fall from a top-story window, or balcony?

The thought pinched at her like a mean girl in class. She shook her head slightly, trying to shake it out of her, but this never worked. The thoughts persisted, intrusive, relentless.

I wonder what it feels like to fly?

To be weightless, just for a moment?

Free of responsibility?

Free of this unending exhaustion?

At worst, you would be a bad mother, a bad wife.

At best, you might stand a chance at...

Being happy.

Barbara fought back tears. Fought, and lost. A trail of them spilled down her face abruptly, betraying her.

'Hey,' a voice whispered.

She started. Baltimore was standing close by. His hand was out, offering her a packet of tissues. The packet was open, and he'd pulled one tissue out ever so slightly, to make it easier to get hold of.

She pulled at it with hands that shook a little, dabbed at her face, and smiled.

'So where to now, Boss?' Baltimore said out loud, and Barbara knew he was being extra jovial to cover for her, to distract the others from her tears.

The Tour Guide, who cut a long and vigorous figure against the marble and stone around him, answered without losing a beat:

'You'll see.'

'Sounds ominous.'

The Tour Guide did not to reply.

The group walked, and seemed, by some strange feat of design, to somehow transgress floor levels to the point where they suddenly all realized how high up they were. Noah, who had cycled through his favorite playlist until his headphones had run out of charge and were now effectively acting as ear-muffs rather than transmitters, glanced out of a large sash window set into an alcove in the Gallery as he passed it, and saw, between the thick spread of cedar needles, glimpses of Lestershire laid out below like a model town on a display board. In the middle of the town he could make out sections of the peculiar, sprawling cemetery that the entire place seemed to be built around. Valleyview Cemetery, he thought it was called. He'd wanted to explore it when they first arrived to Lestershire, but his parents had vetoed this, not wanting him to indulge in what his father sneeringly called his 'morbid goth predilections'.

Turning a corner, it became clear that they had seamlessly progressed to the third level of the Chateau without taking any stairs. Noah liked how the house was constantly turning them about, subverting their sense of direction the longer they remained. This unreliability of dimension appealed to him, for Noah liked chaotic, nonsensical things. He'd been planning on sowing a little chaos himself, back in the Library, but his father had stolen his thunder by acting all weird with the walking cane. He had time, though. Time. He would take any chance he could to disrupt the day, even if it was in a way that was not immediately obvious to his parents. He'd do something. He *needed* to do something. His urges to steal came and went in waves, and his anxiety ramped up the longer between takes—not to mention his libido. Once he successfully filched something that did not belong to him, he felt better. It was instant relief, like masturbation, almost. He felt pleasure in the act, and then guilt. The guilt dissolved over time, to be replaced with the urge to steal again.

And so it went, over and over.

The Gallery widened out without warning into a large landing from which three staircases went off in different directions.

Terry whistled, and yanked on his bow-tie.

'It's like an Escher lithograph in here,' he said, awe in his voice. 'The House of Stairs.'

'Quite,' the Guide replied, and he led them down one staircase in particular. It ended in a high, arched door made of glass that was richly etched with plants, flowers, and vines. He opened the door with a weariness born of repetition, and held it wide.

'Well come on then,' he said, an impatient mother scolding her children once again. 'We haven't got all day.'

The tour party did as they were told, without argument, and found themselves in a large, green, bright and humid space that came to a three-sided glazed peak in what seemed to be the epicenter of the house.

A GREEN AND PLEASANT PLACE

'This is the Atrium,' the Tour Guide pronounced.

This, out of all the rooms they had visited so far, seemed to affect the Guide the most. Noah watched as the man did a quick headcount, tapping each of the guests lightly on their shoulder as they passed him and filed into the space.

'We've lost nobody yet, that's something, I suppose,' he said, after completing his count, but Noah knew this was a lie. Linda Louise, the outspoken woman in the green dress, had not been with them since they'd left the servant's passage. Noah had noticed this almost immediately, but said nothing. He figured she'd had enough of the tour, had maybe slipped away along another passage, and he wished he'd displayed the same initiative.

Strange how no-one else had noticed she was missing, though.

The Atrium more than made up for the lack of light the guests had grown accustomed to up until this point on the tour. Capped with a pyramid of glass that was wholly invisible from the outside and so, the guests assumed, must be sunk below the line of the tiled mansard roof visible from the drive, it was a hothouse, of sorts, a large humid greenhouse that held a multitude of plants.

The contrast between the staid, formal colors of the rest of the house and the green, lush shades of the Atrium was enormous, and, as with most things in the Chateau, it was also slightly disconcerting.

Don was the first to voice his discomfort.

'God*damn*,' he said in his nasal voice, a voice that had years' worth of stress and inertia woven into it, 'It is hotter than goddamn hades in here!'

The Tour Guide smiled his razor-sharp smile, allowing it to sit on his lips for his standardized three seconds before switching it off again. This particular group of tourists, he realized, did nothing but complain, more so than was usual for the average tour. Complain, and try and teach him how to do his own job. The sooner today was over with, the better, he thought, glancing at his wristwatch and then frowning. The second hand was now stuck over the number '5', jarring back and forth over the mark by tiny increments, instead of progressing slowly and steadily, as time is wont to do, around the watch face. He tapped the glass of the face and popped out the winding crown, ratcheting it around until the second hand began to move once more in the right direction. The Guide pulled his sleeve back down to cover the watch, glancing as he did so a set of initials inlaid into the center of the watch face: *CL III.*

To make much of time, he thought, bitterly, *for having lost but once your prime, you may forever tarry.*

'Wonderful,' Terry said, clapping his hands together in delight. 'Simply wonderful.'

Barbara could not disagree. Exotic plants of all descriptions sprouted from huge ceramic and terracotta pots crammed into every available standing space, corner, nook and cranny, and the diversity of life on display before the guests was dizzying, not least because of the heady, mingled mass of scents that tickled their noses the longer they stood there. Ferns, cycads, anthuriums, carnivorous plants, mosses, grasses, climbers and creepers, spread themselves far and wide across the generously proportioned space, which had a red brick courtyard style floor that was pierced in the middle by a large triangular pond, a mirror image of the glass pyramid that rose above it. In the center of the pond a spectacularly ornate working fountain that was tiered like a wedding cake stood. It was topped with a pair of chubby, naked winged cupids holding urns from which water dribbled at a soothing pace.

Baltimore took his cap off, scritch-scratching away at his head. It was a wonder he had any hair left there at all, Noah thought, with disgust.

'Who keeps all these watered?' Barbara murmured, admiring a picture-perfect orchid that was a deep, luscious purple with dark violet spots that clustered around a white nub, a nub that looked exactly like a clitoris, she realized suddenly, yanking her head back and blushing as she made the connection. Terry, who stood close to her, mopped his brow with a neatly pressed handkerchief, and tweaked at his bow-tie again, making sure it sat level against his collar. His eyes twinkled as he looked at the orchid.

'Now you can see why that lady artist painted so many pictures of flowers, eh?' He chuckled, winking at Barbara. 'Of course, the parts of an orchid *are* outrageously sexy, I don't blame her one bit. This thing here-' He used his right pinky finger to point at the white nub— 'Is called an Anther cap. These pointed petals are called Sepals, the bit under the cap is called the Stigmatic Surface, and this delicate little flap here is called the Lip, or Labellum.'

Barbara wished she had hung onto her soggy tissue so she could wipe the sweat that had suddenly beaded on her brow.

Don, suddenly aware that someone was talking to his wife, his property, in double-entendres, interjected.

165

'You seem to know a lot about all this stuff. You after the Tour Guide's job?'

Terry remained pleasant and affable, despite Don's sudden hostility. 'Plants are very much my specialty, after art and textiles. And you needn't worry, I wasn't being salacious. My personal tastes and preferences are... Diametrically opposed to anything remotely orchid-like, shall we say.' The bearded man chose his words with careful amusement. 'In case you were feeling uncomfortable,' he added, winking at Barbara again.

It took her a moment to register what he was saying, but when she did, she relaxed a touch, allowing herself to gaze at the orchid once more.

'It *is* remarkably beautiful,' she admitted, wondering how nature could come up with something so distinct and unusual by stint of pure evolution alone. A flower like this looked designed, planned, intentional from the get-go, rather than the result of multiple accidents of morphology that had just stuck, over time.

'Orchids are the most beautiful and fascinating of all flowering plants, in my humble opinion,' Terry said softly, and he wiped his face again, although this hardly made much difference. Terry was not the only one sweating, and one by one, the guests began shedding jackets and sweaters. Barbara was reminded of the parable of the north sun and the wind, who had a competition to see who could get a passing traveler to remove his cloak first. The sun won without effort, and for some reason that fable had always stuck in her mind, but for all the wrong reasons, because to her, it implied that a person didn't have to try very hard at all in life to make someone else uncomfortable, and when she thought about her son, and how awkward and displaced he made her feel without even going to much effort, she understood that fables can be anchored in awkward truths, but this was all part of parenting, she assumed.

Wasn't it?

'And this one really is lovely. It's called Starry Night, I believe. Wonderful coloring, isn't it? The violet really contrasts with the tropical green in such a striking way.'

The Guide, annoyed at Terry's superior botanical knowledge, waved them through the Atrium, flapping his hands towards the fountain, and beyond that, towards a door almost completely smothered by ivy that was set in the far wall. He seemed in a hurry to get in and out of this room as quickly as possible, but the guests were too busy spotting things that grabbed their attention.

'What is that?' Baltimore had seen something sitting in a shaded spot, surrounded almost entirely by nodding ferns and a couple of enormous broad-leafed plants that Terry confirmed as 'Fiddle-Leaf Figs.' The object nestled amongst the greenery as if it were shy, and trying to hide from the group.

'It's a chair, look- it's carved from the roots of a tree.'

'An oak tree,' The Guide confirmed, eyeing the item askance. 'It dates from 1820, and was presented to the family by a travelling Methodist theologian and scholar who befriended the Lesters long before this house was built. He travelled to Sunshire all the way from Bristol, in England, dragging that chair with him, and had some...interesting views, for the time.' The Guide thought suddenly of Linda Louise, who would have understood the significance of the twisted oak seat, and wondered idly if she had gone mad, yet. It took some folks longer than others, but she had been inquisitive, and intelligent, and feisty, and the house ate those types of people up greedily, as entrees. Was she still in the passages, or somewhere else in the house? She'd find her way out, one way or another, but her mental state upon doing so was down to whether or not she had encountered any of Sunshire's other lost wanderers.

Or whether or not she'd touched something she shouldn't have.

The Guide clicked his neck again, side to side. Cartilage popped. Barbara winced.

'Lester inherited the chair rather reluctantly, and called it a 'monstrosity' on more than one occasion. He decided this was the best space for it, and so here it stays.'

'Kinda ugly, isn't it?'

'Beauty is subjective. It's what it represents that is the beautiful thing,' the Guide said, quietly.

'And what does it represent?' Don puffed out his chest, suddenly more belligerent than he'd ever been. The heat was getting to him, as were the other guests. Not a single one of them worth his time, in his opinion.

The Guide looked at the chair, and then motioned for the guests to continue walking on. 'Nothing that Lester would have liked,' he replied, and nobody could persuade him to explain this cryptic statement.

On the other side of the fountain, stood two enormous plant pots, almost car-big, made of terracotta, and home to two huge, people-sized plants that were, the guests realized, actually giant flowers, fluted like lilies on the verge of opening and crested with massive, pointed stamens. Blood red on the inside, the gigantic petals were green on the outside and frilled, like an old-fashioned petticoat.

'Oh my...*Titum Arum*', Terry said, looking up at the plants with sparkling eyes. '*Amorphophallus titanium*.'

'What is it with you and plants with rude names,' Baltimore laughed, and Barbara joined him before catching herself and pulling up short. Don, who had been fastidiously brushing dropped pollen off of his sweater, shot his wife a dirty look.

'Most plants have something a little saucy about them,' Bow-tie replied, gleefully. 'It's just nature, doing her thing. I think it's marvelous. Some of these flowers can grow over twenty feet high, did you know that? And weigh over thirty pounds. This is the largest flowering structure known to mankind, and the flower only opens for forty-eight hours every seven or eight *years*, so do you know how lucky we are? Often they don't flower in cultivation at all, they have to be carefully hand-pollinated.'

'Doesn't look much like a flower,' Don sneered.

'Well, the petals are more like frilly leaves, really. They're adapted to protect the actual flowers that blossom at the base of the plant.'

'Ugh, what is that *smell?!*'

'Ah, yes. They don't call it the Corpse Flower for nothing, you know. Smells like rotting flesh, apparently! Not that I would be able to confirm that.' Terry seemed completely unphased by the appalling stench that suddenly enveloped them all. He was so enraptured by the plants, he looked as if he were about to throw himself at one of them and embrace it.

'Mostly they smell worse at night, because they sort of heat themselves up, you see. The heat helps them spread the smell further, to lure in beetles and blowflies that usually feed on carrion. Clever, isn't it?'

Barbara felt faintly sick. Noah, on the other hand, was genuinely enraptured, and shuffled forward, finally slipping his headphones off of his ears and leaning in for a better look, sleeve clamped over his nose to help with the smell.

'Cool,' he said eventually, and Barbara was astounded.

Finally, she thought, *finally I brought him to something that he likes.*

Terry bounced up and down on his heels, enthusiasm fairly spilling out of him.

'It *is* cool, young man, you are correct! What an absolute treat this is to see! Do you...is there a resident horticulturist working here? I saw the Gardener outside, is he responsible for this?'

'Not yet,' the Tour Guide replied, his eyes flickering to the plant for a split second. Then he cleared his throat. 'I mean, not anymore.'

Terry did not notice the shift in tense. 'Remarkable. Remarkable! So much diversity in one space. Whoever looks after all this has green fingers, indeed.'

The Tour Guide yawned and examined his fingernails. 'I am happy to see you so gratified,' he said, in a voice devoid of any warmth or happiness whatsoever. 'Can we move along now?'

'I might just...I'd like a little longer to look at them, if that's okay?'

The Guide shook his head. 'It's not a good idea to separate yourself from the tour, it really isn't.'

Terry pouted. 'But...just for a moment, you see, this is such an *event* for me, I-'

The Guide cocked his head to one side, like a bird eyeing a worm. Barbara felt sure he was about to give him the same ice-cold dressing down he'd given the two old ladies at the beginning, but he didn't.

'Two minutes,' he said instead, and Barbara realized that Terry had been right earlier on. He was not berating the other man because he was, in fact, a man, and that seemed to make a difference to the Guide. This realization astounded her, although it shouldn't have. It was a degree of deference to gender that came from another era, although when she thought about it, that era didn't seem so far removed from what she went through with Don day in, day out, not really.

'The rest of us will wait outside that door.'

'Thank you!' Terry's eyes shone with gratitude.

He really does like plants, Barbara thought, fondly.

'Thank me later,' the Guide replied, curtly, and he led the others out of the Atrium without further ado, cutting as wide an arc around the titanic plants as possible.

'Two minutes!' He repeated, before closing the door behind him. 'Not a minute more.'

Terry nodded. 'I promise!' He said, and they both knew it was a lie.

Bow-tie took a moment to enjoy the peace and quiet left behind by the tour party as they exited the Atrium. He hadn't realized, but the small crowd of guests and Guide were noisy, noisy to the point that he now felt his ears ringing faintly in the wake of their departure. He was not opposed to noise, generally preferring a nice hubbub around him, for it was indicative of life, and people going about their business, and things happening, and he was a sociable creature who enjoyed meeting new people and experiencing new things, especially as he got closer to his twilight years, but still. A little peace was a vastly under-rated thing, he thought, and he breathed deep in the silence, almost choking as he then inadvertently sucked up lungfuls of the foul stench the Titums emitted.

Coughing and spluttering until his eyes watered, Terry mopped his face with his handkerchief and surveyed the twin Titans in their pots. The terracotta planters at the foot of each plant were large enough for a man to crawl inside, comfortably, with room to spare, and the Arums inside looked almost small by comparison, despite their colossal size.

Oh, how Simon would have loved this, he thought, sadly. It had been a year since he'd lost him, a year in which he'd felt progressively smaller, and less real. Simon had loved anything like this, anything which displayed what an incredible artist Mother Nature was. As a child, Simon had collected leaves, pressed them between the covers of books, framed them when they were flat and dead and crisp, which is a little how Terry felt since the love of his life had left him for another, more aggressive partner—cancer. His house was covered in leaves, now, leaves all over the walls, leaves on the furniture, appliqued on with clear glue, leaves as bookmarks and coasters and mats on the dinner table. A house of dead leaves, and nobody to kick through them with.

Terry sighed, and mopped his face again, brushing away a few tears. He was even more glad to be alone, at that moment. Grief was unpredictable, at best, and downright sordid in its timing at worst. He'd been having fun, until now. He had to remind himself, clearly, that it was perfectly acceptable to have fun. His dead love wasn't going to be mad at him for trying to enjoy his life a little after he'd moved on to the next.

Was he?

'One minute!' The muffled voice of the Guide came to him from the other side of the far door. Terry rolled his eyes. The bastard was timing him, of course he was.

He moved closer to the biggest Arum, admiring its size, its structure.

He wanted to touch it.

Terry knew he shouldn't, but he could not help himself. He had never seen a flowering Titum in the flesh, not in all his years of visiting botanical gardens and hot-houses, and the thing looked so real, so delicious, so...so...*human*, almost, fleshy and tactile, that he couldn't resist. He ignored the smell, and stood on tip-toe, reaching up to peer over the cusp of the plant's petals, aching to touch the long, phallic stamen, more correctly known as the spadix, that thrust its way out of the top of the petals like a grotesque parody of an erect member. Being quite a short man, he found he had to lean in, and even then he could barely touch it, but Terry was a determined soul when it came to the things he loved, and though he felt as if his arm was about to pop out of its socket, he stretched and stretched until his fingers brushed the peculiar squashy mass, sighing in bliss as he made contact. Gently, for he did not want to damage the plant, he stroked the spadix up and down, his fingertips feeling the strange sponginess of the thing as if making contact with an alien, and as his legs began to shake from the awkwardness of his pose, he could feel the plant heat up beneath his touch, heat up and—

The Gardener was digging when Charles Lester III emerged into the green, pleasant space of the Atrium. Weak fingers of dawn filtered down into the foliage-infested room, and it took a moment for Lester's eyes to adjust from low light to the natural glow of the slowly rising sun, but when they did, his heart sank. For, grubbing around in a giant terracotta pot easily the size of a small elephant and home to an enormous, peculiar plant that was one of a pair his wife has insisted upon purchasing, ugly, twin things that looked like long, green pupas or spears and never seemed to bloody flower, the young man worked, turning over soil that was bound tightly around the roots with a shiny new trowel-soil that Lester, having thought long and hard about it, had designs on. Charles saw that the Gardener was already covered in muck, scratches and fragments of greenery, for his day began earlier than most. By dawn's break, as was his habit, he had watered, trimmed and tended the vast array of plants that had been so diligently selected and installed by the architect in this glass-vaulted space that usually, only his wife frequented, the place being too hot and humid for Charles Lester III's tastes.

Charles, being generally disinterested in such things, had no idea the Gardener would be about so early. Thus when he appeared from behind the fountain, dragging a bloody, rolled-up Persian carpet behind him, it was something of a shock to find he was not alone.

It was a shock for the Gardener, too.

For a moment, the two men said nothing, simply looked each other up and down. The Master was red from his roots to his heels, and there was a pair of feet sticking out of the carpet-cigar behind him. It didn't take much to put two and two together: there was a body in the rolled up rug, and Charles Lester III was trying to get rid of it.

Once is a mistake, Lester thought. Twice is a coincidence, thrice is a…a habit.

Lester knew he could not wait to act. He was tired, he was sore, and he was feeling his age, but he was also still angry. Angry at his Valet, for betraying him. Angry at the Housekeeper, for barging in when she was not wanted.

Angry at this Gardener, for doing his job.

His anger would carry him through, he knew.

The young man straightened up, the trowel in his hands. Although it was coated in soil, Charles could see it was slender, and pointed at the tip, more of a trowel-shaped knife with a long tang. His wife could have told him, were she present, that it was a rockery trowel, but she was not. She was safe abed, he hoped, sound asleep and snoring, as she always did.

'Good morning, Master,' the Gardner said, eyes fixed on the rolled carpet and the pair of feet that protruded from the end.

Lester, who was able to talk his way out of most situations, dropped the body in the carpet and straightened his back.

The Gardener, who was no fool, tightened his grip on his trowel.

'It seems we have a little problem here,' the Master said, pleasantly. He began to cross the distance between them, slowly.

The other man shook his head as his employer approached. 'No problem here, Master. Not from me.'

'Are you sure?' Charles was smooth as silk. 'Because if you're thinking of using that, well...I'd urge you to reconsider. How would it look? The Master of the house, slain. His Valet, brutally murdered and callously concealed in a rolled-up rug. Yes, it's the Valet. I caught him stealing from me, in case you're curious. His behavior was unacceptable. I corrected it.'

The Gardener swallowed, his eyes darting about, looking for an escape route. Lester was blocking one path, and the giant flower pot he stood next to blocked the other.

'Just imagine the furore. Prominent benefactor and businessman, founder of the town, slain by a member of his own household! You'd be hunted in every corner of the state, in every state! What sort of life would that be? A fugitive on the run? You'd never work again, and you know it.'

The young man licked his lips, and Charles edged closer.

'On the other hand, you and I could come to some sort of arrangement.'

'Arrangement?'

'Yes, arrangement.'

175

The Gardener stared at him. Lester could see the wheels turning in his head.

I could make some money out of this, the wheels said.

'Yes, an arrangement.' Charles repeated himself, a neat trick he'd learned from years in business. He tried to sound calm, reasonable. 'You forget what you've seen here, this morning, and I pay you handsomely for your trouble.'

'How much?' The Gardener was a business man too, it seemed. He got straight to the point.

'How much do you want?' The Master was close enough now to reach out and shake the other man's hand, but he held back, curious to hear what the Gardener would say.

The Gardener thought about it, wondering how far he could push his advantage. His hold on the trowel never loosened.

'Five thousand dollars,' he said, eventually.

'Done,' the Master replied, promptly. 'Shall we shake on it?'

The Gardener assessed his master, looking for lies. 'How do I know I can trust you?' He asked, eventually, and Lester had no answer for that.

'You don't. You'll just have to take my word for it.'

The Gardener shook his head. 'I need a guarantee.' He spotted the Master's cufflinks, winking on his wrists.

'Give me those,' he commanded, although he was bad at asking for things. Not a natural, like Lester, who smiled.

'I think not,' he replied.

'Then no agreement!' The Gardener brought the trowel up like a small dagger, and levelled it as his Master's chest.

Lester could see he was on the verge of losing him.

It would not be the first man he'd lost over the cufflinks that day.

Fine, he thought. If I can't do this the easy way, I'll do it the hard.

'As you wish,' he said out loud, and, lightning fast, he grabbed hold of the Gardener's hand, the one that held the trowel, and he swung it upwards as hard and as fast as he could, before the younger, fitter man had a second to think, or react, or tense, or flex, or resist, and the momentum of this action carried the trowel blade fast through the air, up towards the Gardner's right eye, where it sank neatly into the socket with a grinding, slick noise.

The Gardener sagged to his knees, clutching at his ruined eye, from which the trowel now stuck at an acute angle. It looked ridiculous, in Charles' opinion, so he ripped it out and thrust it back into the socket again, so deep it sank into where the tang met the turned wooden handle, and embedded itself in the Gardener's brain.

The Gardener collapsed backwards onto the floor and lay, twitching, blood pouring from him like rain.

Lester knew he could leave him there, and the man would die, eventually. There was no way he could survive such a horrible injury.

Lester knew this, but still ripped the trowel free a second time. Because the Gardener, he reasoned, had interrupted his plans. He had thought he could be blackmailed, he had thought himself as clever as Lester, as smart, and he had put himself on equal footing with his superior.

Charles Lester III could not reconcile with that, so he stabbed at the Gardener's face with the trowel over and over again, until his anger had thinned out, and then, before dawn became morning and he would truly be in trouble, he used the trowel to start digging around the base of one of the giant, ugly plants.

And he was glad, suddenly, that his wife had insisted on these two monstrous things, for the pots they rested in were amply sized: a perfect place to hide a pair of ruined bodies, and—

Terry removed his hand slowly, slowly, and stood, his entire body shaking, the feel of another man's soul sliding into his something that he knew would haunt him for the rest of his life. He gazed down at the pot beneath the Arum, the enormous, body-sized terracotta planter, and he thought:

Are there still bones beneath those roots?

He was on the verge of digging down to find out with his bare hands when the Tour Guide materialized behind him.

'It's been two minutes,' the tall man said, quietly.

Terry, who now had tears freely streaming down his cheeks, looked up at the Guide with a pleading expression.

'What's buried down there?' He asked, and the Tour Guide sighed, and lay a hand gently on the small of Bow-tie's back, steering him towards a different door to the one he had led the others through, a door Terry had not noticed, until now.

'Nothing of any consequence,' the Guide replied bitterly, and Terry, who could feel nothing except the crunch of bone and the resistance of flesh beneath a brand new, stainless steel rockery trowel, allowed himself to be led.

'I want to leave, now,' he whispered, miserably. 'I would like to go home.'

'I know,' the Guide replied, and he was almost kind. 'Trust me. I know.'

UP HIGH

'What is this place?'
'It's where I come to feel better,' Alice said, pushing open a large hatch. 'When I'm sad.'

They were somewhere on the top story of the house, now, and Ned felt a little giddy at how high up they were. Alice had made him climb a lot of stairs, and then, a small access ladder, which he was pretty sure he wasn't supposed to climb. He wondered what the Guide would say if he caught them, and smiled inwardly at the idea of annoying the other man.

'And what do you have to feel sad about?'

'A great many things.' The hatch fell backwards, and they were greeted by blue sky. Ned realized, with a soaring sensation of relief, that he had not looked at a blue sky in what felt like a long time.

'Such as?'

'Things. Like the dreams I had, that I'll never fulfil. The family I lost, who are long dead, now.'

'Your family is dead?'

She nodded, and hoisted herself through the hatch nimbly. Then she held a hand down to help Ned up the ladder. Her hair clouded around her face as she looked down at him, a red haze, curls held aloft by the fresh breeze. 'But it's alright. We all die in the end, I know that. I just wish I'd been able to do a little more living, first.'

He found himself surrounded by leadwork, chimneys, bird droppings and slate, for they were up on the roof of the Sunshire Chateau. The sky stretched wide and clear overhead, and Ned saw they were above the reach of the cedar trees. He hadn't realized quite how dark they had made everything down below. Being out of their shadow was liberating, like shrugging off a jacket that was too tight across the shoulders.

He frowned at something Alice had said as he took in the view. From here, the entire town of Lestershire spread out below them, much of it dominated by large boxy factories and processing plants that belched out foul smoke from large, tall chimneys. In the center of the town, Valleyview Cemetery sprawled out, with its great monument in the middle. The Tour Guide had told him Charles Lester III was buried beneath that monument, which his wife had erected in his honor. Ned tried not to feel bitter about the romantic gesture, but he found other people's love stories hard to hear, even now.

'You know,' he said, taking in a deep breath and filling his lungs with The Outside. 'You speak a lot like you're dead yourself, sometimes. It's very dramatic.' He winked, to soften the words, but her face remained serious.

She didn't answer him directly. 'This way,' she said, instead, starting to pick her way carefully across the many lead hips that crisscrossed the roof. A long ridge beam split the area in half, and she was headed for a flat depression in the center of this ridge, from which a large glass pyramid-shaped skylight rose. The sun glinted off of the unstained panes of glass that made up the pyramid, and Ned thought: *who comes up here to clean those? Not her, surely?*

'What's down there?' He asked, stopping in front of the pyramid. Up close, the glass was clean, but clearly old. Some of the triangular panes were fractured, chipped, on the verge of collapsing through. He bent forward carefully and peered through a single pane to see what lay below. He could see plants, plants of every size, shape, and description. A fountain that looked like a cake decoration—*get out of my head, Jo*—pots, creepers. Polished tiles, flowers in a dazzling array of colors and variety.

And the tour group, who were gathered around two gigantic terracotta planters which held two peculiar blood-red flowers easily as tall as a man inside of them.

'Some kind of hothouse?'

'The Atrium,' Alice replied.

'Amazing. And so much light, too. What a clever design.'

She shrugged. 'Plants won't grow anywhere else in the house. The trees block out the sun, don't they? Except for up here, and in there.'

'And that's why you come here to feel better,' Ned smiled. 'That makes a lot of sense. I feel better, too.'

In front of the skylight was another shallow platform, and on that platform a little wooden bench was bolted down, ornate and pretty, not tacky or ostentatious like a lot of the furniture inside Sunshire. It felt like the kind of thing a woman with good taste would buy. Perhaps it had been a secret place for Rose Lester, a place where she could relax and reflect away from the aggressive masculinity of the interior of the Chateau.

'It's funny, but from the ground, I thought this roof was almost flat on top. You can't see any of this,' he said, taking a seat next to Alice on the bench.

'The thing about this house,' she replied, staring into the distance, 'is that there is more than one. House, I mean. There is an inside house, and an outside house. A house within a house, if you like.'

Noah laughed. 'I feel like I'm talking to a cryptic crossword puzzle with you, sometimes.'

She looked blank, as if she did not understand the reference.

'Tell me about her,' she said instead.

Ned froze. 'What?'

'The woman who left you at the altar.'

He shook his head, the memories suddenly knocking again at the lid of their box, and it was like a cloud passing over the sun.

'I shouldn't have told you about that.'

Alice bit her lip. 'Well,' she said, after a moment or two. 'Whoever she was, I'm not entirely sure she deserved you.'

Ned said nothing. He looked out at the view, wondering where in the world Jo was, right now, and what she was doing, and hating himself for caring.

Because he knew very well what she was doing. She was not missing Ned.

Ned knew this because fourteen months after his aborted wedding, he was scrolling idly through his phone, mindlessly flitting through his various social media accounts, when he noticed an old school friend of his, tagged in a photograph. Without knowing what he was looking at, he tapped on the image to make it larger and came face to face with a group of his former friends and colleagues all grouped around a smoking barbeque, smiling at the camera. In the center of this group, a happy, grinning Jo cuddled up next to a tall, bearded man. She looked good: relaxed, tanned, less frown lines than he remembered. And then Ned saw why: she held a fat, bouncy baby, a baby who so clearly looked like his father, the man who stood next to her, that there could be no doubt what Ned was looking at.

He was looking at betrayal, and his heart, already down to its last few weak beats per minute, stopped altogether.

And Ned didn't smile again, not properly, not a truthful smile, for a long time.

Until he met Alice.

Alice, who continued to watch him closely.

'I overstepped,' she said, eventually. 'It is not my place.'

'Sorry,' he mumbled, scratching at the back of his neck. 'You didn't, not really. I'm just...I'm not used to talking about my feelings. Nothing good comes of it. Trusting someone with this stuff. Anyone.'

Alice considered this. 'I understand,' she replied, gently. 'But not all of us are as cruel as the woman who hurt you. I also used to place too much trust in people. Some of us are just like that. We like to believe in the best of things.'

'She wasn't cruel. She was...selfish, perhaps. Cowardly. Unhappy. I don't know. But not cruel, not intentionally.'

Alice folded her arms, unimpressed. 'That's a mighty fine pedestal you built for the woman who broke your heart and danced all over the remains.'

He thought about that. How all this time, he had assumed it was *he* who had not measured up, *he* who had not been good enough. He *had* put Jo on a pedestal. Did she deserve to be there? Did anyone? Pedestals were lonely plinths, when all was said and done. Maybe he'd been in love with a version of her that simply didn't exist, had never existed.

Maybe that's why she'd left.

'I think some people sometimes don't know how to stop being the worst versions of themselves,' he said.

'Charles Lester's life, for example. Driven by avarice and ambition, by owning things, winning things, achieving things. I can't imagine a man like him dying, not willingly. I can't imagine any peaceful 'crossing over,' or 'letting go'. Can you?'

Alice nodded curtly. 'He was not a man who gave up on anything easily. Giving up was not in his nature. Giving up on living wasn't really in his nature either. Why did you mention him? We were having a nice time, before that.'

Ned shook his head. 'You can see his grave from here.' He pointed at the memorial.

Alice sighed. 'Well, that's spoiled it.'

A bird landed on the roof not far from the couple, its beak stuffed with bugs and insects. It ignored them as it concentrated on gulping down its meal, then preening itself.

Ned, who was happy to think of anything but Jo, let his mind run on. He peeked over his shoulder, craning his neck and peering down into the Atrium again through the triangular panes of glass. The tour group had gone now, off to see another of the many magnificent sights Sunshire had to offer, no doubt.

'Think of all the effort that went into building this place,' he said, thinking aloud. 'Curating the collections, decorating it with accomplishments. The sum of a man's life, encapsulated within these walls. Why would the afterlife appeal, when a man has all this?' Ned swept his hand wide, gesturing to the Sunshire Estate as a whole. 'If it were me, I would haunt the hell out of this mansion.'

'Oh?' Alice fiddled with a strand of hair that tickled at the nape of her neck, and Ned had to stop himself from reaching across, winding the soft filaments around his finger.

Instead, he said:

'Alice, I saw something in the Blue Room.'

'Go on.'

'I saw...I think...I know this is going to sound absurd, but...I think I saw a ghost. Not Lester. A woman. I can't...I can't stop thinking about it.'

Or Jo, he thought, but he kept that to himself.

'I know you did,' she replied, sadly. 'You saw Isabelle.'

Ned froze in shock. 'You know about her?'

Alice rose from the bench, as if preparing for something. She stood with her back to him for a moment, and he could see her shoulders moving up and down, a telltale sign that she was crying.

'I know about all of them,' she said.

'There is...more than one?'

Another jerky series of movements as she brushed tears angrily away. 'It is a full and violent house, Ned. A terrible place. An unnatural place. A prison, really.'

'I...don't know what you're trying to say.'

'It's easier to show you.'

And Ned, who was beginning to get an odd, sick feeling in the pit of his belly, watched, almost hypnotized, as Alice turned to him. He gasped. Her face had become an odd, shifting mess, in much the same way that the face of the ghost of the Blue Room, Isabelle, was an indistinct, blank, sketchy place where nothing remained obvious for very long.

'What is happening?' He breathed, getting to his feet sharply and moving to put the bench between himself and Alice, who no longer looked like Alice. She looked like a woman with a papier mâché head, only the head was melting, dissolving. Unable to look away, he saw droplets of crimson red start to lift themselves away from her scalp, drift off into the sky like bubbles blown by a child. He knew it was blood. He knew he was looking at a version of Alice that related to violence, to her death, and he knew, by that logic, that Alice was not alive. Just like the Blue Room ghost. They moved the same way too: as if their bodies were being dragged about by a strong, unseen current. Her hair started to float up from her hairline and splay outwards, drift around her, tangled, matted, caked in gore. She seemed to be trembling, shivering, or was it just that her form was moving too quickly for his eye to follow properly? Both moving, and static.

As if the laws of the living no longer applied.

'What is happening?' He asked again, in a small, frightened voice.

'We who live here choose who we show ourselves to carefully, Ned.' She spoke even though he could no longer make out the shape of her mouth. She spoke formally, as if recanting something she had been taught. 'And we choose *how* we show ourselves.' As she said this, he heard the distinct sounds of bones breaking, and saw her arms snap just below the elbows, and contract, and then hang uselessly. He saw her chest cave, and a bloodied, broken rib work its way out of the smart, clean fabric of her tunic. He saw her legs buckle at the knees, and draw up to her chest, and then, as he backed away another step, mesmerized in the worst possible way, Alice bundled up into a strange, floating fetal shape, knees tucked up to the ruined chest, feet crossed, head resting against her thighs and bent awkwardly at an angle, arms dangling by her sides, and Ned was reminded of a child's doll stuffed unceremoniously into a too-small shoebox, and he could bear it no more.

He turned and tried to run.

He did not get far. His foot caught on a zinc roof rib, and he tripped, flying forward. The bird, who had finished preening itself, burst into the air near his face, frightened wings flapping ten to the dozen as it made its way to safety, away from the commotion. Ned flapped his own arms, desperately windmilling them around in vain to try and restore his balance, but it was too late, the stumble too forceful. Before he could save himself, the glittering glass surface of the pyramid skylight came rushing up to meet him, and then, there was the distinct, awful sound of old, weakened glass shattering, and a thousand splinters sliced at him, and he was falling, suddenly, falling down, and it looked as if he were a man falling from a plane into the jungle, for green, luscious things rushed up to greet him, and one image in particular imprinted itself on his terrified mind before he landed with a sickening *crunch*, and that was the sight of a giant, red plant with a huge, weird spear of a stamen, one of a pair, racing up to greet him, and for a second he thought he might become impaled on that strange, alien thing, but he was a man, a substantial man falling at many feet per second, and the plant stood no chance.

Neither did the pot it was planted in.

There was a crack, and a heavy thump, and then silence.

As the dust and shards of glass settled on the floor of the Atrium, Ned, who lay on his back dying, his clouded eyes staring at a blue sky he would never fully appreciate again, a blue sky with strands of red flying across it, had a second to think about a woman, a woman who had always had flour on her face from baking, a woman with long thick hair, a woman who's waist had fitted perfectly into the circle of his arm, a woman who had married another man, and given him a perfect baby.

A woman called Jo.

I can haunt you properly now, some part of him either living or dead realized, and then, without ceremony, his light went out. A wet final breath rattled out of him.

His eyes remained fixed on the sky.

And any visitor to Sunshire who stumbled upon this scene might have noticed, after the initial shock, the following things:

A large hole in the Atrium skylight, through which a shaft of sunlight fell.

A man's body, broken and leaking blood, head cracked wide open like a split fruit.

A dead plant, as big as the man, smashed into a pulp, its own red flesh soaking into the man's remains.

And a pot, fractured in two from the force of a heavy impact, regurgitating its soil and contents all over the floor of the Atrium like a volcano spewing lava.

Amongst the clods of pot-bound earth and roots, there lay bones. White, old, longer than average. The bones of a tall man.

Lying amongst them, rusty from years of exposure to damp earth, a set of keys threaded on a large loop nestled up close to the moldy, splintered remains of a once polished ebony walking cane.

THE MASTER'S STUDY

FOUR DOWN, FOUR TO GO

The Guide closed the door to the Atrium behind him softly.

'Well,' he said. 'Next stop- who's ready?'

Barbara cleared her throat.

'Um...Where is Terry?'

'Terry was tired. I left him in the Atrium, so that he could rest.'

Something about the way the Guide said this did not sit right with Barbara.

'Shouldn't we go back for him? You said we should all stay together, and I'd hate for anyone to get lost after-'

'Terry will be fine. We, however, are running out of time.'

'You keep saying that. But I can see your watch. It's broken. It's been broken all along.'

The Tour Guide sighed. There came a point on every tour where the guests began to mutiny. It was unsurprising, given the circumstances, but it was tedious. The Guide felt as if he were living out the same tired show at the Lester Opera House, over and over again.

'If it would make you feel better,' he said, 'Terry wanted to go home, so I pointed him in the direction of the exit.' He held her gaze forcefully, and Barbara felt her suspicion dwindling the longer she looked into his eyes, which were dark, she realized. So very dark.

'Oh,' she said, feeling disappointed and suddenly a little sleepy. 'That's a shame.'

'Yeah,' said Baltimore, who looked around to find that the remaining members of the tour aside from himself were all related to Barbara somehow. He was beginning to feel like a fourth wheel on Barbara's family car. He frowned, then. Was someone else missing too?

'There's someone else, too,' Noah said, softly echoing his thoughts. 'The lady in the green dress.'

Baltimore whistled through his teeth. 'Shit, yes! When was the last time…'

'Linda Louise!' Barbara looked mortified.

'The historian lady?'

'How did we not notice?'

'How long has she been gone for?'

Barbara shook her head. 'I don't know, isn't this awful of us? I feel terrible. She must have slipped away after the Library, that's the last time I remember seeing her.'

'She was behind us in the servants' passage,' Noah said.

The Guide remained tight-lipped.

Barbara's anxiety spiked again.

'Oh God, what if she's still down there, wandering around, lost?'

'Maybe the ghosts got her,' Noah added, a small, mean smile on his face.

'There won't be any of us left, soon,' Baltimore said.

'Oh dear,' the Guide replied, lightly. 'What a *pity* that would be.'

Don, who appreciated sarcasm, grinned. It was a malicious grin, almost the twin to the smile on Noah's face, and Barbara felt that sinking sensation again when she saw it. She was outnumbered, and the feeling of being an outsider in her own family got worse as the days, hours, moments passed.

What would it be like, she wondered, *to punch my husband square in the teeth? Wipe that awful expression off his smug, bloated face?*

Not now, brain! She shook her head again, minutely, not enough to draw unwanted attention to herself, but enough to kick start a separation from the intrusion. Noah caught her doing this, and gave her a steady, unreadable look. Barbara was thankful that he had no idea of the thoughts that often ran through her head. Imagine how much worse he would be, if he knew. What kind of mother was she to think in such a way?

The failing kind, that's what, her thoughts whispered.

'We should go look for her,' she said, out loud, and Baltimore nodded in agreement.

'No,' said the Tour Guide, walking away from the now much smaller group. 'We should not.'

Don, who was good and bored of the conversation, began to follow. He didn't give a rat's ass what happened to anyone else on this never-ending tour. A strange, gray fog had settled in his mind since his experience in the Library, which he could no longer remember. He just wanted to see the next room, get another look at Charles Lester III's extraordinary wealth and good taste. He wanted to imagine what it would be like to be lord of the manor for a bit, away from the annoyances of his wife and kid, away from a mediocre wage and his mediocre job as a technician at a manufacturing plant in Tennessee. He wanted to put himself in Lester's shoes, feet up on a leather Chesterfield, whiskey in hand, a roaring fire going, maybe a lewd serving maid bending over to stoke the fire, ass on show. Maybe she'd be wearing one of those little kinky aprons, pressed, white, with a lace trim, and maybe, he could reach out, grab the edge of her tunic, flip it up to reveal...

'Don? Where are you going?' His wife, as she so often did, interrupted his daydream.

He shrugged, and kept on walking. She'd be along presently, he knew it. Barbara always followed him, even when she didn't really want to.

Because where else would she have to go?

The other three remained behind, unsure of what to do.

'Hey!' Baltimore, his affability evaporated, called out after the Guide. 'What, we're just going to leave her to her own devices?'

'She'll be fine,' the Guide replied, his form retreating along yet another corridor towards yet another landing from which too many doors led. *Hallways and doors,* Barbara thought, feeling her anxiety intensify. *This place is mostly hallways and doors.*

They can't all lead somewhere, that would be impossible.

This made her think of those wooden puzzle toys you got sometimes at Christmas. You had to try and navigate a small steel ball through a balsawood maze without falling down a hole, or meeting a dead end, or finding yourself in an endless loop, or even worse, right back where you started. She'd never been fond of puzzles. They required energy, and hers had been sucked out of her.

In the meantime, Noah, who had no idea any of this turmoil was taking place beneath Barbara's composed exterior, looked instead at his father, ambling off without a thought for the rest of them. He felt a hate twisting in his chest, wriggling around and around as if trying to find a comfortable home in his dried reedbed soul.

Why did I have to end up with such shitty parents? He thought, furiously.

Why me?

Why not some other kid? Like Jackson Barnes, from next door? Jackson Barnes was a deep-fried, chili-flavored piece of shit through and through, yet *his* mom and dad seemed perfectly normal, and in love, and able to function as a unit.

He looked back to his own mother for reassurance, and saw how close to the loser with the expensive baseball cap she was standing.

He was on his own, he knew it.

He threw himself after the Guide too, vowing to slip away at the first opportunity. If the Bow-tie guy and the lady in the green dress could do it, so could he. He was going to blow this whole thing off and go to town, sit in the cemetery a while, smoke. Try and figure out his next steps. He was pretty certain he was going to run away, but he needed a plan, first.

He needed funds.

His fingers spasmed by his sides. The urge to steal was now almost overwhelming, but for the first time in a long time, it came with a purpose: if he could fund his own escape, he could start over. Alone. His rules. His terms. He could make something of himself, no matter what his father thought of him.

He left Barbara and Baltimore alone. The two looked at each other, and it was a look that lasted maybe thirty seconds longer than it should have.

'Guess that's our answer, then,' Baltimore said, eventually.

'I guess so,' Barbara agreed, but she stuck her head back into the Atrium before they left. Terry was nowhere to be seen, so she assumed he'd done as the Guide said— returned to the start, and made his way home, somehow. This made her think of her own home, which she did *not* want to go back to.

So don't, the whispers in her head said. *Don't go back.*

'Shut up,' she muttered to herself, and she hurried to rejoin the tour, which seemed to wend its way inwards, downwards, for an interminable length of time, towards the heart of the Sunshire Chateau itself, if a house could be said to have a heart at all, that is.

Behind them, minutes later, the sound of shattering glass echoed around the empty corridors.

A PAIR OF YELLOW CUFFLINKS

'And this is the Master's study. Take a moment, and breathe it all in. It's quite something, isn't it?'

The tour group filtered into the room and stood to one side of the door, waiting for the Guide to take his position in the center of things. The tall man did so with his usual sense of proprietary belonging, casting a quick glance around to see if anything were amiss, damaged, out of place or otherwise not as he had last left it.

It *was* something, he was right. As Barbara walked into the square, warm space, Baltimore at her back, nose wrinkling with the musty smell of leather, dust, and old oak, her first thought was: *Don will love this room.*

She was not wrong. Don did love this room, for one reason: it was the single most masculine space he had ever encountered.

Firstly, as with most of the rooms at Sunshire, there was a color theme, and, true to the nature of the man who had spent most of his time here seeing to business, this theme was red. Blood red. Scarlet wallpaper with a dark red diamond pattern adorned the walls, and the thick oriental rug underneath was a shade of merlot that made Don think of drinking, and ripping into raw steak with hungry teeth, or maybe even into the soft parts of a woman whose hands were bound above her head. It had a deep pile that made his slippers sink under his weight, and it sucked at his feet as he walked across it.

The red theme extended to the furniture, which was fashioned from leather and mahogany, and included a pair of chesterfields, much to Don's delight, arranged on either side of a large stone fireplace. The desk, also mahogany, was topped with three large red leather blotter panels, tooled by hand with gold leaf, as the Guide informed him. It was piled high with books, papers, pen stands, a letter knife, a cigar box, stacks of folders, envelopes and an open leather briefcase. A banker's lamp sat on top of the desk, its glass shade predictably crimson.

To one side, near a tall dresser, another long, life-sized portrait of Charles Lester III stood on two legs with clawed feet that ended in small castors, so it could be wheeled about, for whatever reason made it necessary to do so. In the portrait, the Master was wearing red, and he posed in front of a red velvet backdrop, his hands on his hips, legs braced wide apart, as if he were trying to balance upon the deck of a ship at sea. Behind the dresser, red drapes accented the walls at various points around the room, wherever there was space to do so, for space was at a premium here: it was a busy, crowded space.

All in all, Don felt like he was inside the living, beating heart of someone, and he loved it. Red was his favorite color too, although he had never told anyone that. To him it symbolized drive, ambition, passion, a fighting chance at being something greater than average. His car was red, as was his underwear, which Barbara complained about a lot—his smallclothes often ruined a wash by staining everything else as the color ran. He liked the thought of that, liked the thought of ruining the prissy, boring whites his wife enjoyed so much, so he kept buying red. Little acts of chaos, sown about like wild seeds, whenever he saw an opportunity.

He pivoted, drinking in the rich, musky smell that hung heavy in here, a smell that could have been pipe-smoke, mildew, wet dog, or wood polish. Or perhaps, all of these things mingled together. His eyes went to the top of the room, to where trophies were displayed on custom-made trophy shelves capped with little glass domes to keep the dust off and stop them from tarnishing too quickly. Hunting trophies, he realized, and this was backed up by the rich and varied display of dead animals and exotic game that were stuffed, taxidermied, and hung upon the walls for all to see: deer antlers, a lion's head, two tigers, a boar, an elk, a gazelle, an antelope, a springbok, anything with horns, in fact, and more—birds of all description, from finches, to gulls, to an albatross, their feathers tattered and purposefully splayed to mimic flight, an alligator, suspended from the ceiling, its stiff, lifeless legs sticking out like stubby tree branches. A huge skull, resting on the floor in one corner of the study: elephant or whale, Don couldn't tell which. A pair of polished and carved ivory elephant tusks that hung, crossed like the bones of a Jolly Roger flag, above the large executive desk. A snake, or rather a python like the pythons depicted on the staircases downstairs, stuffed and almost completely stiff, lying across one of the bookshelves.

And on the shelves, none of the philosophy books or fiction or history or Latin or theosophy that dominated the bookcases in the Library or the Blue Room. No, each shelf in this room carried one cargo: rank upon rank of red, leather-bound folders. On the spines, in gold lettering, a different year was stamped.

Those are the accounts, I'll eat my hat if they aren't, said Don to himself, and the word 'hat' made him suddenly look for Baltimore, who was, as usual, standing too close to Barbara. He found that this no longer bothered him like it had earlier.

The only thing that interested him now was taking a look inside one of those red leather folders.

How much was the old bastard worth? He wanted to know. *How much, to live large, to live like a king?*

Don had never had much money. His own mom had run out on him when he was eighteen months old. He became a latchkey kid while his dad worked shifts. He learned real quick that if you're born poor, you tend to stay poor. Only a lucky few—like Charles Lester III—worked their way up out of being hungry. Grafters. They replaced one type of hunger for another type: hunger for success. Hunger for respect. Hunger for permanence. Being poor meant things didn't tend to last long, which was the truth Don had grown up with. Food didn't last. Love didn't last. Families didn't last.

Money lasted, however.

Or at least the things you bought with it did.

As the sole breadwinner in his family, success and money had been thin on the ground for Don, and that situation was unlikely to change any time soon. Part of this was his fault, he knew, although it would take something drastic for him to admit to that publicly. He'd kept Barbara from working when she'd shown an interest in it. She'd wanted to take a secretarial course, find a part-time job working for someone else, and Don knew what that meant: microwave dinners. An untidy house. Him, having to do childcare.

He had vetoed it.

But he wondered about the extra money, sometimes. How nice it would have been. He didn't feel guilty about it, he just realized, when he gave it a moment's thought, which was not often, that he had probably cut off his nose to spite his own face, and that feeling made him a little angry.

Don was angry a lot, these days.

Baltimore eyed the portrait. 'Damn, that's a realistic one,' he said, taking off his cap and peering in. 'Feels like he's about to walk right out of that frame.'

'That this was both a functional and highly personal room for the Master of the house should be immediately obvious,' the Guide said, ignoring Baltimore and throwing Don a knowing and almost deferential look. Don frowned. The Guide had dipped his head as he looked at him, almost as if taking a small bow. Was this guy jerking him off? Or had he mustered up some newfound respect for his guests late in the day? Don didn't know, but he liked it. He liked the deference. He felt broader, and his back felt straighter. He found himself nodding, just once, a smart dip of the head, by way of acknowledgment, although he had no idea where that gesture, which felt like practiced, ingrained behavior, had come from.

'Not only are the walls and shelves redolent with the Master's personal and professional trophies of achievement, but this was where he chose to dress, answer calls, deal with business correspondence, host billiard parties for his associates…' He pointed to an enormous billiards table that Don had somehow missed, which dominated the far end of the room. 'And unwind at the end of a long, arduous day.'

'Lucky him,' Baltimore said, a little envious. 'Only place I have to unwind at the end of the day is an empty hotel room, usually.'

Barbara looked at him.

'I travel a lot,' he explained. 'For work.'

'Your wife must love that,' Noah said, trying to appear innocent.

Baltimore chuckled ruefully. 'She didn't, much. I guess that's why we're divorced.'

Barbara filed this fact away as Noah scowled.

201

The Tour Guide cleared his throat, irritated by the interruption.

'In fact, the Master spent so much time in here that he barely used his bedroom for anything except sleep, and sometimes not even then. He began his day in here, and ended his day in here. He even had this dresser custom made by an Italian master joiner so that he could wash and shave in here.' He stopped next to the piece of furniture in question: a tall mahogany dresser and shaving stand, upon which stood an elegant chrome bowl, shaving brush and ivory-handled razor set. Next to this, a comb, a jar of pomade, a bottle of Baldpate Hair Tonic, a folded pair of spectacles in a case with the lid open for display purposes, and a small black velvet cushion, which rested upon a small cut crystal platter.

And in the middle of the cushion, a pair of glittering cufflinks lay, both of which were fashioned from a thumbnail sized, pale-yellow jewel. They looked like cat's eyes staring out of the dark, and Noah was instantly fascinated by them.

'What are those?' He breathed, unaware of the naked greed that had suddenly crept across his features.

'Ah, yes. The Master's favorite—and famous—cufflinks,' the Tour Guide explained, and for some reason, although nobody present knew why, his voice rose as he spoke, until it was almost an uncomfortably high pitch. He rubbed the back of his head absently again, wincing as if in sudden pain.

The group crowded around the dresser. A brief silence settled on them all as they looked at the cufflinks.

'What's so special about them?' Don said, sniffing. He was unimpressed by jewelry. He wanted to know about the trophies, the dead animals.

The accounts.

Noah shot him a look. His father was an idiot.

Anyone with half a brain cell could see these cufflinks were rare, rare and expensive as fuck.

His eyes began to glow with excitement. *How far could I get with those?* He asked himself, but despite the sudden quickening of his heartbeat, he managed to maintain his cool, feigning indifference.

The Tour Guide switched on a pained smile. Barbara, who was looking right at him as he did this, thought she saw something flicker around his face, something so fast and transparent, almost, that she blinked, assuming she had something in her eye—dust, or a stray fiber. She rubbed them with the backs of her index fingers, and when she had finished, the Guide looked as he had before: solid, thin, dissatisfied with life.

'These cufflinks are,' he said, solemnly, 'as far as I am aware, at any rate, quite possibly the most expensive cufflinks in the entire world.'

'Go on,' said Noah, who was struggling so hard not to snatch them from the cushion that he had begun to sweat.

'Made of eighteen carat white gold, centered with two flawless ten carat, Asscher cut canary yellow diamonds in an octagon setting, surrounded by another ten carats of baguette cut white diamonds each, with elegant whale flip-back latches on the reverse, these cufflinks were gifted to Charles Lester III himself by an undisclosed mystery benefactor. The Master loved them so much he never really took them off, unless it was bathing time. Until, of course, he died. Why he was not buried with such treasured personal items we are not entirely sure, but his loss is the Chateau's gain, you could say.' The Guide rubbed the back of his skull once more, and then touched his wrists, first the left, then the right, softly, as if subconsciously mimicking the act of pushing cufflinks through holes in his sleeves.

Noah watched him do this, and understood.

The Tour Guide coveted the cufflinks too.

'What are they made of?' He asked, his own pitch wobbling wildly out of control for a second. Barbara smiled inwardly, knowing better than to register any outward amusement over her son's voice breaking. The sound of his adolescence hurtling towards adulthood made her feel things she didn't understand. She missed her little boy. She missed being the apple of his adoring eye. But she was also, trepidation about his current behavior aside, looking forward to seeing what sort of man he grew into.

Whether he was still talking to her by then was another matter.

She suspected that his coming of age would coincide with his leaving her behind, but she couldn't blame him. He deserved a better life than the one he had, currently. He was an outsider, was Noah. A loner at school. At home, he was never seen, never heard, and when he was heard, when he did muster the energy to talk to them, Don usually shot him down in flames. Nothing she said or did seemed to make him happy, so increasingly, she left him alone, for that was what he seemed to want.

She looked at him now, as he leaned into the cufflinks, intently focused upon them.

Watch him, Barbara, the nasty little voice in her head whispered.

He's going to steal those.

The Guide was of a similar mind. He rested a hand lightly on Noah's shoulder.

'Have they caught your eye? Of course they have. You have taste. The Master had taste. He might have liked you.'

Baltimore huffed. 'And they're just...sittin' there, plain as day, on that raggedy old cushion? No glass display case, no alarm? Aren't you worried someone will steal 'em? How much are they even worth?' His Baltimorese ramped up with this little speech, the word 'on' coming out like 'awn', and Barbara found she liked the sound of it.

The Tour Guide smirked into his clipped beard and shot Noah another inscrutable look. Noah, who was a million miles away, didn't see this look. His eyes were fixed on the cufflinks, and nothing else existed for him in that moment, just the gleaming, beguiling yellow accessories that sat on their little cushion self-importantly. Noah realized with a fierce jolt that he had never wanted to own anything as much as he wanted to own these bright yellow things, and he also knew, as a cold wave of adrenaline surged through him, as his cheeks flushed red and his mouth ran dry, he knew with the inarguable surety of a young boy about to walk blindly towards his own fate, that he would not be leaving this room without the cufflinks secreted away in the small lined pocket he had fashioned on the inside of the jacket he wore over his hoody. He was going to steal them, and sell them, and use the money to get out of his parents' lives, get out of town, get out of the damn state, and he was going to start a new life, a life where only he was in charge of himself, responsible for himself, answerable only to himself and nobody else, and he would get a job, a decent job doing something useful, something where he could lie about his age, where he could use his hands, maybe fix cars, or dig holes in people's backyards, or stack shelves, or maybe drill holes in pieces of metal, some kind of job where he felt like he was fucking making something that was worth something, but he would also study, he would read, he would write, if only to prove his dad wrong, because fuck him, that's why. And school could get fucked too, who had time for school anyway? He could do everything he did at school on his own terms. School was an exercise in adolescent torture as far as Noah was concerned, where the kids around him formed hostile little groups and cliques that closed ranks whenever he tried to approach, and the teachers were all on power trips, and honestly, what could he learn at school that he couldn't find out on the internet anyway, if he needed it? Who the fuck needed trigonometry to live a long, fulfilling life? Or the periodic table? Or the history of impressionism in art? Fuck all that shit.

All he needed was the price of a ticket out of town, and enough left over for rent, and he would be golden.

Out loud, he said, in a far-away voice: 'Yeah... how much *are* they even worth?'

To the Tour Guide's eyes, the cufflinks seemed tarnished, dirty, flawed, caked in filth and old dried blood and mud, but he knew the power they held over those who were seeing them for the first time.

He knew only too well.

He remembered trying them on, once, on a day like this nearly seventy years ago, give or take.

Back when he was a Valet, instead of a Tour Guide.

He remembered being caught red, or yellow-handed, as it were, by his employer, Charles Lester III himself.

He remembered the look on the Master's face as the realization sank in that his right-hand man, his most trusted employee, his Valet, his attendant, was stealing something that didn't belong to him.

Something Lester had worked for, something he bought and paid for with his own blood and sweat and cunning and nous, something that did not belong on the wrists of a man who was born into servitude and who, by stint of touching that which did not belong to him, would damn well die in servitude.

The Guide wished he could remember being a free man, before he laid his fingers on those alluring yellow diamonds, but he couldn't. He had spent his entire life being owned by one entity or another, whether it was a man or a house, what did it matter? But he wondered, particularly on the mornings when he opened the doors to the Sunshire Chateau to let in those who dwelt on The Outside, when he saw their sun-blushed skin and the ease in which they moved around, assured of their independence, *what would that feel like*, he always wondered, *what would it feel like to be free?*

Truly, completely free?

And in that respect, although he was not aware of it, the Tour Guide and Noah had a lot in common.

IN THE RED

The Guide let none of these thoughts show to the guests.

'Well?' Noah demanded, growing impatient. 'How much would they be worth?'

'Oh, they would be virtually impossible to sell or profit from if someone *did* somehow manage to steal them,' the Guide replied, remembering the feel of a long wooden cane as it came down hard on the back of his head. He touched his hair lightly, in the exact same spot that the first blow had struck him. The pain had been indescribable, he could remember that much. There had been blood, a lot of blood. He remembered falling to the ground, twisting in time to receive another blow to his face. He remembered seeing things from that point on out of one, single, swollen eye. Movement, and pain, and the sound of his Master breathing heavily, swearing, and grunting as he struck him. Again, and again, and again. Like a cobra striking, over and over.

He thought about that: how quickly it had all happened. How it had taken him fifty-six years to reach a point where he was comfortably employed, comfortably fed, and comfortably stabled, as it were. He'd had his own rooms, away from the servants' quarters. He'd had his own clothing allowance, own meals, served in his room, and access to an auto car. He'd even had his own set of keys, keys that unlocked every single door, cupboard, box and lock in the Sunshire Estate.

And all of it had dissolved in the blink of an eye, in the switch of a cane.

How we are undone, he thought, his heart bleak. And then, because he still valued poetry:

When he shall die,
Take him and cut him out in little stars.

That was Shakespeare, from the play *Romeo and Juliet*. Rose Lester had stolen a copy of Shakespeare's collected works from the Library for him to read, and it had been his single most important possession, once. She had taken a silver pencil and written on the inside cover:
Love, Rose.
And yet, he had still coveted the cufflinks.
How we are undone.
There are no stars for me. Just these walls, these corridors, these rooms.
His words came out weary and rehearsed.
'As far as we know, or so we have been reliably informed, there is only one pair of cufflinks like this in existence, and the highly distinctive diamonds have an equally distinctive and highly traceable provenance, which any jeweler or dealer worth their salt would be immediately aware of as soon as these came their way. Therefore anyone naively looking to trade them in, or fence them would have a horrible time trying to get rid of them, even on the black market. In that sense, I suppose you could say that this renders them both priceless and worthless at the same time, which is rather amusing, when you think about it.'
And with that, the Tour Guide chuckled. There was no warmth in the sound whatsoever.
Barbara, who had wandered close to the desk so she could keep a better eye on her son, noticed that one of the leather-bound folders was lying open there, as if abandoned by someone halfway through the act of reading it. Without thinking, she maneuvered around the

desk so that she could see the contents of the folder right way up. She knew immediately that it was a ledger book, and that she was looking at the Sunshire Estate's accounts, circa 1919. She could just about read the writing within, although it was scrawled in an untidy, antique hand, slanted, with lots of loops and flourishes, but mostly legible. She could make out the word 'balance', and a receipts or expenditure column, populated by row upon row of figures. Some of the numbers were written in red ink, and some in faded black ink.

Her eyes scanned down to the bottom of the column, where a larger number than all the others sat. Someone had circled it angrily with red, and the number itself bled onto the paper, imprinted there by a shaky, furious hand that had pressed so hard the pen nib had sputtered and splattered droplets of ink all over the bottom of the page.

She put a hand out to bring the ledger closer to her, already fully understanding what she was seeing, but wanting to be sure. As her fingers touched the page, a woman's voice, intrusive, but not intrusive in the same way all the other voices in her head were, whispered vehemently in her ears:

He has used up all my money!

Barbara snatched her hand away, staring at her fingertips, which had a new white film on the skin, as if she'd been burned for the briefest of moments, not enough to hurt yet, not enough to do proper damage, but enough to sear the very top layer of her skin like a steak hitting a hot pan. She stared at them in shock, then back at the ledger.

'What's that?' Baltimore said, moving to peek over her shoulder. This act put his body in close proximity to hers, and Barbara felt warm, suddenly, flustered. To cover for this, and to hide her reaction to the secret, whispered voice nobody else had heard, she hardened her voice.

'It's the accounts, I think,' she said. 'For 1919.'

'The same year Charles Lester III died,' a new voice said, and Barbara gasped.

'Linda!'

As one, the rest of the group turned.

Linda Louise, who had been hovering near the open door unseen by anyone, entered the Master's Study. She looked like she had been running: her hair was a mess, sweaty at the temples, springing out of its hair tie at the back. Patches of sweat marked her green dress, she had cobwebs attached to her, dust smeared down one arm, and her slippers were ragged, and torn. Her knees, which peeked out just below the hem of the dress, were scraped, and leaking blood. A long, red mark ran along the line of her nose, as if she had been hit hard in the face by a solid, sharp object. A crust of dark red had gathered about her nostrils.

'Are you alright?' Barbara forgot all about the ledger and rushed over to her.

Linda Louise gave the other woman a blank look.

'Why wouldn't I be?'

Barbara stuttered. 'Your clothes...your knees! Your face! You look like you've fallen.'

Linda Louise looked down at herself, confused. 'Huh,' she replied, after a moment, touching her face gingerly with fingertips that looked swollen and sore. 'It does look like that, doesn't it?'

'Did you...maybe you hit your head?' Barbara asked, but silently she was thinking that she'd seen that look in Linda Louise's eyes before. She'd seen it on Don's face, in the Library, and immediately after. It was a dazed, stunned expression, as if a bomb had gone off in close range.

Linda Louise dismissed Barbara's fussing, and looked around the room. 'Where's Terry?' She asked, frowning.

'He went home,' Baltimore said.

Don, who had sidled over to the desk to look at the open folder, annoyed that his wife, who didn't understand money—largely because he kept control of their finances and information about their accounts (which were all verging on red) away from her—had seen it first. He scowled down at the marching line of numbers.

'What am I looking at here?' He asked, frustrated with himself and uninterested in Linda Louise's return. Numbers swam in his vision, but they refused to add up. 'What does this mean?'

Because his head couldn't make head nor tail of it. He could see money going out, but not that much coming in. He knew he must be reading it wrong. For a person as wealthy as Charles Lester III, these numbers did not make sense.

Barbara, openly irritated with Don for the first time since her arrival at Sunshire, shot him a look.

'It's hardly the most important thing right now, is it honey?'

The Guide, who had been watching all of this from his position by the dresser, laced his hands together demurely, waiting.

Linda Louise rubbed absentmindedly at a long, deep scratch on her arm, and said: 'I'd like to know, too. Those are the accounts, aren't they? They look like accounts.'

Baltimore leaned down and whispered into Barbara's ear.

'Is this all starting to feel...off to you?'

Barbara nodded, swallowing. It did feel off. The conversation happening around her seemed surreal, disjointed, and nobody was behaving normally, in her opinion. Rather, the other guests were speaking as if reading lines from a script, only she wasn't entirely sure they were all reading from the *same* script.

She did a quick check on Noah, to see where he was. He was still by the dresser, staring at the cufflinks.

'It does,' she whispered back.

'Hey! What are you two getting cozy about, over there?' Don spat, and Barbara could see he was about to turn nasty.

'What you're looking at,' she blurted, in a vain attempt to turn the tide of his anger and buy herself some more time while she tried to make sense of the weird atmosphere in the room, 'is a whole lot of debt. If those are Lester's accounts, then he was in trouble.'

Don stared at her, his face suddenly pale. 'What?'

'Lester was in debt. It's there, plain as day on the ledger.'

Linda Louise, who seemed to be slowly waking up from a dream, snorted. 'Why does that not surprise me? Lester was a known fraud, through and through. He inherited his wife's fortune upon marrying her, didn't he?'

'He did?' Don looked as if he were about to spit loose teeth.

'Sure he did. Rose had been married before, but her first husband ran off with another woman, and so she was considered an undesirable divorcee. Handing over control of all her wealth was a condition of Lester marrying her, according to records. Her father, who couldn't wait to get her off his hands, brokered the deal behind her back. By the time legislation caught up with the idea of women having unfettered autonomy over their own money, Lester had spent all of hers. On bad investments. Do you know she was not allowed to open a bank account without

Lester's permission? Women didn't have that right until the Sixties.'

There was silence following this little speech. Noah stared blankly at the cufflinks, the rest of the world outside of their sphere of influence gray, and insubstantial. Don, his illusions about Lester as a successful businessman rudely shattered, stared down at the ledger, feeling angry, feeling duped. Linda Louise, who hardly knew where she was or what she was saying, but was aware she was waking up from a strange dream, slowly began to look around her, taking in the decor of the Master's Study, and curling her lip as the extravagance sank in.

Barbara, who felt sick thinking about Charles Lester III's wife, stripped of assets by way of matrimony, heard the voice in her memory again:

He has used up all my money!

Her fingertips throbbed.

Baltimore took his cap off, and scratched his head.

The silence stretched for a full minute.

Then it was broken by the sound of someone screaming.

'Help!' The voice yelled, getting closer as it sounded out. 'For the love of god, *help!*'

'Is that- Terry?' Baltimore asked, and then he strode out of the room into the corridor, where the noise was coming from. Barbara followed unthinkingly, as did Linda Louise, who was glad to leave the oppressive atmosphere of the Master's Study.

Don, disgusted with the whole charade of the Tour, the house, the Lester 'fortune', hawked up a gobbet of phlegm and spat onto the open ledger. The small spit-bullet hit the page with an audible splat, and sat there, soaking into the yellowed paper.

Then he ambled after the others, not wanting to be left out of anything, despite himself.

The Tour Guide and Noah remained, side by side near the dresser. The Guide's hand still rested on Noah's shoulder, although neither of them had noticed this. Noah was rooted in place as firmly as if he were a tree. He swayed a little on his feet. He was sweating all over now, and he clenched and unclenched his hands repeatedly. All he could think about were the cufflinks. All he could think about was the new life they were going to afford him.

All he could think about was his glittering, yellow freedom, freedom that shone like cat's eyes in the dark.

The Tour Guide thought about cautioning the boy for a moment, knowing what was about to happen. He thought about it, and remained silent. The kid was too far gone. The house had sunk its claws in, and his words of warning were rarely taken in the spirit in which they were intended anyway.

And he knew better than to try and intervene when the house had made its mind up.

Not when Sunshire had really set its heart upon a person.

He let go of Noah's shoulder and followed the party, stopping by the desk first to blot at the patch of wet on the ledger with a neatly pressed handkerchief, his mouth drawn down at the corners in disgust, then drifting slowly across the room on feet that perhaps, if a person were to look very, very closely, didn't quite touch the ground, but walked upon the thinnest margin of air between his brightly polished shoes and the rich, deep carpet.

And Noah, who was finally, blissfully alone, reached out a trembling hand.

A REUNION

It was Terry. He was running down the corridor towards the tour group as fast as his legs would take him. He was terrified, his skin ashen, his hair a mess on top of his head. His eyes had an odd, filmy look to them.

'Just like Linda Louise,' Barbara whispered into Baltimore's ear.

He nodded. 'I see it,' he replied.

'We thought you had gone home,' Barbara said out loud, as Terry drew himself up to a hard stop in front of them.

'Please,' he breathed, his bow-tie skewed at a ridiculous angle. Sweat poured down his pale cheeks, disappearing into his neat beard. 'Oh please. I heard a crash- I turned back, and...Oh, you have to come!' He covered his face with shaking hands, then, and Barbara made an effort to comfort him as he dissolved into hysterics.

'What's the deal?' Baltimore asked, struggling to make himself heard above Terry's noise. Subconsciously, he moved closer to Barbara, as if to shield her from any bad news.

'There's been...there's been a terrible accident!'

'What kind of accident?' Linda Louise scanned Terry up and down, the whole length of him, and then turned her scrutiny on her own stained dress, scratched skin, grazed knees, cobwebbed shoulder. She ran a hand over her hair, realising what a disarray she was in.

'What..?'

'I don't mean to interrupt, but I think something is happening to us,' Barbara interjected. 'It happened to Don, it's happened to you, it happened to Linda Louise. You disappeared for a while, then came back with the same look on your face. You can't remember anything after you left us, can you?' She was talking to both Bow-tie and Linda Louise, but Terry was in no fit state to answer.

Linda Louise held up a hand, slowly. It shook a little. 'What do you mean, *after I left you*?'

'You left us, in the servant's passage. When we got to the Atrium, you weren't there. We didn't...we didn't realize until later. We were worried about you. I wanted to look, but...' Barbara glared at the Tour Guide, who lazily joined them. He seemed wholly unconcerned with the news Terry had brought them.

'Atrium?' Linda Louise gazed at Barbara as if she had grown three heads.

'What kind of accident?' Baltimore said, trying to bring the conversation back round to what he thought was more pressing at that particular moment in time. 'Is someone hurt?'

Barbara snapped her mouth shut.

Terry, who shook from head to toe, hiccoughed miserably, and quietened down a touch.

'It's easier to show you,' he said, in a small, scared voice.

'Show us *what?*'

'Yes, show us what, exactly?' The Tour Guide asked, examining his fingernails as he did so.

'It's the bookie. Ned. He's...it's easier to show you,' Terry repeated, and then he started to cry.

A MAN'S PROPERTY

Noah closed his eyes, shuddering as he made contact with the cufflinks. They felt warm to the touch, which surprised him a little, but he found the sensation of flesh meeting diamond exquisite. His fingers closed around the jewels.

'Finally,' he breathed, and he shifted from foot to foot as the blood rushed to his groin. This always happened when he stole. He'd never figured out why, exactly.

He dropped the links into his sweaty left palm and gazed at them. They felt heavy, comfortingly so, in his cupped hand. Red light from the nearby desk lamp hit the flawless surface of each diamond and was absorbed, as if the jewels were hungry for light, which in fact they were, hungry as the Chateau was hungry, for everything that lived inside the walls of the Sunshire Estate had once been eaten by the house.

Noah closed his hand into a fist, and felt the diamonds press into his skin. If he squeezed hard enough, they would cut him, he knew.

Worth it, he thought.

He turned, and caught the eye of the oil version of Charles Lester III, who posed stiffly in the large portrait that stood nearby. The other man was sporting the cufflinks in the painting, Noah could see. They were two little yellow blobs in a sea of red velvet, for Lester had decided to dress ostentatiously for this particular portrait. Noah thought he looked ridiculous, and held up the cufflinks for Lester to admire.

'Mine now,' he said, smiling. 'Mi-'

Charles Lester knew someone was in his study before he pushed open the door quietly, so, so quietly, to see who it was. He had heard a person moving about in there, rummaging through drawers, shuffling papers, and he had paused, light as a cat, in the corridor outside, listening. A quiet muttering came from behind his study door. The voice was familiar.

The voice was treachery.
So, he thought to himself.
The Valet, is it?
The thieving bastard Valet.
Lester had known that someone had been stealing from him for some time. Little things, at first, things that the thief thought wouldn't be missed immediately. A silver spoon, a tie-pin with a small emerald mounted on it. A silver-plated pencil on a chain. Then the things that disappeared got bigger. A paperweight. A pair of fur-lined gloves. A special edition of the collected works of Shakespeare. That last one hurt a lot. Lester had paid over the odds for it at auction on the recommendation of several experts. He had shelved it in a particular place in the Library where he thought it might remain out of sight and touch. When he'd discovered it missing, he had begun to inventory everything else in the Chateau, and realized.

Someone was taking his things.
Charles Lester III was not about to stand for that.
So he'd set a trap. The most expensive cufflinks known to the world, gifted to him by a business associate in Russia. Usually, if not wearing them, he would lock valuables like that in one of the twenty-five safes installed throughout the house by his architect at his behest when the Sunshire Chateau was first built, for Charles Lester III did not believe in banks, and preferred to keep his riches close, like his

enemies. Usually, anything with value beyond definition was kept secret, and safe, and out of harm's way.

But the cufflinks had represented an opportunity. For which thief would be able to resist their allure? They were so small, so easy to secret away.

He left them out in plain sight. It hurt him to do so, but it was necessary. Softly, softly, catchy fishy.

And the bait, it seemed, had worked.

Charles peered through the tiny gap he'd made around the door's edge, using the doorframe and his walking cane to hold himself steady so he did not make any creaking sounds on the floorboards below.

What he saw when he peered into his study made his blood boil.

The Valet held himself erect in front of a long standing mirror that was positioned near his desk. Lester had installed it there because he sometimes liked to look at himself while he worked. He also dressed in his study often, and the mirror was essential. He had appearances to maintain, for no really successful businessman ever brokered a deal looking like a sloven.

Inside the reflection, the Valet admired his own appearance, as he held his wrists up to the light from the banker's lamp on the desk. Yellow flashed.

The Valet, Lester saw, was not stealing the cufflinks outright.

He was adding insult to injury before he did so.

He was impersonating Lester, shamelessly.

The Valet straightened his back, and peered down his nose at himself, mimicking the way Lester peered down his own nose whenever he spoke to anyone he considered beneath his station.

'Do it NOW,' the Valet said, and then he smiled, shaking his head. His face grew serious. His shoulders rounded out, *and he carefully knelt down, until he rested on one knee, his other knee up before him. He removed the cufflinks and placed them in the palm of his right hand, then offered this up, as if offering a gift at an altar.*

'Rose,' the Valet whispered, peering at himself intently. 'Will you run away with me?'

Charles Lester III's rage filled every spare part of his body.

Rose?

Why was his wife's name in his Valet's mouth?

He had seen enough. He pushed his way into the study, walking cane held before him like a sword.

'I think those are mine,' he said, cracking the Valet across the back of the head without a second thought.

The Valet cried out, tried to defend himself, but the Master, who was covered in livid red spots of anger, thrashed him again.

'I wasn't stealing them!' The Valet tried to shout. 'I was only trying them on!'

'Mine! Mine! Mine!' Lester roared, bringing the cane down hard once more. The Valet, who had scrambled into survival mode, rolled to one side at the last moment, and—

Noah understood, too late, that he'd been lured into a trap. He opened his hand, turned it upside down, and tried to shake the cufflinks out of his palm.

He found he could not let go of them.

With horror, he saw that his hand was bubbling like melted plastic, and the cufflinks were sinking into the charred flesh, burrowing in like strange, beautiful little burrowing beetles, like gold bugs, and they dug deeper and deeper into him, wriggling their way between his tendons, slicing through ligaments and rupturing veins, and Noah screamed in agony, for the pain was the fiercest pain he had ever experienced in his short life, but it was not only the pain that made him so scared, it was the sensation of another man staring out at the world through his eyes, or was he staring at the world through someone else? It was so blurred, the boundary between himself and this other entity, and around the edges his of vision, in the direction of the portrait of Charles Lester III, he sensed movement, but he could not bring himself to focus on it, he couldn't seem to focus on—

'I just wanted to see what it felt like!' The Valet croaked. His face was almost obscured behind a veil of blood, and Lester could see a large split now running up one cheek, from his mouth to his eyebrow.

Lester stopped beating the man for a moment, if only to catch his breath. He realized that the cufflinks were now back where they belonged, on his own wrists. He did not remember attaching them to his sleeves, but that hardly mattered anymore.

'You will never know what it feels like to be me,' he spat. 'You are lower than I will ever be. Do you understand? You are a low, pathetic creature.'

The Valet's eyes were wounded beyond the physical damage his Master had done.

'But when I came to you, you said...'

Not this again, Lester thought.

'You think you can blackmail me with that pathetic lie about us sharing blood?'

'My father was your father. I have the documents to prove it!'

'You had *the documents. Whether or not you still have them is down to how effective my lawyer was when he went through your things. I have lived too many years to let a lowly, common worm like you blackmail me.'*

223

The Valet, who was no longer a young man himself, persisted.

'I have just as much right to these things as you do! We are family. I have a birthright, I have-'

Lester jammed his cane's tip into the center of the Valet's chest and pushed, hard, forcing the other man to lie flat on his back.

Then he stood heavily upon the Valet's neck, cutting him off mid-sentence.

'I gave you a job all those years ago because I admired your courage in coming to me, and because I saw potential in you. I saw the same thing I saw in myself. Yes, you were a little long in the tooth, but you kept your ambition. You kept your drive. You wanted to make something of yourself. I indulged you. I trusted you. I treated you like the family you say we are. And this is how you repay me?'

The Valet, who could sense his own death looming, forced his next words out painfully, defiantly, his voice box creaking under the weight of Lester's foot.

'She loves me. She told me so.'

With that, Charles Lester III was done talking. He was done arguing, and reasoning. His anger welled up like blood from a new wound and he thought: Why not let this cane do the talking instead?

And so he raised his arm, and brought it down hard on the Valet's face.

And he kept doing it until the other man was dead.

He was dimly aware that in killing the Valet, he was crossing over into new territory, walking through a door that had until now been closed to him. His previous experience of doors was limited to those that opened upon opportunity, wealth and status, doors that led to success. In that respect, and based on his personal opinion that the world was a crowded and ambitious place with finite resources and opportunities, it was every man for himself. In his mind, doors should be simple mechanisms, and if a man could not find a door to take him to where he needed to go, he could simply make one, smash a hole through whatever barrier stood in his way and pass through, at his own leisure.

A door did not need a fancy handle to serve its purpose, in his opinion.

Not when it was every man for himself.

Not when murder was the door through which Charles Lester III had just stumbled, headlong, and—

'Take your filthy fucking hands off my things, boy.'

Noah came to his senses with a jolt.

The voice, which came from somewhere no further than a few hand spans away, was unexpected. Noah thought he might be hallucinating, perhaps in pain, but then he felt a harsh, stinking breath on his cheek.

He looked again with streaming eyes at the full-length oil portrait that stood on a wheeled legs next to the dresser.

Only, now that he looked at it, he could see it wasn't a full-length portrait at all.

It was a full-length mirror.

And climbing out of it, hovering half-in, half-out of the glass, was the figure of Charles Lester III himself.

The Master snatched hold of Noah's wrists with cold, clammy hands. Noah screamed.

'You like these, boy?'

Noah let go of his bladder. Warm piss ran down his leg and soaked into the thick carpet, which had seen so many terrible spills over the years, yet somehow remained as pristine as the day it had first been laid.

'I'm...sorry...' Noah tried to back away. The pain in his hand was indescribable, and he found it hard to think, hard to speak, hard to move.

The ghost of Lester sneered at him, his long, cruel mouth turning down at the ends. His grip on the boy tightened.

'Did you earn these? Did you work for them? Have you worked for anything in your life?'

Noah began to cry, shaking his head.

'I'm sorry!' He begged. 'Let me go, I'll never do it again, I swear!'

'*THEN GIVE THEM BACK, BOY!*' The ghost roared, and he let go of Noah's wrists and pounced, digging his cold, ferocious hands deep into Noah's palm, long, sharp fingernails digging for gold in his tender flesh, and the mirror, huge, heavy, poorly weighted, rocked on its feet violently, back and forth, back and forth, as Noah struggled with the frenzied entity within, and then, with a slow and ponderous crash, it tipped over, and fell to the ground, the weight of it smashing Noah flat against the floor of the Master's study and covering him like a tombstone, until the only part of him left visible was a hand, bloodied, a hole ripped clean through the middle of the palm like a stigmata, and it twitched once, twice, three times, then lay still.

And blood began to slowly spread from beneath the mirror.

The Sunshire Chateau drank it thirstily.

MATTER AND DUST

Ned woke, but it was a strange sort of waking. Not like rising from sleep, because he hadn't felt like he had been asleep. He'd been...away, for a while.

Yes, that was it. It was not waking, but returning, through a door he hadn't realized he'd passed through in the first place.

Returning.

To what?

He rose up from the floor of the Atrium, and came face to face with a man. The man stood still next to the remaining unbroken giant terracotta pot, the sister to the one Ned had smashed, and faced him, as if he'd been waiting a long time.

They looked at each other, and Ned noticed something sticking out of the man's eye socket: a trowel. Slim, sharp, it was buried into him up to the hilt. Ned was strangely unmoved by this, although he knew he should have been terrified.

'That's the Gardener,' Alice's voice said, from behind him. 'He's shy. He doesn't show himself to Outsiders often. Many of us don't like to.'

He turned, and realized he was pleased to see her. She felt safe, and familiar, and...Trustworthy. He found he was not afraid of her anymore. He didn't really know why he had been afraid of her in the first place.

Her hair gleamed red.

It was odd, but all he felt now was...calm. As if he'd accomplished something, a task that had been hanging over him.

'You'll see a lot more of us, now that you belong to the house,' the Housekeeper continued.

'Belong?' Ned asked, although it wasn't really like speaking. It was more like thinking directly into another person's mind.

Alice pointed to the floor. 'I'm so sorry,' she said. 'But it would have happened sooner or later. That's just how it is, here.'

And Ned saw his own body then, saw how ruined it was, saw blood, saw bones that had shattered, saw parts of him disassembled, and many things clicked into place all at once for him, like the individual components of a complex locking mechanism sliding together and springing open a long-locked secret door.

'Are you alright?' Alice took his hand, although it wasn't really his hand, it was only a memory of his hand. An approximation of his hand. It was dust, matter, energy, settling and resettling, like the small swarms of flies that had begun to settle on his bloodied corpse.

And Ned, who had secretly vowed to never fall in love again, not while he was alive, looked at Alice, who was the same as he was, who had been this way for many, many years, and he felt his heart crack apart, as if he were a geode, unremarkable on the outside, yet full of dazzling crystals within, only those crystals were his feelings, feelings that he was terrified of, feelings that he'd hidden for a long, long time behind a granite layer of agreeable, good-natured cheer, and he found that inside of himself, those feelings were still violently sparkling, and that somehow, despite everything, after all this time, love had found a chance to creep back in, now that he was dead.

He looked at her, and she glowed under his scrutiny.

'So...we died,' he said, for clarity, and it felt like a silly question to ask, but he had to hear it from her.

'Yes. And now we live here. Sunshire is a place for people like us. Some of us stay for a long time. Some of us leave quickly, move on to find a different place to live. It's not so bad, really. The house understands us, at least.'

'You said it was a prison, before.'

'It is. But there are degrees of imprisonment.'

'And Charles...the Master. Does he live here too?'

A cloud passed across her. 'Yes. He lives here. But he can't hurt you, not now. He just has to relive his own pain, over and over. Some of us are able to come to terms with it. I have. The Gardener has. Others, like Isabelle, like the Master...they cannot find their way out of their own deaths. They hang, you see. No control.'

Ned didn't see. 'So...am I dead too?' He kept repeating himself because he wanted to be absolutely sure.

Alice smiled. 'Do you *feel* dead?'

He shook his head vehemently. 'Not when I'm with you.' His eyes went back to his own corpse, which hardly looked like the body of a human at all, it was so distorted, so flattened so...rearranged.

'What happens now?' He asked, turning away from his own decay.

Alice laughed. The Gardener, who had been observing all of this, ambled off, looking for work.

'What?' Ned did not understand what amused her so much, but he did understand that he found her beautiful. Not just the form of her, but everything. In this state, he could see *everything*. He realized how intimate the situation was. They were laid bare, now. He had seen her body in death, and she had seen his. It was a shared secret, a relationship ritual.

This is what I look like, on the inside.

'Do you like to dance?' She asked.

THE MAP ROOM

NOAH IS LOST

It took five minutes before Barbara realized Noah was not following them. She stopped mid-stride as she made this discovery, and Baltimore ran right into the back of her.

Stupid, stupid woman! She said to herself furiously, wheeling about. *You've done it again! You don't deserve a child! You don't deserve a damn thing!*

Baltimore tugged on her sleeve and caught her as she tried to push on by. 'Hey! You okay?'

She shook her head, close to tears, and shrugged him off. 'No. No I'm not. We left Noah behind! I…I lost him!'

Baltimore looked confused. 'He seems a bit old to be lost, Barbara. He's probably just behind us.'

They looked back down the corridor they'd hurried along, but there was no hint of Noah to be seen. Then they looked the other way, to where the Guide, Don, Linda Louise and Terry were rushing along, intent on seeing what Terry's fuss was all about.

Barbara swallowed, beginning to panic.

'Lost, behind, whatever you want to call it- I had him in my sight, and now I don't. I'm so stupid!' Furious with herself, she tugged at her hair, hard, and started marching back down the corridor, returning to the Master's study.

'Hey, hey, go easy on yourself!' Baltimore hopped after her, and quickened his pace to keep up. 'Kid's a teenager, right? They're pretty self-sufficient.'

Barbara had no time for reassurances. She walked faster.

'You don't understand,' she said.

Baltimore panted a little, trying to catch his breath.

'Well he can hardly have gone *far*. He must still be in the Study. You just got distracted, is all. It's understandable, in this place.'

'I can't *afford* to get distracted, not with Noah.'

'Okay, but what about Terry?' The others had disappeared from view now, and Baltimore knew from experience that this was not a good thing.

'Whatever is going on elsewhere, it's not more important than my son. We're supposed to stay together, or we'll end up lost. This place is huge, and old. What if he falls, or breaks something? I'm so angry with myself I could cry!'

'You know, there is such a thing as letting them grow up and make their own mistakes.' Baltimore said it gently, trying to lighten her distress.

'I know what you're thinking,' she said, as she marched. 'Overprotective Mother, uptight, relax, he'll be fine. My husband thinks the same. But you don't know Noah, not like I do. He's...He needs watching. You can't trust him on his own.'

'Oh?'

She bowed her head, feeling suddenly exhausted. 'We've...we've been having issues.'

Baltimore went quiet as he realized what Barbara was trying to tell him. Not wanting to intrude on her private business, he held up his hands. 'Say no more,' he replied, kindly.

But now that Barbara had broken her own self-imposed silence in the face of unexpected sympathy, she had a good deal more to say. She strode along, arms swinging like an army major on parade, and a deep flush of red spread across her face. She flushed easily, Baltimore realized, but it made her seem more honest, somehow.

'It's just that...since he hit puberty, I don't know...Noah *changed* so much. He is so angry all the time, he throws his weight around the house when he doesn't get what he wants. He punches walls and plays loud music just to piss us off.' She began to wave her hands around as she spoke, finally giving into her agitation.

'Well, I mean mine does that too,' Baltimore reasoned. 'It's just hormones, right?'

Was it his imagination, or had the carpet in this hallway suddenly changed color?

'I know, all normal teenager stuff, right?' Barbara laughed bitterly. 'Well, he steals things, too. Small things at first, but they got bigger and more expensive as the months passed. He didn't need those things, I mean, we aren't rolling in cash, but we tried to give him everything he needed, you know? He just stole things because he could. He got a thrill from it. I once caught him with someone else's dog, just walking down the street like it belonged to him. He took it out of our neighbor's front yard in broad daylight. Do you know how *embarrassing* it was to have to return that dog to its owner, and explain that my son just walked on into their property, untied it, and sauntered off? And that was just a warm-up. After that, he got sophisticated. He stole another neighbor's car keys and jacked their car. I didn't even know he could drive! Don never gave him lessons. He said he learned off the internet. Luckily he didn't damage it, returned it a few hours later. They didn't press charges. We had to move not long after.'

'Wow,' Baltimore replied, sympathetically, but he was only half-listening now. He eyed the corridor around him warily. What he really wanted to do was interrupt Barbara, and tell her they were walking the wrong way, down the wrong corridor, he was almost certain of it. How they had ended up here, he couldn't say. He didn't remember turning any corners, crossing any junctions, passing through any doors, but just the same.

This was not the corridor they had just walked down with the group.

In fact, he had no idea where they were anymore.

He wanted to be more upset about this, but he was too tired. He had walked too far, and taken in too much information. His brain was beginning to feel like a bowl of overcooked pasta, limp and slippery.

And try as he might, he could not find the right moment to tell Barbara about this new development. Every time he thought she might take a breath, more words spilled out.

So he slowed his pace, hoping she would do the same, until he could squeeze into the conversation.

'I had lived on that street eighteen years.' Barbara, lost in her own grievances, realized she was on the verge of tears, and rubbed her eyelids angrily. 'I knew everybody, but our name became dirt after that.'

'Uh-huh,' Baltimore said, slowing even more.

'And we tried to be firm with him,' she continued, trying to keep her voice steady and not quite managing it, 'But he is just so smart and persistent, he has absolutely *no* respect for our boundaries, or rules. He flatly refuses to accept anyone else's point of view, and I am convinced he thinks I hate him, even though I try, you know? I try to tell him I love him. In small, subtle ways. I change his bed, I wash his clothes, I make sure the cupboards are full of his favorite things to eat, and...And...'

'Barbara?' Baltimore could see she was not going to stop.

'You know, when you have a kid, your entire body changes?' Barbara grew suddenly quiet, lowering her arms and voice. 'Men don't get this. They don't understand the enormity of it, the extent of the changes. Your entire body inflates, like a balloon that's pumped up too tight, and then you have this moment, this delivery moment, where this tiny creature is given to you, and it's incredible, and then you deflate, slowly, over time, and you think, stupidly, *oh, well, now I can get my body back,* but you never do. You're left with scars, and your breasts are no longer your own, and you have loose skin in places you never thought possible, but it's all part of the sacrifice, the thing they don't tell you about when you get pregnant. Your body belongs to someone else until they decide they're done with it. And aside from that? Your hormones become these bewildering, nonsensical things that dominate your whole life, your hair falls out, or grows in weird places, and you're either bleeding or you're not bleeding, and-'

'Barbara.' Baltimore waved a hand in front of Barbara's face, desperate to get her attention. Truth be told, he was growing a little frightened of the Pandora's Box he had just opened, but Barbara had the bit between her teeth, now. It was rare that anyone took enough of an interest in her and her affairs to allow her to openly talk like this, and now she had begun, it was as if water had started to flow from a rusty old gummed-up tap for the first time in years.

And she hadn't realized how much she needed someone to talk to, until now.

'And they say '*Wear your scars with pride, your body is a beautiful, brilliant, resilient thing. It brought new life into this world. You have tiger stripes now, love them, embrace them, they are part of who you are, you are mother, you are woman, you are amazing.*' But I don't *feel* amazing. I haven't felt amazing for fifteen years. I don't feel beautiful.

I don't feel resilient. I don't feel like the bringer of life. I feel diminished, broken, stretched, and my body is a thing that I hide from, you know? As if, when I look in the mirror, I am afraid I'll...it's like being afraid of finding a ghost in the reflection. Only the ghost is me. And whenever I summon the courage to look at myself, I see glimpses of the woman I was before, and she...she *haunts* me with her unblemished skin and tight, smooth abdomen, and bright eyes that never knew what it was like to nurse a baby for hours and hours into the night, alone, into the small hours of the morning, and do you know how lonely that can be? Sleeplessness? Staring into the dawn day in, day out, while your partner sleeps blissfully in bed beside you?'

What Barbara didn't realize was that her sudden desire to talk wasn't entirely down to Baltimore's politeness and the kind, worried look in his eyes. Rather, it was the house. The Sunshire Chateau was particularly good at wrestling the secrets of guests out from behind their protective wrappers. The house craved high emotion, being gluttonous in nature, gluttonous as the Master had been gluttonous, but instead of riches and opportunities, it fed upon secrets, and feelings, and the struggles of those who walked within its walls.

Barbara didn't know this, and so she kept on talking, giving the house what it wanted.

'*But looks are not everything,* they say, and I know, I know, I know, I *fucking know, but...*'

'Barbara!' Baltimore reached over, gripped her by the shoulders and gave her a little shake. 'We're going the *wrong way.*'

She looked at him with eyes filled with tears, eyes that searched for understanding, and compassion, and sympathy. Her voice cracked as she continued on, unable to stop.

'Grow old gracefully, they say, but there is nothing graceful about me. I'm a slow, useless, worn-out thing.'

'Did you hear me?' Baltimore began to look worried. 'We're headed the wrong way. This is a different corridor to the one we walked down. We got turned about, somehow. You need to stop. We need to turn around, go back on ourselves, before we get too lost.'

'He was kicked out of school, you know. That's why we're on this trip. We wanted...*I* wanted to try and reset a little. Regroup before he started a new one. It...It hasn't been going well.'

Baltimore cleared his throat, and looked down at his feet, unsure of what else to say or do. He couldn't be angry with her. None of this was her fault. She wasn't reachable. She was in a daze, drowning in words she'd bottled up for a long, long time. He sensed that anything he *did* say wasn't really necessary at any rate, for Barbara just needed to talk, just needed to be heard.

Next time you have some downtime before an important meeting, go sit in a diner, he told himself, ruefully.

'Do you feel better for getting that off your chest?' He asked eventually, good-naturedly deciding to ride it out. He'd get through to her in the end, he knew he would.

'I'm sorry. I'm...I'm so sorry. I don't know where all that came from.'

'It's alright. We all get a little het up from time to time.'

'I just...don't want to...I don't want to deal with any more consequences of my kid's shitty behavior, if you take my meaning,' she continued, hesitantly, sensing that she had overstepped and feeling mortified at how familiar she had allowed herself to be. 'I didn't go through all that just to...Not now. I love him. I want him to be happy. I want him to have a good life to look forward to. He's a good kid, underneath the bullshit. I want to enjoy him. I want him to enjoy *me*. I just need...I just need a little break from it all, for a while.'

Baltimore smiled, wanting suddenly to make this tired, pretty woman smile too, for she seemed so heavy and careworn, and he didn't think it was fair for a woman to be run into the ground like this. She was soft, yet resilient, and he could see people took advantage of both qualities.

'I catch your drift, Barbara,' he said, and an instinct of sorts rose up inside him. It had been a long time since anyone had let him play hero, and he rather liked it.

'You do?'

He nodded.

'I do.'

'Thank you.' Finally, she wound down, like a clockwork toy. She'd run out of words.

Got there in the end, thought Baltimore.

'No problem. Now. Did you hear anything I just said?'

She shook her head.

'Never mind.' Baltimore took her gently by the elbow and steered her through a one-eighty. 'Let's just keep walking. We'll find your son in no time.'

'Thank you.' She had no energy left to say anything else. She was utterly depleted, drained. She walked alongside him and enjoyed the sensation of someone else taking care of things, for a change.

'You can call me Mike, by the way,' Baltimore said, with a twinkle in his eye. 'Not that you ever asked.'

'Mike,' Barbara said, allowing herself a small smile. 'I like that.'

CLEVER DESIGN

'This is it, right? I'm sure this is it!'

Barbara and Baltimore—or Mike, as she had to call him now that they were on a first name basis with each other—stopped outside the dozenth identical mahogany door and looked at each other.

'It *looks* like the door to the Master's Study,' Baltimore said, cautiously, 'But then we said that, before.'

The pair had been walking for an hour, give or take, and had tried every single door they had passed by.

Not one of them had led them back to the Master's Study.

They were lost.

They both knew this, but they had kept walking anyway, trying door after door in vain hope that they would eventually find themselves somewhere familiar, because what else was there to do?

'Maybe we'll get lucky this time.'

'Maybe.'

Barbara gripped the handle. 'You ever feel like this house is turning us around and about on purpose?'

'Every minute that goes by.'

'I hope Noah's okay,' Barbara replied sadly.

'Noah will be fine,' Baltimore said. 'He's a smart kid. Right now, I'd be more worried about how lost *we* are.'

'Oh, I've been lost for a good long while,' Barbara sighed, and she pushed the door open.

The room behind the door was not the Master's Study.

Instead, it was an empty, nondescript chamber with one lonely chair in it, some dust sheets draped over an indeterminate object in the corner, and a large bay window that looked directly out onto the thick dark foliage of the cedar trees.

Barbara slammed her hand into the corridor wall in despair. 'I don't understand!' She cried, frustrated. 'We retraced our steps exactly; I know we did! The Study was right here, I was so *sure* this time!' The image of a wooden puzzle toy sprang to mind again, and she felt like the little steel ball inside, rolling around, crashing into dead ends while some giant, unseen hands manipulated the game. She yanked on the door handle, slamming it shut with force.

'Mom?' A voice called out from behind the mahogany paneling. 'Mom, help!'

'Noah?' Barbara gasped, scrambling for the door handle once again.

'Mom! *Mom!*'

'I'm coming, just give me a- come *on!*' Her fingers slipped and fumbled on the handle.

Baltimore slapped a hand down, stopping her in the act of re-opening the door. 'Barbara,' he said, shaking his head, 'I don't like this. We just saw that room. There's nobody in there, remember? You just saw it a second ago.'

'*Mom!*'

'That's my son!' Barbara cried, renewing her efforts to get into the room. 'Maybe he's not in there, but he could be in another passage close by, or a room next to it, or...or...'

The door burst open again, and Barbara hurtled though it, nearly falling flat on her face and taking Baltimore with her. He swore as he came through after her, and then corrected himself, bending down to pick up the cap that had fallen off his head and freezing mid-act as he got a good look at the floor beneath him.

Slowly, he straightened up and took in his surroundings.

The door had opened up onto a completely different room.

'What...what the fuck is going *on* here?' He asked, wide-eyed.

'Noah?' Barbara called, but Noah wasn't there.

Instead, they found themselves in the Map Room.

A SMALL GOLDEN KEY

They didn't know if that was its official name, but that was the first name that sprang to mind, because the entire room was papered with maps. Maps on the walls, maps on the arched ceiling, maps in frames, maps on tables, maps on stands. The windows, of which there were twelve set high up, three on each wall, reminiscent of a church or chapel, were all glazed with stained glass versions of street maps that Barbara didn't recognize, but Baltimore did—they were sections of plans depicting the town of Lestershire. The biggest window, in the middle of the wall opposite the door, held the biggest portion of town, and he could make out the Valleyview Cemetery in the center of the map, represented by a dozen little crosses cut out of milky white glass on a small, emerald green square. The cemetery had been expanded long after the house was built, Baltimore assumed, and was easily three times the size it was on the window, proportional to the rest of town, but he didn't have much knowledge about that. He was not the historian in the group.

What he *did* know was that he was impressed, despite himself. That was the thing about this house, he realized, as his eyes scoured the room looking for Noah. No matter what your mood, what your situation, whatever other preoccupation you had, the house demanded attention, craved it, and won.

His eyes lit on the numerous globes dotted around the place, globes of varying degrees of artistry and accuracy, some made from wood, some from papier mâché, some from brass, showing different versions of the world he knew depending on the age of the globe.

But it was the floor of the Map Room that was the highlight, for him. The floor looked like a center-spread in an atlas, and was an exquisitely detailed delineation of the world picked out in the most incredible array of inlaid hardwoods, each piece hand-cut and worked to perfection, from birch to beech, oak to ash, maple to mahogany. It was a dizzying display of craftsmanship, laid out in a giant, burnished circle, the lines of each country contoured with gleaming brass strips, and there was a large brass disc set into a recess in the middle of the map, somewhere just beneath Britain and flirting with the Atlantic Ocean, which picked out the middle of the room. Inscribed on the disk, the following phrase:

'Earth's crammed with heaven...But only he who sees, takes off his shoes'

Coming out of the disc, rising up like a strange, gilded flower, a slender plinth, and on top of that plinth, another small globe. This one had star constellations engraved on it, the individual stars picked out in what looked like diamonds and rubies. Above it, a large brass lantern that looked North African hung so low from its plaster ceiling rose that it almost kissed the top of the golden globe.

'How is this possible?' Ned breathed. 'This whole room...it wasn't here a moment ago.'

'Maybe...maybe it's a design trick. A perspective thing. Or another secret section like the servants' passage. Perhaps we...triggered a mechanism...or...' Barbara trailed off unconvincingly.

'Maybe,' Baltimore muttered, but they both knew that wasn't it.

Below the Valleyview Cemetery window, a small, modest portrait hung. This one was not, Baltimore saw in some relief, of Charles Lester III—goddamn, but he couldn't stand the sight of that smug face anymore—but of Lester's wife. What had been her name? The Guide had been possessive of it, down in the Reception Hall. Rose, that was it. Rose Lester. She looked much the same as she did in the portrait he'd seen earlier: tired, kind eyes, a figure obscured by folds of unflattering satin and crinoline, hands folded demurely on her lap, a small, hesitant smile above a soft, weak chin. A small golden key hung from a delicate chain around her neck, and she looked more comfortable with this than she had with the heavy choker she'd been wearing in the other painting.

Beneath her portrait, a gramophone box rested on an antique dresser. It had a shiny silver horn protruding from the top of the box next to the turntable, upon which an old record rested. A crank handle stuck out of the side of the box, and next to that, a stack of records in yellowing old paper sleeves.

'Noah?' Barbara shouted, but her voice faltered. They were the only living people present in the Map Room, and she could see that, plain as the nose on her face. She kept trying anyway.

'Noah? Are you here?'

Only silence replied.

Baltimore, who had a strange, prickling sensation crawling down the back of his neck, carried on with his assessment of the room. He realized he was looking for any potential threats, and made an effort to drop his shoulders, loosen up his hands. He thought he was right to be cautious, for Baltimore had good instincts, and trusted them. Things were 'off', as he liked to say. Way off, way outside the realms of normal.

But he needed to keep a rational, cool head. If he didn't, Barbara certainly wasn't going to. She was barely keeping a lid on her panic, and he couldn't let himself dip, not even for a moment, or she would collapse.

But she was right. They *had* heard Noah's voice, coming from this room.

The room that had changed, in the blink of an eye.

Funny how quickly you can get almost used to something strange, he thought.

'I heard Noah!' Barbara echoed his thoughts, frantically scanning the room. 'I know I did!'

'I heard him too,' Baltimore replied, 'But he isn't here, hon. Look.'

He was right.

'So what did we hear? An echo? Something else?'

Baltimore shook his head. 'I wouldn't like to say. I really wouldn't.'

'I'm tired,' Barbara said, then. 'I would really like to leave this place.'

'I think that's a fantastic idea,' Baltimore confirmed. 'But first, we have to find your kid. And ourselves. We're lost, Barbara.'

She thought about that for a moment. Then an idea came to her.

'Maybe...'

'What?'

'Well. This is a room of maps, right?'

'Yeah.'

'Well...' She spread her hands out, instead of finishing the sentence. It took Baltimore a moment or two.

'Oh, right! You mean there's probably a map of the Chateau here somewhere?'

'Yes,' said Barbara, pleased. 'A floor plan or schematic, maybe.'

'Smart woman,' he replied, impressed. Barbara dipped her head.

'Occasionally.'

They spread out, each taking a different side of the room and exploring it: Barbara went west, and Baltimore east. They checked the framed maps, shelves, alcoves, found nothing. Baltimore even checked the gramophone sleeves.

They came together at the top of the room, beneath the cemetery window. They stood and looked at the portrait of Rose Lester for a moment.

Barbara thought how nice she looked. Like a kind, unassuming woman. The kind of woman who put up with a lot from other people. The kind of woman who—

A voice hissed: *he has used up all my money!*

She shuddered, and then noticed something. A small brass plaque with a raised edge on the bottom of the portrait. It had what she assumed was the artist's name painted on it in black enamel, and was oval shaped, and slightly smeared. As if a thumb or finger had left a print there, recently.

Without thinking, she reached out, and pressed it. Because she knew instinctively that the brass oval was not a plaque, but a cunningly concealed button.

And as her finger depressed the button, she heard a small, low, grinding noise, and felt something shift behind the portrait, felt the picture's frame start to move sideways. At the same time, the tiny golden key around the painted neck of Rose Lester detached itself from its painted chain, and fell. Barbara gasped, and caught it before it hit the floor.

'Would you look at that,' Baltimore whistled, looking back to the portrait. There was now a blank white space on the painting where the key had been sitting. 'Think she's real too?'

'I don't know,' Barbara muttered. She held the key in her hand, a far-away look in her eyes. It felt warm to the touch, as if it had fallen from the still living, breathing chest of Rose Lester, not her canvas counterpart. The sensation was unnerving, it wa—

I cannot bury her in the grounds, Charles Lester thought. The Housekeeper lay beneath him, staring up with blank eyes, eyes that had seen things they should not have before the sight was robbed. Her red curls were dull now, and matted. Her mop and pail lay abandoned in the doorway of the Study. He would use it to clean the blood trails he would no doubt leave as he got rid of her. Then, he would dispose of the mop and pail. Loose ends. Details. He would make sure he was safe. He would make sure Sunshire's reputation was safe.

But how? He hadn't quite figured that part out yet.

His eyes flicked about his surroundings, looking for inspiration. He was tired. It had taken longer to dispose of the Valet and the Gardener than he would have liked. He was thirsty now, after his work in the Atrium, and he longed for the whisky he kept in the Blue Room, but he still had this pressing issue to attend to.

Where?

I cannot carry her to the wine cellars, not now. It had been exhausting work, digging two man-sized graves in two pots, cleaning up the blood, disposing of the carpet by cutting it into strips and burning it. He was on his last reserves. He was not a young man anymore. Anger and adrenaline could only carry him so far. It had to be somewhere close by. Somewhere easy to get to.

I cannot...where?

His gaze went around and around, touching on all surfaces, all corners, his mind ceaselessly working until abruptly, he had an idea.

His hand went to his waistcoat, where a concealed silk-lined pocket was hidden in the lining. He had all his waistcoats tailored to this exact specification, for one reason: to keep the small golden key that rested inside close to his person at all times.

The key was a master key. There were twenty-five safes hidden in the walls of Sunshire, and this single key, which was the only key, fitted each one. As such, it was his most prized and secretive possession.

Twenty-five strongboxes, built into the brickwork, concealed in various places around the Chateau.

And the closest was in the Map Room.

The Map Room was only a moment or two from where he was now.

'Come on then,' he said, smiling down at the House-keeper. Alice, he thought her name was. He let his wife hire the domestic staff, and remember their names, but hers had caught in his memory for her pretty red hair.

A large gash now snaked across both her eyes, and the jagged end of the broken walking cane had ripped her eyelids clean away. It made her look as if she were staring at him, unable to stop looking, horrified by what had become of her.

He shook his head at this fanciful notion, and bent down one last time, bracing his knees as he collected the weight of another dead corpse in his arms.

'Shall we dance?' He chuckled, and dance he did, all the way to the Map Room.

Barbara gripped the key with fingers that had turned bone-white. Another man's memories swilled around inside of her like sewage water, and she opened her mouth, retching.

Before her, the portrait of Rose Lester continued to slide sideways, and she could see it was mounted on two brass tracks. Behind the painting, a large, square metal door.

'It's a safe,' Baltimore said, but Barbara could not hear him, could not—

Charles Lester III fixed upon a single portrait hanging on the wall at the far end of the Map Room. It, unlike most of the other oil paintings in the Chateau, was not a portrait of Charles Lester III himself, but of Rose. It was a painting he had always despised. The artist had been an admirer of his wife, something Lester did not allow or approve of, but he'd found himself forced to be sycophantic with him, despite his better judgement, because the idiot had been the oldest son of an important business investor. When the painting had been presented to Rose during a Christmas soiree the year the house was completed, Lester had gritted his teeth and pledged to hang it in a prominent place. And he had kept his word, because business was business, but it didn't stop him from hating the picture, and the look on his wife's face within, which the artist had captured brilliantly: placid, trusting, a little vacant and sad about the eyes, like a cow chewing the cud.

But the portrait and the ire it aroused was not the important thing. The important thing was the large, cavernous cast-iron safe embedded into the wall behind the painting, a safe that was lead-lined, airtight, and 'invincible', according to his architect: impossible to get into without his golden master key.

Charles Lester III felt suddenly very pleased with himself.

He lay the body down, having tired of dancing, and moved the painting of Rose to one side. Then he took out his key, slid it into the exposed safe lock and tugged on the brass pull-handle next to it vigorously. Once open, he removed the bundled notes and documents and the generous stack of gold and silver ingots that rested inside.

As a hiding place for a corpse went, it really was perfect, he realized, congratulating himself on his quick thinking.

The Master then proceeded, with some difficulty, to stuff the body of the maid into the deep, dark hole that yawned before him.

It was hot, fiddly work, for although the safe was large and the woman was small, he had somewhat miscalculated the size and dimensions of both, and he found, after putting the bulk of her into the coffer, that folding the Housekeeper into a small enough ball to ensure nothing obstructed the door when he tried to slam it shut was damn near impossible. Charles was slippery with blood and sweat and fatigue, and every time he thought he had it, an arm or a knee or a hand or a foot would flop out, obstructing the door seal. Desperate, aware of time ticking ever on, he gave thought to the idea of dismembering the woman, but he discounted the notion quickly. As much as he would no doubt have enjoyed the process of hacking this limp, useless thing to pieces, he did not have the time, tools, or patience for meticulous butchery.

Which meant there was nothing for it.

He was going to have to make the stubborn creature fit, no matter what.

The Master, who had spent his life up until this point perfecting the singular craft of compulsion, bullying and railroading, took a moment to gather his waning strength. He rolled his head around on sore shoulders, held his breath, puffed out his chest, and with a final, herculean effort, he violently shoved the body of the woman hard to the back of the safe with every ounce of his remaining energy, feeling things shift and crunch crack and break as he did so.

Then he waited to see if anything would slide out of place.

Nothing did. Alice, folded and squashed like a ragdoll crammed into a shoebox, was finally contained, and remained still, and silent.

Except...

Wait a moment.

Charles Lester III stared at the bloodied, broken bundle of bones and hair and skin before him, and heard a noise.

A faint, wet, rattling noise.

Like a breath, whistling past broken teeth.

He slowly poked his head further into the safe, wondering if he was running mad, for there was no way the woman could possibly have survived the beating he had given her.

Or was there?

'Stronger than you look,' he mumbled, and then, there it was: the Housekeeper's lips trembled, the last few ruined lashes on the scant remains of her eyelids fluttering against her bloodied cheeks.

Still alive.

Still alive, definitely dying, but somehow, despite everything, not yet dead.

Her eyes fluttered again, and her left hand, the only one visible, twitched.

Still alive, after all that.

Charles Lester III saw this, and a broad, frantic smile grew upon his face.

'Well, not for long,' the Master said, out loud. 'Not for long.'

He slammed the safe door shut, turned the key in the lock, pulled the portrait back into place, and turned his back on the Housekeeper, his wife, and the last vestiges of his frail, worn humanity, all the while hoping, for practicality's sake, that no-one else got in his way that night.

Barbara wiped her wet cheeks. She felt sick. 'I need to sit down,' she whispered.

'What's wrong?'

Barbara answered by collapsing slowly.

Baltimore grabbed and held her arms as she lowered herself to the ground. The key slipped from her grasp and clattered daintily to the floor.

He picked it up, and slid it into the newly exposed safe's keyhole.

Barbara stared at her fingers, barely registering pain. They were seared, singed with the form of the key, like her fingertips had been seared earlier by the leather folder in the Master's Study.

She folded her hands carefully into loose fists, then tucked them under her armpits, rocking herself gently back and forth.

Baltimore turned the key in the lock, then worked the handle next to it.

The door swung open.

'Fuck,' Baltimore said. Then: 'Fuck.'

Inside the safe, seated in a fetal position, was a half-mummified corpse. Dry, brown, shiny skin stretched thin over delicate bones. A yellowing cotton apron dangled from a shattered rib cage. Splintered fragments of bone littered the floor of the safe.

Thick, faded orange hair still clung to a papery scalp.

Baltimore examined the inside of the safe door, to check for something. He had a hunch, looking at the skeleton, a feeling that he knew what he would find.

Dried blood, smeared across the door.

Handprints.

The unmistakable shape of a curled fist, frantically, desperately banging against the cast iron.

Baltimore didn't know who the body in the safe belonged to.

But he could tell that person had been alive when they were locked in there.

'We're leaving,' he said, making a sudden decision. 'We're going.'

'But...Noah,' Barbara whispered, weakly. 'I have to find Noah.'

'He's not here,' Baltimore replied, and he hauled Barbara to her feet, and hurried her out of the Map Room as fast as her exhausted feet could take her.

OUBLIETTE

'And last, but not least, the Map Room,' the Tour Guide said, glancing at his watch, which was still frozen. They had run over time by quite some way, but the Guide knew that didn't really matter. Time was a convention he was habitually attached to, but it accounted for little in Sunshire. The night would come, as it always did, and then it would slip away again. He wasn't even entirely sure, as he wound the tour down, that he hadn't taken this particular tour party around the property already, that he hadn't had the exact same conversation he was about to have with them, or whether it was yet to come. They all blurred into one event, in the end. A long parade of Outsiders, blissfully ignorant as to the vagaries of time and space, the intricacies of life and death. Occupied with their petty dramas and small grievances. With things like love, and hate.

It was all immaterial, when you came to Sunshire.

His grip on his appearance began to slip in accordance with his now tired mindset. Usually, he managed to stay in character for the whole tour, but as he looked down at himself, holding out an arm, he could see bits of flesh detaching, floating off. He could see his contours shifting and blurring. He knew, without looking, that his head would be flitting between a solid and temporal state, and his feet would not walk upon the floor, but he didn't think his guests would care that much, or even notice, not now.

It had not been difficult to distract them away from the Atrium. They had all experienced things beyond their understanding, and as a result, their brains were cotton-wool, children's brains, easily led off track. After ten minutes of wandering the ever-shifting corridors, Terry had forgotten all about whatever it was that had roused him into such distress. The others took a little longer to forget, but by the time he ushered them into the Map Room, they all wore the same tired, blank expression. They had no idea of where they were, what time it was, or even what their own names were, anymore. The Chateau had been feasting on them all day, and no normal person could withstand that drain for any extended period of time. Not without consequences, at any rate.

This would be the last room, the Guide decided. The house was done with the tour party, well and truly, he could tell. They huddled together, looking at but not really seeing the display of maps, the array of globes, and the stained-glass windows. Linda Louise, who looked as if she had a broken nose, did rouse a little as she stared at the portrait of Rose, but quickly sank back into a waking stupor, working the same strand of hair through her fingers over and over again, until she looked ready to pull it clean out of her head.

The Tour Guide also let himself look at the portrait of Rose that hung on the far wall. He knew what lay behind it, for there were no secrets from those who dwelt at Sunshire, no secrets at all.

He wished Rose still lived here too, but she didn't, not anymore. She had done what he never could: she had left Sunshire, left it as an old woman, and she had passed beyond his reach forever. He had watched her every single day she was alive inside these walls, right up until the very day she packed up and moved out, and he had a feeling she had known he watched her, too. He used to leave the collected works of Shakespeare lying around for her to find. He could have shown himself to her, could have spoken to her, touched her, if he'd wanted, because the dead could do that at Sunshire, but what would have been the point? They were in different states. Time moved separately around them. Their futures were no longer entwined. Soon enough, she was an old woman, while he remained as he had the day he had died.

The house remembered her at her best, though.

The Guide allowed himself one final indulgence. It had been a long day, and a hard one at that. The guests had been fractious, demanding. So had the house.

He walked to the middle of the room, to where the small golden globe sat upon its plinth. This had been Rose's addition to the Map Room, a pretty, devious addition. It was the one place where he knew he could still come and experience her, feel close to her. Everything else in the house had been reclaimed by the Master.

But not this.

He laid his hand upon the globe, and let the memories flood him throughout.

'Charles? Where have you been? I've been looking for you.'

Charles Lester III froze in the door of the Map Room, mop and pail in hand. He had swabbed the floor once in here already, having gone back for the cleaning implements immediately after disposing of the Housekeeper. He had thought he had scrubbed out all evidence of his activities, evidence like the thick trail of splattered blood that he'd left behind in the corridor, but thinking about it later had made him paranoid. He'd decided to revisit the Map Room and the hallways that led to it one last time, with fresh water, and make absolutely sure there were no traces of blood left anywhere at all.

Working a trail methodically backwards from the Study, he had swabbed and swilled away any scraps of red he'd neglected to clean the first time, and as he arrived at the Map Room, panting with exertion, he realized he was still covered in dried blood, sweat, gobbets of flesh and earth, and now drenched with dirty mop water. He knew his appearance was wild, to say the least. His hair stuck out madly from his head, and his shirt, long since washed with red and brown, had come unbuttoned and untucked, ripped in multiple places. He was also starving, and feeling faint from exhaustion.

But he was close, he knew he was. Just this last thing, and nobody would know any of it. Nobody. He had covered his tracks. Just this last thing.

Or so he had thought.

'Charles?'

Wholly unprepared for the sight of his wife waiting for him, he closed his eyes and rested his weary forehead against the mop handle.

So close. He'd been so close to getting all the details finished. He'd dragged the body of the Valet to the Atrium, where he had also disposed of the Gardener, his tools, and his walking cane. He'd slashed the bloody carpet and burned it, returned for the Housekeeper, gotten her into the safe, cleaned up after himself, retired to the Blue Room, rid himself of Isabelle in the meat cupboard, stashed the bloody door stopper in the back of the fireplace to deal with later, and gone back over the entire Chateau one last time to be sure nothing incriminating remained.

And now, he was going to have to kill his wife.

His wife, her hair worn up in a loose chignon—an old-fashioned style for the time, but Rose refused to adapt and grow with couture as other, younger women did—a large, ugly amber broach at her throat, and her usual fur stole clutched at her waist, inside of which her hands were buried, looked at him. It was evident something awful had happened, something awful that he was responsible for. She did not seemed to be much surprised by this, and Charles Lester III began to wonder if she had, in fact, been sound asleep in her bed the entire night after all. Had she heard something, seen something she shouldn't?

Either way it made no difference.

Fifth time is a...

Charm?

At least the muffled screams from the safe had subsided. He was grateful for that, at least. He had left it long enough, although not intentionally. Isabelle had interrupted his plans.

All these bloody, meddling women, he thought.

'Hello, Rose,' he said out loud, heavily. He knew he would take little pleasure in killing his spouse. For one thing, she was the same class as him, if not higher born, particularly in terms of wealth, which galled him to say, but he cared about things like that. He did not consider her on the same plane when it came to matters of freedom of movement, or of expression, or of learning, but when it came to birthright...that was another matter. He cared about the natural order of wealth. Secondly, killing Rose would create more problems than he knew how to adequately plan for. She was a notable person, and she would be missed, unlike the others. There would be a furore. People would start asking questions.

Third, there was the child.

His heir, growing in her belly. He was convinced it was a son, and he was aware that his existing son, already taking over large areas of the Sunshire Estate's business, was not perhaps as well equipped with financial acumen as he had hoped for. Harry kept talking about shoe factories, for one thing. Shoe factories, as lowly an investment as he could imagine.

Yes, killing his wife would bring him no pleasure, but he knew he would have to do it, child or no child. But he wouldn't enjoy it. Not like he had the first four times. This...this would be tricky.

Lester would have to make it look like an accident.

Perhaps he could lure her to some stairs, trip her up so that she stumbled down them. Perhaps he could open a window, and push her out. Something that he could explain away as a tragedy, as poor luck, as the hand of fate, showing an ace.

Perhaps. He was so fatigued he could not see a clear path ahead, for the first time in his entire existence.

'Hello,' Rose replied, sweetly, as if they were taking tea in the drawing room. 'Whatever are you doing?'

He stared. She could see very well what he was doing. She could see, and yet...

She was not shocked. Not in the slightest.

An absurd thought popped into his head. He wondered remotely if she was wearing a corset today. He had lavished her with American lady corsets, back when they were first married, and gossard corsets, and a whole array of fine silk and cotton nightgowns, envelopes, petticoats, camisoles and bloomers, all trimmed with exquisite laces and embroidery and in some cases, even studded with pearls and crystals, but Rose had always refused to wear them. It had been a continued source of discontent between them, but why he chose to think of it right now, he could not explain.

Perhaps he was finally running mad. He thought he might be. The mechanics of his brain had changed, since he'd first struck the Valet.

'Cleaning,' he replied, wearily. 'What are you doing here? I thought you would be abed.'

'Yes, I was,' she replied, coolly. 'But then the Valet didn't come to me, not like he usually does.'

Charles Lester III blinked. The Valet's voice came to him, unbidden:

'She loves me. She told me so.'

A cold, rushing feeling tore through his head.

Was the child in her belly even his?

Isabelle's face drifted into his mind's eye. A horrible thought occurred to him.

Had he killed his real heir earlier that night?

Rose continued, calm as the ocean on a still day. 'And so, I went looking for him.'

'You...went looking for the Valet.' He was aware he sounded stupid, repeating her words, but he lacked the energy to correct this.

'Yes. I looked in all the usual places, and do you know what I found?'

'What?' It wasn't a question.

'Nothing. I found nothing except absence. Like the carpet, missing from your Study. Like the doorstopper, missing from the Blue Room, the one shaped like a dragon. Like the cufflinks, from your dresser. And the Valet, who was supposed to come to me. All gone. Where, Charles? Do you know?'

'Oh,' replied Charles, wondering how to navigate this. Denial, or admission?

Rose, who was no longer the Rose he had grown accustomed to all these years, but a sharper, sterner, more alert woman he'd never encountered before, pulled something from her fur stole and levelled it at him.

It was a pistol, pearl-handled, delicate, a Smith and Wesson, if he had to guess.

'What did you do with him, Charles?' She asked, coldly. 'Is he dead?'

'Yes.' Charles Lester III shrugged, seeing no reason to conceal it anymore. The bitch was going to die anyway, so she may as well know her lover had already departed this life, before she could. 'Dead.'

Without a moment's pause, Rose shot Charles Lester III, once in the right kneecap.

'Evil made a home in you a long time ago, Charles,' she hissed, as the gun's report echoed around the Map Room, and he could hear no emotion in her voice. Only emptiness, the devastating emptiness of loss. 'It dwells as comfortably there as you dwell in this huge, ugly, impractical house you insisted on building for us.'

Charles Lester III swayed on his feet, feeling pain, delayed momentarily by shock, suddenly tear through him. He veered sideways and fell, landing hard on the floor, clutching his knee. He tried to form words with his suddenly swollen tongue—swollen because he'd bitten it, in surprise.

All he could manage was a furious, spittle-drenched stutter.

'Bi...bi...bi....'

'Bitch?' Rose finished the short sentence for him, and moved to stand next to the odd golden globe she'd insisted on having installed in the middle of the room. He'd allowed it, because the architect had assured him it was no bother, and because giving into her occasional whims had made him feel magnanimous.

Now, he wondered if there was some ulterior purpose to the globe.

'You do love using that word, don't you?' Rose continued. 'You think I'm a dog, when all is said and done. You certainly treat me like one. A pet dog, but a dog nonetheless. If it were not for my money, you would never have looked twice at me, would you?'

Charles rolled onto his back. His heart had begun to pound erratically in his chest. He thought he might be having an attack, for a band of tightness suddenly clamped down across his upper body.

Rose glared at him, then studied the globe. On it, star constellations were picked out with precious stones. She frowned for a moment, as if remembering something, and then pressed one of the stones in with her index finger. It retreated into the globe, and she pressed another stone, and then another, and finally, a large red ruby.

The floor beneath him began to shake.

Rose watched dispassionately as the individual components of the wooden floor atlas began to shift and splay apart, moved by an unseen mechanism hidden beneath the floor. The brass inlay strips delineating each country's boundary retracted fluidly into the center, like so many tiny worms pulling back into their holes, as something clever and sophisticated wound the metal inwards, like a reel.

'The thing about dogs,' she continued, keeping close to the globe, her feet within the circumference of the round brass disc at the base, 'Is that you can only beat them so many times before they turn on you, Charles.'

Charles saw that her disc had become a pillar, which didn't make sense until he realized that the floor around her had contracted, retracted, disappeared altogether, leaving her standing like a statue on a plinth in the middle of the room.

He had a moment to appreciate the visuals of this, a moment when he thought, for the first time, that she looked grim, and rather beautiful, up there on her column, and then he felt the ground open up beneath him, and he was falling, into darkness, into a large circular well that had appeared where the wooden map had been only moments before, into something he had no knowledge of, something his wife had cooked up with his architect, behind his back, and—

The Valet, who had a new job these days, and called himself Tour Guide, pulled his hand back, cutting the connection with the past. He was not sure how much good it did him, coming back here as often as he did, reliving a memory that did not belong to him, but it was the only way he could see her, now she had left the Chateau, and so he did.

But you're missing the best part, he told himself, and it was true, he was.

He placed his hand back on the globe, and allowed himself to enjoy the experience.

'*Do you remember our wedding night, Charles?*'

Charles opened his eyes. He was lying on his back at the bottom of a long, deep circular shaft. His leg, the one that had been shot, splayed out before him, useless and limp. His other leg was folded awkwardly beneath him, for this is how he had landed. The pain was indescribable, but it kept him conscious, and for that, he was briefly grateful.

Above him, high, high above him, stood the dark, skirted figure of his wife.

She called down to him, and her voice echoed around the shaft.

'*I was twenty-eight years old, and you were thirty. You were the happiest man this side of Lestershire, for you had just married into my money. And I never saw a dime of it, from that day to this, did I? You took everything my family gave you in exchange for me, and you used it to build your little empire. You frittered it away, on antiques and collectibles, on bad business decisions and bad people, on bribery and deception and terrible investments, and here we* live, surrounded by the spoils of your success.' She waved a hand around at the Map Room. 'Are you enjoying your success, Charles? Does it feel good?'

He mustered up enough energy to scream:

'Let me out of here, you crazed woman!'

'Of course I'm not going to let you out of there,' she replied, in a matter of fact tone. 'Don't be silly. We have plans for your town, Charles. Harry and I want to turn your cigar factories- which are hemorrhaging money, by the way- into shoe factories. Much more profitable, so I hear. The Lesters will make shoes, fancy that! What a step down for your legacy. I rather like that.'

'You're fucking crazed!' Lester roared, knowing it would not help his cause.

'No, darling, what I am is pragmatic. I knew you couldn't be trusted with my money, and I knew you couldn't be trusted with this house. So I made my own plans, as any sensible woman should. Did you think I would stand by and let you run my family's name into the ground with debt, and scandal? I know about the scullery maid, Charles. I know about her, because of the servants' gossip. You couldn't keep your seed in your cup, could you?'

He could think of nothing else to say.

'Well, you weren't the only one with special requests for the Architect, darling. As you can see for yourself, now.' Rose allowed herself a small laugh, and Charles realized, with horror, that she meant to leave him down there.

In the dark, at the bottom of a shaft.

Like a dog that had stumbled into a well.

She meant to leave him here, to die.

'Do you know what I call this? I call this the Oubliette. They were commonly found in castles, oubliettes, during the medieval ages. In French, the word oublier means 'to forget'. And that is precisely what will happen to you, Charles. You *will be forgotten. This trapdoor is the only way into the Oubliette, and also the only way out. You won't be able to reach it by climbing, because the walls curve inwards, you see- you won't be able to support your own bodyweight under the overhang. There also isn't much room in there, as you'll no doubt find. Yes, I'm going to leave you here, to rot, and I shall invent a tragic story of your financial woes, of your noble suicide. I might even erect a monument in town in your name. I can just about afford it, if I'm careful about it. I might have to sell a few things, first, some of your collectibles, perhaps, but I can make it work.'*

'How...how...'

She knew what he was trying to ask.

'Did you think you had control of all of my money? How naive. I've been bribing your accountant for years, darling. He siphoned off a portion of your dividends each year, and I paid him a percentage by way of thanks. How else could I afford to commission the architect, privately? I had to make it worth his while, didn't I? Besides, I rather think he liked the challenge. Didn't he do excellently?'

'Please,' Lester begged, for begging was now his final resort. His voice echoed around and around the long, narrow well-shaft. 'Please, please don't leave me down here. I beg you. Please.'

Rose pressed a series of jewels upon the golden globe, and the floor began to slide back into place above him, countries, oceans, brass inlays all.

'PLEASE!' He screamed, as the circle of light above his head shrank, and shrank, until the only thing he could see was the hem of his wife's skirt, barely visible through the remaining gap. 'PLEASE, FOR THE LOVE OF GOD, I-'

'He was worth ten of you,' she spat, before disappearing from view, and he knew she meant the Valet, and he howled.

The floor closed up with a rumble, and all lights went out for Charles Lester III, who roared, and screamed, and beat at the stone walls until he was blue in the face, but nobody came for him. Nobody would ever come for him, ever again.

And as he began the slow process of rotting to death, alone in the bowels of the Sunshire Chateau, his pride, his joy, a house that had betrayed him as surely as his wife did, as surely as his Valet had, and his architect, and his accountant, and his son, all the little pieces of him that made up a whole began to sink into the stone, and the house, which had been greedy for Lester's rage, Lester's avarice, Lester's hard and deadly ambition, for a long, long time, above and beyond all other offerings, consumed him hungrily.

STAY

Alice led Ned to a room covered in maps. Ned suddenly realized he had no use for maps, not as he was now, but that was not why they were there. They were there for the gramophone.

It was a nice room, the Map Room, covered in globes and a large wooden map on the floor and attractive stained glass windows, with a portrait of Rose Lester hung on the wall at the far end above the gramophone, but Ned found he was less and less impressed by the design and décor of the place now that he was to live inside of it forever more. There would be plenty of time for that, later.

For now, Alice wanted to dance.

She wound the gramophone's handle to get the turntable flying, dropped a record lightly onto the spinning table, carefully positioned the ornate chrome tone arm on the outer rim of the record, laid a hand carefully upon the wall next to the painting of Rose, where Ned thought he could see a faint, stained outline, square in shape, box-like, and then she turned back to him. Ned watched this little ritual with his heart in his mouth, for she was so graceful, so sure yet delicate in her movements, and he felt like a clumsy bear by comparison, but Alice didn't mind about that. She walked over to him, slid one arm around his waist, held his other hand in hers, stepped lightly up onto his toes, and said: 'Dance with me, would you?'

'I don't know how to,' he replied, in a daze. Music swelled around him, defiant, celebratory, mingling with the bubbles of blood that drifted off of him, for he could not control his appearance, not yet, not without practice, not like she could, and Alice laughed.

'Doesn't matter,' she replied. 'Just move your body around, Ned. Let go a little. It'll feel good. Trust me.'

And so he did. He held her in his arms, and began to spin, duck, dive, and move, his body matching hers as they got used to each other, and he thought *this is what it should have been like, on my wedding day.*

This.

This is what I have been looking for.

As Alice threw back her head and laughed throatily, the walls of the Chateau seemed to creak and swell by way of response, like a proud parent looking on, and as the clustered crystals in his heart multiplied and became a cave of spires, he thought,

They say that when one door closes, another one opens, don't they?

And then he closed his eyes and rested his cheek on the top of Alice's head, and there were no more thoughts, no more doubts, no more pain, no more cares, not for a very, very long time. There was just the music, and the feel of her weight leaning against his, the sensation of all the tiny parts of her mingling with his, and the knowledge that he had found a new home, a home he hadn't even realized he had been looking for.

'I'd like to stay,' he said, softly, and it was true. 'I'd like to stay here with you. Do you think…do you think the house will have me?'

The Sunshire Chateau, by way of reply, shuddered almost imperceptibly. The picture on the wall rattled as an anticipatory vibration ran along the map-smothered masonry and across the floors, up Ned's legs and into his heart, and he thought about how a person could move and stay static all at the same time, and how none of that mattered, if you were moving or staying still with a person you loved.

MUSIC

Music drifted through the halls and corridors of the Sunshire Chateau, and it moved from room to room, space to space, corner to corner, like a snake weaving its way through grass, and at every turn it encountered a presence, a person, or perhaps the imprint of what had once been a person, the lingering matter and energy that was left behind, for energy cannot be created nor destroyed. It simply changes state, and at Sunshire, itself a constantly shifting entity that straddled some unseen divide between life and death, orderly and disorderly, that energy had space to breathe, space to play, space to simply…

Be.

The music mingled with the scattered parts of the ghosts it met, both living and dead, and wrapped around them lovingly, a silken scarf of rippling piano notes and a mournful oboe teasing beyond the jaunty melody, and the first people it encountered were Barbara and Baltimore, who walked endlessly through corridors that never led anywhere. Their slippers, now ragged on their feet, flapped about them as they walked, and their hands, loosely entwined, were cold, and listless. They had moved beyond hunger, beyond fatigue, beyond all human motivation. Barbara knew, deep down somewhere, that she was looking for something, but she had forgotten what. Baltimore, who had only been hoping to kill an hour or two before his big meeting, couldn't even remember his own name, now. He kept a hold of Barbara's hand, however. Letting go would be letting himself get lost entirely, he knew it, deep down where it was still warm inside of him.

The music brushed past the couple and left them walking, knowing that, at the very least, they had each other, and found its way into the Master's Study next, to the pulsing red chamber where Noah still lay dead beneath a giant, heavy mirror. In the corner of the study, knees drawn to his chest, rocking backwards and forwards, another version of the boy, a scattered, broken apart version, looked on in horror at his own deceased body, and cried out for his mother.

'Mom!' he whimpered, 'Mom, help! I'm sorry, Mom, I love you!'

But she never came, and she never heard him, for the sound of a rippling piano drowned out his noise, and the tune withdrew from the room, moving along, always moving along, knowing that it would only be a matter of time before the boy was reunited with his mother, it would only be a matter of time before they could perhaps start to repair some of the damage done, because their priorities had changed, now, after all. Changed, and realigned to their new circumstances.

Their new home.

The music circled back, as all things do, to its point of origin, passing on its way the Atrium, where three sets of bones now lay, tickling the ear of the Gardner, who bent over a large terracotta pot, one that used to be part of a pair, loosening soil around the roots, passing the Library, where a black wooden cane that shouldn't have been there leaned jauntily against a desk, passing the Blue Room, where a woman called Isabelle had once been bludgeoned to death with a doorstop shaped like a Chinese dragon. She hung there still, jerking and twitching, a tortured soul in a permanent state of injury, but the music kissed her lightly as it passed, lightly and gently, and there was a distant part of her that heard it, heard it and found comfort, for not everything in the living world was terrible, even if she had forgotten that.

And the Tour Guide, who now stood in the Reception Hall, waiting, back at the very start of things, opened the doors of the Sunshire Chateau wide, and let the music, which had penetrated and filled up every part of the house, out into the world, and along with it, three weary guests, who took a last, lingering look around themselves before they went, feeling an unbearable sadness settle upon them, without knowing why.

BACK IN THE OUTSIDE

Dusk had fallen across the Sunshire Estate. It fell with grace, which is more than can be said for most humans, and it brought with it cooler air, and bats, and a heady fragrance as the flowers in the borders of the driveway opened up their petals and breathed into the night.

It was a house the sunlight barely touched, but moonlight had unfettered access.

As purple-greys dissolved into bruised blacks, stars began to poke through the canvas of the sky overhead, and the moon shone brightly, spilling its paint all over the house and the gardens surrounding it.

And into this silvery land, an orange, glowing sliver appeared upon the gravel driveway, accompanied by another. The slivers widened into wedges, and those merged to become a wide, illuminated portal.

The large double doors of the Sunshire Chateau were open again, for the first time since that morning.

Out of it, three shadows spilled. One, a large man with a heavy gait, face lined with meanness and hardship and spite. Behind him, a woman in a green dress, leaning against a smaller man with a skewed bow-tie. They tripped out of the house as if drunkenly rolling off of a ship that had docked after too long at sea, swaying from side to side, stumbling and tripping over themselves.

A slip of paper fell from Bow-tie's pocket as he crossed back over the threshold of the Sunshire Chateau: a yellow entrance ticket, with a red stamp shaped like the house marked onto it crudely. Bow-tie, who had another name, but couldn't remember it, thought distantly that it looked a little like a leaf, this ticket, as it fluttered to the ground, and then he thought: *I like leaves. So did Simon.*

But he had no idea who Simon was, anymore. Or why he had even liked leaves in the first place.

The doors, as so many doors do, started to close slowly behind the three surviving members of the tour group. They turned to watch as they did so, eyes glowing with their shared experiences of the house, and they could see, just before their vision was cut off for good, the shadow of the Guide, standing tall and still in the Reception Hall. He raised a hand, waving a slow goodbye, and had any of them been in their right minds, they might have thought it a sarcastic gesture. As it was, they returned it sleepily, three hands flapping a dazed farewell into the night, and the Guide grinned, and then turned, as if startled.

The final three guests could see that behind him, on the stairs, another figure had materialized.

It was the shadow of another man.

He was also tall, older, by the shade of his hair, and he used a cane.

He looked remarkably like the man who was depicted in fifty-three portraits that hung around the house.

Then, with a soft *clunk!* The doors sealed, and the pair were gone from view.

Don, Linda Louise, and Terry walked silently along the driveway, away from the house, away from the Sunshire Estate. They felt, the further from the place they walked, as if they had escaped something, although they could not recall what, exactly. Their minds felt heavy, used, wrung dry.

They just knew they needed to keep walking.

Behind them, had they taken the time to look, they might have seen the windows of the Chateau, which spilled forth a weird, orange, artificial glow, grow dim, and if they had been looking really hard, they might have seen more shadows silhouetted in the dying light: a woman, hanging, a man, with a trowel, a couple, dancing near the window. More shadows: indistinct, changing, always shifting, small, tall, thin, wide, crooked, standing, spinning, hiding, a multitude of shadows, an ever-shifting puppet show of matter, for the Chateau had a big appetite, and a lot of space in which to accommodate the lost, the disoriented, and the dead.

The window lights dulled, and then eventually grew dark, as the house put itself to sleep.

And the shadows, some of whom were used to each other, others who were not, faded into the night, as shadows do.

It had been a busy day.

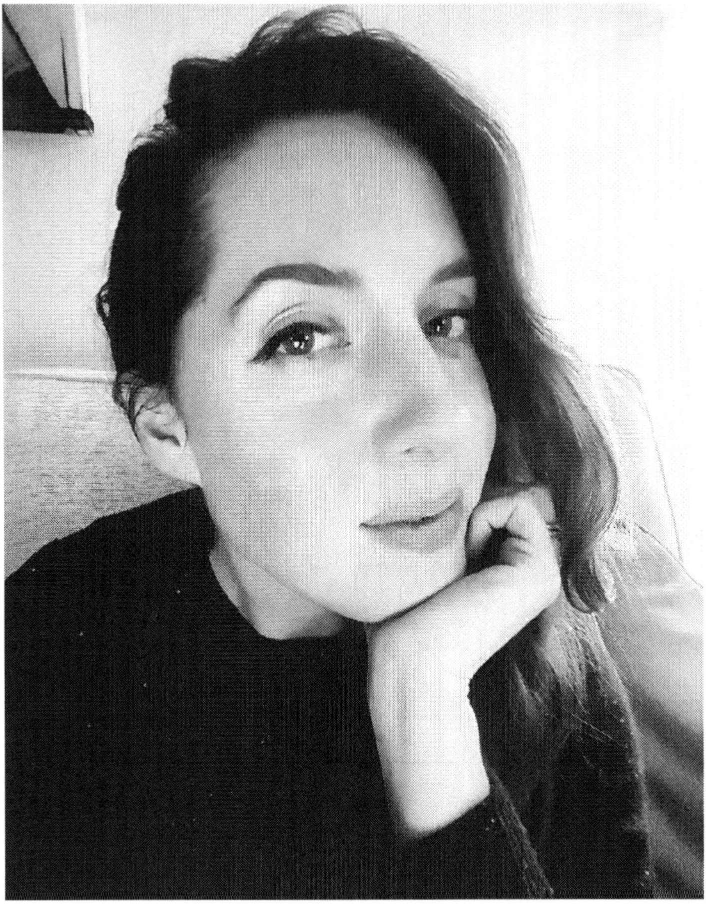

Gemma Amor is a Bram Stoker Award nominated author, voice actor and illustrator based in Bristol, in the UK. She self-published her debut short story collection *CRUEL WORKS OF NATURE* in 2018, and went on to release *DEAR LAURA, GRIEF IS A FALSE GOD, WHITE PINES, GIRL ON FIRE, THESE WOUNDS WE MAKE* and *WE ARE WOLVES* before signing her first traditional publishing deal for her novel *FULL IMMERSION*, due out from Angry Robot books in 2022. *SIX ROOMS* is her eighth published book.

Gemma is the co-creator of horror-comedy podcast *Calling Darkness*, starring Kate Siegel, and her stories feature many times on popular horror anthology shows *The NoSleep Podcast* (including a six-part adaptation of *DEAR LAURA*), *Shadows at the Door, Creepy* and the *Grey Rooms*. She also appears in a number of print anthologies and had made numerous podcast appearances to date. Other projects in development include a video game, a short film she co-wrote called ABASEMENT (2021), and more.

Gemma illustrates her own works and also provides original, hand-painted artwork for book covers on commission. She narrated her first audiobook, *THE POSSESSION OF NATALIE GLASGOW* by Hailey Piper, in 2020—it won't be her last.

Printed in Great Britain
by Amazon